THE AMBER STONE

DARA GIRARD

ISBN: 978-1949764239

THE AMBER STONE

ILORI PRESS BOOKS, LLC

P.O. Box 10332

Silver Spring, MD 20914

www.iloripressbooks.com

Gaining Interest

Careless Rapture

Dangerous Curves

Familiar Stranger

It Happened One Wedding

Unexpected Pleasure

Midnight Promise

Sweet Temptation

Always and Forever

Clifton Sisters

The Sapphire Pendant

The Amber Stone

The Emerald Ring

Fortune Brothers

A Tempting Proposal

A Seductive Arrangement

Novels

Honest Betrayal

The Daughters of Winston Barnett

Remember My Name

Illusive Flame

Winterwood Lane

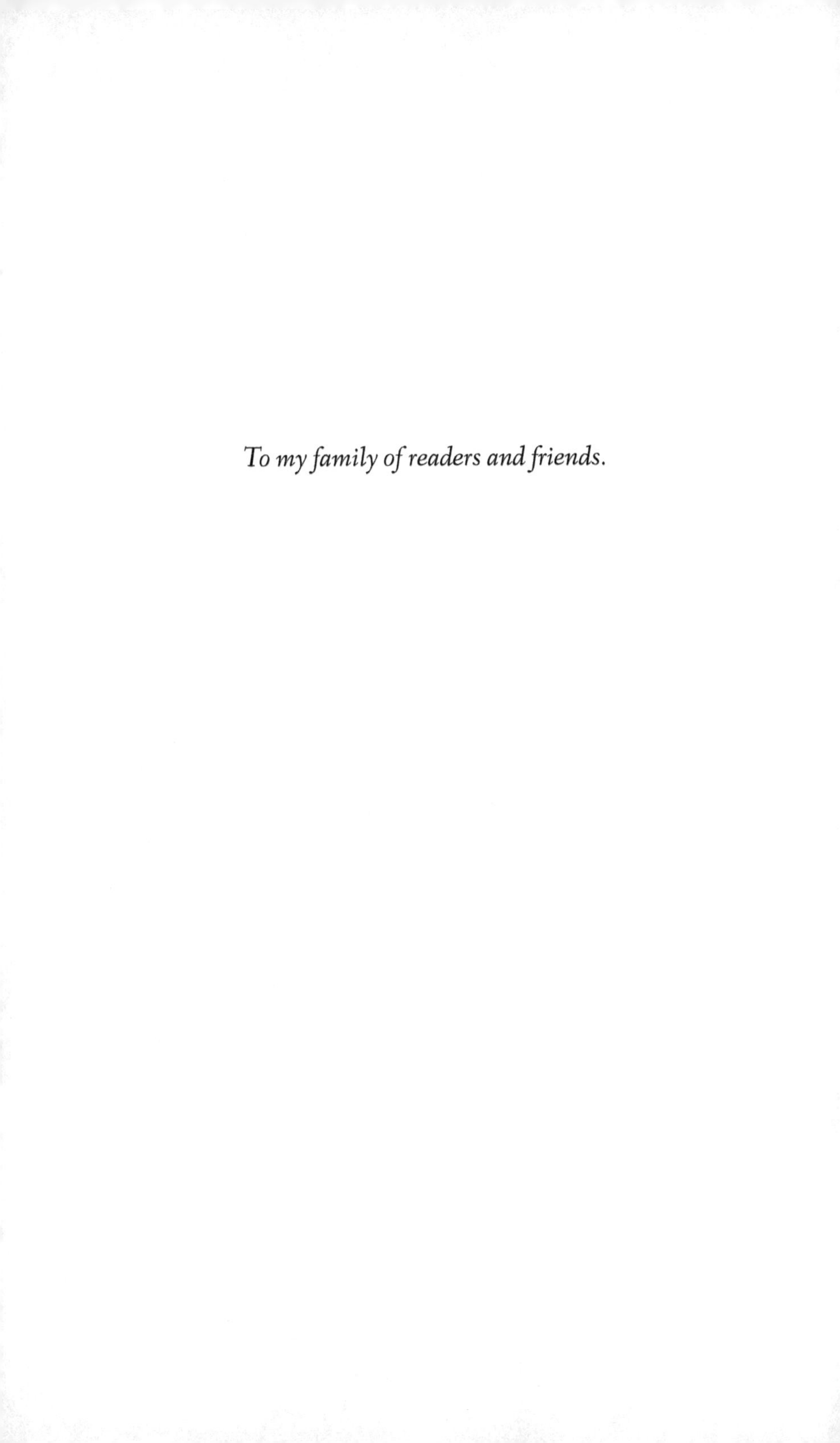

To my family of readers and friends.

PROLOGUE

LATE 1700S

Martin Hamilton could feel the hard earth against his bare feet as he ran towards the cool, dark allure of the Caribbean Sea. Behind him he heard the sound of dogs, and the yellow glow of torches shone against the night sky. The rebellion was lost and there was no way to escape the island. He'd soon be captured and his life would finish at the end of a rope.

But he'd rather die by his own hands. If he could get to the water, that would be his victory.

"Not that way," a voice said.

He halted, but when he looked around he saw nothing.

"Come," the voice said, then he felt a hand on his arm.

He knew the rough grip of that hand. When he looked up, he could barely make out the dark features of his friend, BC. They'd once worked on the same sugar plantation, but Martin never knew his full name. He wondered if he'd even been given one.

BC turned sharply to the right and Martin followed him. He knew better than to ask questions, but when they reached the sea, his courage left him.

"I can't swim," he said, knowing there would be no escape for him.

BC smiled, his teeth white in the moonlight. "I can. Just hold your breath," he said then dragged Martin into the water.

Martin held his breath until he thought he couldn't hold it anymore. Soon he thought he'd see his mother again in the afterlife.

His mother. A woman who'd died with memories of Ireland—the land she'd never see again—on her lips. A servant since the age of six, she'd been bred by an African rebel and the master of the house. Her offspring had been scattered, but Martin had made his way back to her, their time together too brief.

He reached the surface, painfully gulping in the air he needed. Then his eyes adjusted to the dark, damp stillness around him and knew he was in a cave. He pulled himself out of the water.

"Continue down this tunnel," BC told him in a hushed voice. "It will take you far, far from here. If they catch you, you were not there."

Martin stiffened at the suggestion. He knew that he must never admit to being part of the rebellion if he wished to live. But he didn't want to deny his rage; the deaths he'd witnessed.

"It's a new battle you'll fight," BC said, as if reading his mind.

Martin nodded, understanding the meaning.

"Go," his friend said, then pressed a smooth, round object in Martin's hand before he disappeared into the water.

CHAPTER 1

MIDDLE 2000S

"I told you not to come back here."

Teresa Clifton wasn't surprised by the cold reception. The Wright Herb Shop was the last place she wanted to be. When she entered the store, what always bothered her the most was what was missing. She saw rows of jars and potted herbs and heard the light hum of mood music playing, sometimes a flute, sometimes a harp, but she didn't smell anything. Not the faint fragrance of lavender or vanilla, or even fresh mint or wood. The lack of any fragrance made the atmosphere feel hollow—like a sham. Synthetic rather than genuine. But the atmosphere wasn't the only thing wrong with the store. Helene Wright was the other.

The moment Teresa entered the shop, Helene had made her way over to her with the focus of a heat-seeking missile. She was a stocky woman who could never be thin, the curves of her body exuding a warmth she didn't have. She and her husband, Dr. Thomas Wright, owned the store and had run it for years. She had a face as cute and cuddly as a teddy bear and a personality as prickly as thorns. Few saw past her bright smile to the iron behind it. Teresa had once fallen for her charm, but now knew better.

The Wright Herb Shop was located in Bedford, an upscale part of town perfectly situated in a place where people could easily afford the marked up prices and the advertised classes for yoga, aromatherapy, massage and acupuncture that hung on the wall. It was expertly designed to give a homey, earthy feel, the tones muted, with crystals near the window catching the thin winter light peeking through the grey clouds. She had helped with the design.

But despite the prime location, the rows of jars filled with fancy leaves and oils, the polished wooden floors and railing that led to the upper level, Teresa felt a lack of true care for its patrons. She hadn't stepped inside the herb shop in years, but had come for one reason.

She looked at the bottle in her hand and held it up. "I'm worried about this company. Two months ago I suggested Marla Wessler at the nursing facility take valerian root to deal with her anxiety and insomnia. Instead she still hasn't been able to sleep and developed a rash."

Helene blinked, looking bored. "And you're telling me this because—?"

"Another friend of hers at the home is taking garlic supplements, but also wasn't seeing improvements until I showed her how to use garlic cloves in the kitchen. Her doctor has been amazed by her improvement."

"Again, I fail to see—"

"I don't think these supplements are real."

Helene quickly looked around the room to make sure no one else had over heard them, then grabbed Teresa's arm and shoved her towards the door. "Get out."

"I think Valley Ray Supplements are fraudulent."

She opened the front door. "Do I need to repeat myself?"

"Why are you using them instead of Marchant like you used to?"

"Because they are a popular local company and no one else has been complaining."

"But—"

"Are you a doctor?"

Teresa gritted her teeth. "You know very well that—"

"You don't want to mess with me, Teresa. That would be a mistake."

"This isn't about you. People could get hurt and—"

"You may have gotten away with fooling my aunt and most of the people here," Helene smoothly interrupted as if Teresa hadn't spoken. "But I know the truth," Helene smiled. It was one of her signature expressions and she only used it when she wanted to offer a warning instead of a threat. The smile was simple—it emphasized the smoothness of her skin ('due to our special line of creams,' she liked to say without mentioning that she'd never had problems with her complexion), and the light in her eyes had enough mystery to make one nervous about her intentions. "Come back here again and I'll make your life hell." She removed imaginary fuzz from Teresa's coat. "Think about that."

"If you're not careful, one of these bottles could make someone sick. And they could possibly die."

"Yes, well you would be an authority on that, so I'll keep it in mind." She looked past Teresa at two clients coming to the door and smiled. "Excuse me, I have work to do. Some of us have to earn a living."

Teresa gripped the bottle in her hand. Helene was right. She had no proof, only her suspicions and there hadn't been other complaints. Perhaps Mrs. Wessler and her friend hadn't been using it correctly, but something felt off. She didn't know what. She left the shop feeling defeated.

The following morning she sat on a boulder, lost in her thoughts, as she stared out at the waters of Hollow Cove, glancing at the older couple several yards away who'd braved the winter chill to enjoy the view. She was about to turn away when she saw a man rise out of the water like a son of Poseidon, an immortal warrior ready for battle, with the arrogance of expected victory swirling around him like a cloak. His body—the color of cocoa butter with a dash of cinnamon—cut through the fingers of the wave like a seal, producing a series of little ripples.

Teresa clutched the rock she sat on, her knuckles paled as she watched, mesmerized, wondering if her mind was deceiving her —creating hallucinations as a result of sleep deprivation and anger. She watched the man shake water from his ink black hair, which curled over his forehead like ivy, and wipe water from his beard. Water dripped from it, shining like diamonds in the cool morning sun.

Teresa shook her head, trying to analyze what she had seen. She had only recently begun coming to the bay again to calm her sudden restlessness and feelings of helplessness. Her confrontation with Helene was just one of a series of recent failures. It had been four months, but she still felt shell-shocked by the death of her friend Bess Richman, who'd collapsed from a massive heart attack at only fifty-three. It opened up the wound of losing her parents nearly three years before from pneumonia. And then there were the nightmares that attacked her sleep in their vicious and haunting ways. She sought solace here, desperate to find a way to calm her nerves.

Hollow Cove was a hidden alcove off of Catlon Bay and was not a place frequented by many. After hiking a harrowing rocky path down a nearly vertical hill, the beach itself was rocky except for a small section of soft sand for people to laze on. In the distance, rocks rose up like monolithic sculptures varying in shape and size like new recruits to the army. Further down the cove, caves created great hiding places for children and lovers wanting to find a private place.

Though not a place of beauty, Teresa came to this part of the bay to drink her morning or evening coffee and to collect different debris that washed up on the bank—shells, twigs, bottles. She sometimes hoped to find that proverbial note in a bottle carrying a message from a distant place—a sailor lost at sea, a lover waiting for his darling to return. Or she would write poetry in the little notebook she kept in her pocket and try to make sense of her life. Most of the time her trips were uneventful —until today.

Today was the first time she had ever seen a swimmer. If people wanted to be by the water, there was the commercialized area located downtown, with boardwalks, restaurants and a meticulously clean beach. Now, it was a dot in the distance, with buildings rising like concrete trees. Wealthy homes were spotted around the water like great toy houses.

However, Teresa preferred the quiet, the feeling of being alone in a special hidden place; hearing the morning tide crawl up the sandy beach and sink back like an indecisive guest. Who was this intruder that swam on a day that was probably 50 degrees? She acknowledged the coming hints of spring that whispered its arrival, with buds stretching their arms, green grass appearing under the slush of dirty snow, and warmer afternoons, but it was still a cold late February.

Teresa wrapped her blue wool coat tighter around herself. February mornings at the cove were brutal, but the cold wind invigorated her. She watched the man tread towards the shore, his blue trunks clinging to firm legs and a nice solid bottom.

Taking her eyes off him, she saw what at first looked like a moving rock come up to greet him. It turned out to be a little grey cat.

The cat nuzzled against his wet leg and he sprinkled it with some water, which it seemed to delight in. It stood on its hind legs to catch the falling drops as if performing a dance. The man bent down to stroke the cat, then looked up to the sky—a clear blue sky that for many days had been white with clouds. The sun was continuing its ascent so half of his face was hidden by shadow. He smiled gently. The sound of seagulls could be heard above.

Teresa wondered what secret thoughts he hid behind that expression. If she were standing half-naked and wet on a cold winter day she would be thinking she was losing her mind, but the man seemed unconcerned as he wrapped a towel around his neck and stretched out his body, lunging and twisting like an athlete getting ready for a race.

She crouched down, hoping he wouldn't catch her staring. He could be an athlete, she reasoned. His torso was heavily muscled, his shoulders wide, his legs firm. He was hairier than she usually liked men to be—dark hair curled, forming a V on his chest—but he was in excellent shape. He turned back to the water like a merman missing his home and mumbled something to his feline companion. The cat seemed to nod in response.

The man was just about to leave when he turned and looked at her. Teresa gasped, shocked by the awareness that seemed to cut through the distance between them. Her heart pounded in her chest as if she had run a marathon. He did not smile, wave or frown. He just studied her as she had him a few moments before, his gaze questioning her presence there. Teresa grew uncomfortable by the direct way he looked at her. She offered a shy smile, just to break the moment, but he did not return the expression.

She turned away, pretending to find better things to occupy her attention. Teresa had a strange feeling that she knew him;

that he knew her. To her dismay, the feeling of awareness did not leave her. She quickly glanced up to see if he was gone. He wasn't. Her pulse quickened when she realized he was coming towards her. She resisted a wild urge to get up and run, but felt paralyzed in place and anxiously waited for his approach.

"It's nice weather we're having," he said in a casual tone as if addressing a friend.

She peered up at him and smiled, trying to keep her eyes on his face instead of his chest. "Yes, quite."

He stared at her for another moment. She couldn't quite read the expression in his eyes because of the shadows. He glanced quickly at her lap, then back up at her face. A smile tugged at the corners of his mouth.

"Do you usually like spilling coffee on yourself?"

She stared at him with a blank expression. "I beg your pardon?"

He nodded towards her lap. Teresa looked down and saw that coffee was seeping from her thermos and dripping on her skirt. Already a large stain was spreading like a milky brown blob.

She leaped to her feet. She had completely forgotten about her coffee. "Oh no," she cried, trying to brush the stain away.

"You're only making it worse," he said, grabbing her wrist. "Here." He dabbed at the stain using his towel with a gentleness she had not expected. "This skirt needs to go straight into a washing machine."

Teresa didn't respond. She couldn't. The touch of his hand had left her immobile. She felt her restlessness disappear, replaced with an eerie calm. That had never happened before. Usually by focusing and touching someone else—a gift she'd discovered in her early teens—she could sense something about them, at times even seeing visions of their past, but this time, just the feel of his hand around her wrist opened up an unexpected connection and awareness about him.

She knew he had the hands of a healer, that he'd suffered a terrible loss and now saw life through his head and not his heart. His heart had been broken. She suddenly felt shocked and embarrassed by all that she sensed, as if she'd stumbled upon someone's intimate diary.

She stared at his bent head, wishing the waves would wash her and this entire incident away.

He stood, tossing the towel over his shoulder. That's when she saw it. A silver necklace, with a charm—accented with tiny amber stones—glittering in the sun, lying flat on his chest. It was elegantly made with no particular meaning to an observer, but a pattern of lines melding into one. She'd seen it before...she knew it. But how? Where? Why did it fill her with both anticipation and dread? Who was this man?

She took an involuntary step back, tripping over the rock she had been sitting on and falling backwards. Fortunately, she grabbed her skirt before it fell over her head.

"Are you all right?" the man asked, leaning over her. He sounded concerned. Teresa was now certain he thought she belonged in a nuthouse.

She quickly righted herself, ignoring the stranger's offered hand, unsure she could bear his touch again, and brushed sand from her skirt, trying to get her bearings. She briefly looked at the necklace once more then turned away. "Yes, thank you."

"Did my cat scare you? He's harmless...usually."

"No, not at all."

"You're fine then?"

"Yes."

He didn't seem convinced, but shrugged his shoulders in an impatient manner and nodded. "Good day then."

She was about to say 'good day' too before she heard a splash.

He paused. "What was that?"

"I don't know." She knew it was something big, but she couldn't imagine what. The few people around them didn't seem to be bothered, but she sensed something was wrong and he did too. A terrible feeling of dread shot through her a second time, then she looked out and saw something floating in the water. She pointed. "What is that?"

"What?"

Teresa knew he couldn't see the object clearly and she didn't have time to wait. Her heart began to pound when she realized what it was. She slipped out of her coat and shoes and ran towards the water.

"Wait," he called after her.

But she didn't. Instead she rushed into the cold water. Suddenly the ground disappeared from underneath her feet.

She swam over to the body, her arms already aching. She wasn't a very physical person, and her body seemed to protest her efforts, but she couldn't stop. She wished she was a strong swimmer like her younger sister, Jessie, who succeeded at any sport she tried. But she wasn't, and her lungs felt weary; she just had enough strength to reach the body. She came upon the still figure.

She didn't want to think about what that meant—had she'd arrived too late?—she had to have hope. She pulled the body to the shore, hoping that someone would help her. Suddenly, the weight didn't feel so heavy. A moment later she realized the man had taken the limp body and laid it on the beach. Then her heart froze when she saw the woman's face. She wasn't a stranger. She was her cousin.

Teresa watched the man pumping her cousin's chest. "Come on, Louisa," he said.

He knew her too, but Teresa didn't wonder how. She just

wanted to see Louisa open her eyes and breathe. She had to breathe. She couldn't die like this.

Louisa gasped, then vomited water and took another breath. Soon the paramedics arrived and took her away. Teresa felt relieved and a little vindicated. Death didn't follow her; she'd helped save someone. She put on her shoes and coat, feeling the cold air but not caring, a small smile of gratitude on her lips. Then she heard a passing voice say, "She shouldn't be so proud of herself. We still know she's a murderer."

Murderer? *Murderer!* Why did people still believe that?

Teresa followed behind the ambulance, fighting back tears. She hadn't killed Bess. Her death had been ruled an accident, but unfortunately Teresa had been the only person at the house with her. And Bess's family did nothing to stop the rumors. Although Teresa's family was used to her befriending women twenty to thirty years older than herself, Bess's family met her with distrust and they'd never liked Teresa's relationship with the wealthy single woman. Teresa had been her piano teacher. Bess had wanted to play piano since a girl and now, after taking an early retirement and making good investments, she decided to treat herself. They'd become fast friends.

Teresa had been the one to introduce Bess to a more natural way of dealing with her diabetes and high blood pressure, at times spending as much time in the kitchen as at the piano. Teresa remembered Bess's face when she'd created her own herb garden. It was six months into their friendship when Bess introduced Teresa to her niece Helene, thinking that they'd have a lot in common since Helene was a master herbalist, author, lecturer and owner of The Wright Herb Shop.

But the two women had little in common, although Helene did listen to some of Teresa's suggestions. They discussed little else.

Despite what people thought, Teresa hadn't known that Bess had put her in her will and that she'd get a sizable inheritance upon Bess's death. Nobody knew that Teresa would give all the money back to see Bess alive again.

Instead, some people thought that Teresa had taken advantage of Bess. That she may have pushed her down the stairs, instead of Bess collapsing after her heart attack. Others thought Teresa had convinced Bess not to take her regular medication and that may have killed her. Teresa had her own questions and suspicions. Bess shouldn't have been as sick as the coroner deemed. She hadn't sensed anything wrong. But now she doubted herself. She wanted to bring Bess back so that the whispers could stop, so that she wouldn't keep wondering where things went wrong.

She wanted her life back. She'd been a part-time herbalist and piano teacher, but after getting the inheritance, she'd been forced to stop when a number of students, and not so close friends, kept asking for loans and financial assistance.

Now she spent her time volunteering at the nursing facility. She hadn't touched any of the money yet. Wasn't sure she ever would. She didn't feel she deserved it, but couldn't reject the offer of a friend. But her concerns about Valley Ray had started with Bess and grown because of the two people at the nursing facility, but the supplement company wasn't important right now.

Teresa looked at the ambulance, hoping her cousin would be okay. She remembered the last time she'd followed an ambulance to the hospital. Only a few days later she was driving behind a hearse.

"At least she's okay," Jessie said as she, Teresa and their eldest sister Michelle, sat in Rolland's Café three days later. Jessie was treating them to lunch at a place that had once been too pricey for Teresa's budget, though Michelle had frequently visited the place. The food was always excellent and served in an atmosphere of eclectic class. The restaurant had chrome booths furnished with red cushions. Jessie's husband, Kenneth, was the CEO of a large electronics and software company and was a favorite customer, so any time she visited she was given the best booth—a place with a large window overlooking the main street that was well lit, but tinted, free from prying eyes.

After the rescue, Teresa's whole body still ached. But she didn't complain because she knew her sporty sister would just remind her that she was out of shape. She'd briefly been able to see Louisa at the hospital and speak to her aunt. "Aunt Margaret said it was just an accident," Teresa said. "But I know it wasn't."

"Didn't she get the memo?" Michelle said.

"Memo?"

"Yes, black girls don't commit suicide."

Teresa frowned. "You have a sick sense of humor."

Michelle sipped her drink without apology. "I know."

"I wonder why she did it," Jessie said.

Teresa could speculate. She could understand the deep well of loneliness that could grip someone. It had gripped her after Bess's death and nearly choked her after the death of her parents.

They'd had kids later in life, so they were an older couple. But their illness had seemed so simple. She'd cared for the family before whenever someone fell ill, so nothing warned her that that night would be different. That it would be the last time she'd speak to them. She still saw her parents in her dreams, but they never faced her, as if they blamed her too.

She'd punished herself after her parents' and Bess's deaths by never indulging in speaking about her pain. Instead she smiled. She smiled through everything. "You're the heart of the family," her father liked to tell her. "No one wants to see you sad." So no one ever did. She pretended that the rumors about Bess didn't hurt, laughed away criticism about her natural remedies and indulged her sisters' teasing about making strange potions, even when they tore at her heart.

"There was a strange man who was there," Teresa said, almost wondering if she should. "He knew her."

"That's no surprise." Jessie said with a smirk. "Louisa knows a lot of men."

"And strange men aren't hard to find," Michelle added, shaking her head. "Especially if you've ever been downtown. I actually had a homeless man try to pick me up today."

"Old George on Fifth, right?" Jessie guessed. "The man is hopeless. I once saw him propose to a nun walking past. She told him she was already married."

Michelle laughed, adjusting the napkin on her lap. "That's one husband I wouldn't want to handle."

Teresa frowned, not finding the situation funny at all. She felt sorry for poor, harmless George, who preferred the streets to the homeless shelter. Unfortunately, she didn't always understand her sisters' sense of humor. Though they were like night and day, they seemed to have more in common as time passed. Michelle, the eldest, was the queen of cool and today she looked it, dressed in an ice blue suit, tiny gold hoop earrings and sporting an emerald ring, which she wore on her right hand. Her dark brown hair was cut in a chin length bob that swung casually anytime she moved. She ran the Clifton Center for Business and Enterprise in the exclusive Winfield Building.

Jessie worked with their cousin, BJ, at Fedor Malenkov Jewelers. Unlike Michelle, Jessie had a temper that could melt a glacier. Fortunately her recent marriage had curbed some of it, but it flared up when specifically provoked. She looked casual but sporty wearing a pair of grey wool trousers and an off-white jacket.

Teresa on the other hand preferred loose skirts, bracelets and scarves to suits and sneakers. At times she wished she could be cool like Michelle with her steady calm gaze or fiery and striking like Jessie. She didn't have their signature angular features. Instead her face was soft and round like the rest of her. She loved her sisters, but felt more and more out of touch with them.

"You shouldn't laugh at George," she said.

"Why not? It's funny," Michelle replied, unapologetic.

"So tell us about this crazy guy you picked up," Jessie said.

Teresa pushed food around on her plate annoyed. "I didn't pick up a crazy guy. That's not what I meant when I said 'strange.' I meant I saw him swimming in the bay."

Jessie shivered at the thought. "In this weather? He must be crazy."

Teresa shook her head. "That's just it, he wasn't." She paused, tugging on her bracelets. "He helped me rescue Louisa. One moment he was there and then the next moment he was gone."

Michelle stirred her cream of broccoli soup. "You're not creating another fantasy, are you?"

Jessie laughed. "Check her cranberry juice. They might have slipped something in there just for fun."

"I don't create fantasies," Teresa said in a quiet voice,

knowing she couldn't tell them about how his touch had immediately calmed her. "He was real."

"Okay, we believe you," Jessie said, elbowing Michelle before she could disagree. "What did he look like?"

Michelle groaned loudly; Jessie and Teresa ignored her.

Teresa thought for a moment, bringing his image to mind. "He had a beard, curly black hair and a cream-brown body like an athlete. I couldn't see his eyes clearly, but I could feel them. He's very intense." She paused. "I think he's going to be my husband."

Jessie stopped with her sandwich halfway to her mouth; Michelle's spoonful of soup dripped back into the bowl like a leaky faucet.

Michelle was the first one to recover. She put her spoon down and leaned forward. "Could you please repeat that?"

"I think he's going to be my husband," she said.

Jessie put her sandwich down. "Have you lost your mind?"

Michelle touched Jessie's sleeve, warning her not to overreact. "What gives you the idea that this...stranger,"—she stressed the word—"Is destined to be your husband?"

"He was wearing a necklace with a charm that I know from somewhere and it means something."

"I'm sure you've seen a lot of necklaces."

Teresa shook her head. "This man was wearing an important necklace with amber stones. Healing stones. I think I saw it in one of my dreams." She couldn't yet understand why it was important, but she knew it was. She rarely ignored her hunches. "And there was an awareness that happened the moment I saw it that I've never felt before."

"It's called hormones," Michelle said in a flat voice. "You were supposed to go through this phase at thirteen."

"It's not hormones or an infatuation," Teresa said. "This man is part of my destiny."

Michelle pointed a spoon at her. "I don't want you to go to the bay by yourself anymore. There are a lot of weirdos out there and you're too fanciful."

"Dad used to take us there all the time. When I'm there I feel peaceful. Besides, I carry mace," she said patting her handbag.

"This is silly," Jessie grumbled. "The whole thing about dreams, men and destiny."

"I knew you and Kenneth would be together."

"Coincidence," she scoffed.

Michelle nodded. "Personally, I blame all those JS Braden books you've been burying yourself in. Men coming out of the water like seaweed." She sniffed, shaking her head. "Now you're suddenly engaging yourself to a man you don't know because he was wearing a necklace like someone you've seen in your dream. That sounds downright nuts. Like an acid trip."

"What do you know about acid?" Jessie asked, grinning.

"I'm just using an example to state my point."

Teresa pushed the plate away. "It wasn't just a dream." She knew it was useless to try to explain it to them. How could anyone understand how true her dreams were to her and her nightmares? How she feared evening coming when her sleep would be interrupted by nightmares so real, she would wake up sweating and trembling, unable to understand why they scared her so much. She changed the subject. "What's wrong with JS Braden books anyway?"

"They're children's fantasies and, if you remember, that's when your dreams started. Why can't you ground yourself in the mysteries of science or something else, instead of in the realm of elves, fairy princesses and the world under the Tanton Tomb?"

Teresa blinked. "How do you know about that?" she asked,

amazed that a non-Braden reader would know about the Tanton Tomb.

Michelle sighed, resigned, glancing out the window. "All right, I admit it. I read one."

Teresa leaned forward, resting her elbows on the table, eager to hear her sister's assessment. "And?"

Michelle shrugged and turned back to her. "It was a good story. So good in fact that later that evening I stood outside my window ready to fly. Convinced that the stars would come down to catch me."

"That's not fair," Jessie said, watching Teresa's face fall. "You shouldn't tease her. You read romances."

"I'm different. I know they're only fantasies and can come back to reality when necessary."

"I can too," Teresa replied.

Michelle took a sip of her drink, grinning smugly. "Remember when you prayed for a tornado to strike our house so that we could be blown to the Emerald City or," Michelle added when Teresa began to protest. "When you stared into Grandma's mirror hoping to escape through it like Alice? Soon you'll be looking at the clouds and seeing men's faces."

"I was just a kid, give me some credit," Teresa argued. "You make me sound like a lunatic."

"I'm sorry. I just don't want you developing any strange ideas about this chap, okay? There are a lot of men who wear jewelry."

"We just don't want to see you fall in love with a dream," Jessie said.

"He's not a dream," Teresa said, fighting to keep her voice pleasant.

"But he's a man and that can be just as bad," Michelle said.

"What?"

"You put your hopes and dreams on them and you'll find

yourself drowning in disillusionment. I'm not saying men aren't wonderful accessories, but they're only human after all and not Prince Charming."

"You both got your Prince Charming." Teresa looked at her younger sister who had gotten married over a year ago. "Jessie got Kenneth, a man who's successful, attractive and loves her to bits and you have James."

Michelle tucked hair behind her ear. "Unfortunately, I seemed to have misplaced him somewhere between here and Salisbury, England," she said, speaking of her estranged husband.

"I don't know how you can work in the same building his family owns," Jessie said.

"Well, they are still married," Teresa said.

"It's good for business," Michelle countered. "That's all."

"You'll get back together," Teresa said with a smile. "It's destiny. You're both being stubborn right now. If you just tell me what went wrong I could help."

"What went wrong was us, but that's not what I mean by false hopes. People rarely hit the jackpot and women like us can only have certain expectations."

Both sisters stared at her.

"What do you mean, women like us?" Teresa asked.

"There's no use trying to pretend we're like other women. Jessie got lucky that Kenneth looked past her nasty temper—"

"Hey!" Jessie said in protest.

"And unusual gift," Michelle continued. "To the woman inside."

Teresa shook her head. "It wasn't luck, it was destiny."

"Then I guess we don't have the same destiny for happy-ever-after."

"What happened with James? Could he not accept that you—"

"What I am saying," Michelle interrupted, twisting the emerald ring on her finger, "is that you have to be extra careful when it comes to men. Especially now."

Because of the money Bess left me? Do you think no man will want me for me? Teresa wanted to say, but she didn't want to argue with her so she smiled instead. "Don't worry. I will."

They changed the topic and Teresa turned to the window and watched people hurrying back and forth on the busy downtown sidewalks, unaware of her looking at them from behind the glass.

She knew her sisters were trying to protect her, but she also knew she'd felt the touch of the man who'd hold her heart forever.

CHAPTER 3

An hour later, Teresa sat in the dark, hushed interior of Fedor Malenkov Jewelers among a selection of gems, Victorian-aged pins, and an Edwardian diamond pendant, with her cousin BJ, a large man wearing a heavy canvas apron, who rarely smiled. He had beautifully made ebony features that none of the Clifton sisters had inherited. The tools of his trade sat to the side while he looked over the sketch Teresa had given him. It was of the charm she'd seen around the stranger's neck. She knew Jessie was meeting with members of the Historical Society for an upcoming event, and wouldn't be around.

"It means something doesn't it?" she asked.

"Did you ask Jessie?" he said with a note of caution.

"I'm asking you."

"It could have many meanings, but the main one seems to be a connection to Mother Earth. That's what the tree symbolizes and why the branches are created that way," he said, tracing his finger over the lines. "As if the tree and branches were one and the same. And they're connected by the small amber stones.

Healing stones." He handed the sketch back to her. "Why do you ask?"

She hesitated. Her sisters had already teased her about the stranger, she didn't want BJ doing the same.

"Do you want me to make something similar?" he asked, when she didn't reply.

"No," she said quickly not wanting him to go through the trouble. "I was just curious."

Satisfied with what BJ had told her, Teresa went shopping at The Crabapple, the local international market, to get items for dinner. It was the only international store around for miles and bordered both Randall County and the South Bank, so it was usually crowded with people hoping to get the best bargains, though most patrons knew they were getting ripped off because there were no other stores in the area to compare the prices to. (There was the specialty store in Bedford that catered to the rich, upping prices and promising exotic food, but no one was silly enough to go there). The store smelled of hot spices, dry stockfish, and plantains. The floor was usually dirty, giving the place the feeling of an outdoor market. The aisles were so skinny that one had to walk sideways to pass if someone was in the aisle, but they had the best imported food around so she didn't mind the inconvenience.

She took out her list and began strolling through the aisles, smiling at familiar faces. Despite last year's scandal that involved her sister's husband, Kenneth, his battered reputation had rebounded and his name still held weight in the community, particularly in the Caribbean community, which held him in high esteem, and her status had improved simply by association.

Teresa was looking at some melon seeds when she saw the man from the bay enter the store. The normally noisy atmosphere suddenly grew hush as everyone watched him walk towards an aisle. Newcomers were closely scrutinized. In their community it was important to know where everyone stood. Whether he was eligible for the local ladies to marry or a good business associate, or of no consequence.

"South Bank," someone muttered and the interest disappeared like fog. To be from South Bank always warranted a quick dismissal.

The South Bank was really Hamilton County. It was smaller than Randall County and poor, people referred to it by its nickname. Their mother and father would drive Teresa and her sisters there every once in a while to volunteer at the shelter. Teresa was always fascinated by the single lane roads, large trees and tiny pillbox houses that all looked the same in their private misery. The main street used to be a bustling place full of businesses, little shops, and restaurants. Unfortunately, poor management and the promise of success in the neighboring town killed the possibility of growth. Now, most of the buildings were boarded up while owners went to find their fortunes elsewhere. The only buildings that thrived were the churches, the bars and what was called a library but was really a grocery store with books.

The one savior had been the Valley Ray company that had become the biggest employer, but economic recovery remained slow.

The stranger seemed oblivious to the attention and ultimate dismissal warranted him, and walked around the shop, towering over the aisles like a giant. He was dressed in worn jeans and a red flannel shirt, his heavy black boots kicked up dust. He paused in front of the vegetable and fruit section and stared intently at the selection of papayas.

"That's that mountain man, isn't it?" Teresa heard a woman whisper next to her. Teresa recognized the woman as Camille

Faulkner. Teresa inwardly groaned. Camille probably knew who the man was, but asked just to start gossiping, an activity Teresa didn't wish to engage in. Since Teresa didn't respond, Camille's sister, Anna, spoke up.

"Looks like it, doesn't it? He lives in that big, ugly house in South Bank with people living on his property like squatters."

"I wonder what he's doing here." Her voice rose to a scandalous whisper. "I've heard he's got Irish in him you know."

"Yes, got a funny accent."

Teresa wanted to point out the Trinidadian accent they had yet to lose.

"He's single, but won't look at any of the women here," Camille said.

"Thank goodness. You know just a drop of Irish means he probably spends most of his money and time in a bar," her sister replied.

"Yes, and we know Jamaican men can drink."

"Hmm, looks like he's got some Indian in him too, and you know their taste for liquor."

The women laughed.

Teresa gritted her teeth. She knew the women were speaking loud enough so that he could hear. She glanced towards him. His face could barely be seen behind the surrounding facial hair, but she could feel his eyes. Hard, glittering eyes. He could hear what the women were saying and they were bothering him. Suddenly he looked straight at her, as if he was sending her a message, in her heart she could feel his pain as if they were attacking her as well. He quickly looked away, but Teresa couldn't ignore the awareness that had transpired between them. It made her even more certain of her feelings for him. She felt the weight of their inexplicable connection grow stronger. He was the man for her and she'd protect him.

"You know it's funny that you should talk about bars," Teresa said. "How's my elixir working for your mother's hangovers?" It was known that Mrs. Faulkner liked to toy with rum.

Camille turned a cold eye towards her. "So the witch is going to stand up for the mountain man, how sweet. I'm surprised a rich woman like you still shops here."

Some residents called her a 'witch' because of her interest in herbs and visions. It didn't bother her, but it made some people uncomfortable. Teresa decided to use that to her advantage. "You know, it's not wise to anger someone like me." She bent down and picked up some dust from the ground and rubbed it between her fingers then began muttering gibberish under her breath.

Camille and Anna's eyes widened. They dropped their baskets and then ran out of the store screaming.

Teresa smiled to herself then dropped the dust on the ground, wiping her hands together.

"You shouldn't do that," Bertha Walker said. She was Teresa's best friend and mentor. She wore a large purple turban on her head as if to add height to her small frame. Like Teresa, she earned the nickname of witch, but held reverence in the community for her wisdom and foresight. Before Teresa had been seen as her apprentice, but now people weren't so sure. Bertha was an older woman who shared her love of books, tea, cooking and visions. Bertha took out a handkerchief and began cleaning Teresa's hands as if she were five years old. "You only feed their suspicions."

Teresa winked. "Sometimes that comes in handy."

Bertha tucked the handkerchief away. "Be careful there."

Teresa could still feel the man's eyes on her, as heavy as a hand on the back of her neck, but she didn't turn to look at him. She picked up a bag of melon seeds and tossed them in her cart. When she did turn around, he was gone from view.

"There's no need to stand up for him," Bertha said. "You know who he is, don't you?"

"No." She glanced around the store, trying to find him again, but he was nowhere to be found.

"That's the problem. Nobody does. Half the people think he's on parole after being involved with a Jamaican gang. Another half believe he's part of an Irish mob and his headquarters is that strange house he lives in. It's also said that he's a regular at Louisa's place."

Teresa heard the warning Bertha wouldn't voice. Anyone associated with her cousin was usually bad news. She felt her heart constrict with an unexpected pain. It wouldn't be a surprise. Louisa was fun and beautiful, men falling for her charm was expected. But her heart couldn't let her heed her friend's warning.

"I know he knows her and the rest..." She shrugged. "They're just rumors. I know you don't believe them. What's the truth?" she asked, knowing Bertha could see what others couldn't.

Bertha thought for a moment, pursing her lips. "He's mysterious, but his heart is good. However, he has a cloud over his head, the signal of bad news."

"I know."

Bertha looked at her surprised. "You do?"

"I sensed it when he touched me and that's never happened before. He's important to me."

"How?"

"I'm not completely sure, but I plan to find out."

Bertha shook her head. "Remember you may be sorry for the *mawga* dog, but he can turn 'round and bite you."

"He has the hands of a healer."

"And the body of a thug."

"Bertha," Teresa warned in a hushed tone.

"He can't hear me. Have you noticed the size of him?"

"He's not dangerous."

"You don't know that yet. You only had a sense, not the full story." She narrowed her eyes. "And you've been up to something else, haven't you?"

Teresa sighed. "I confronted Helene about the supplements."

"And?"

"It wasn't a good meeting, but I sent three bottles to a friend who works at the university. I trust him and will wait to hear what he has to say."

"Then let it go. Power and money are dangerous opponents."

BERTHA DID NOT LIKE to act feeble. She took pride in being fit and agile. She'd planned to walk the two miles back home, but knew that she would not catch the young man's attention any other way than by showing a strain of weakness. She spotted him in the parking lot and hurried towards him, then debated how she would collapse without injuring herself or damaging her purchases. She decided it was best not to fall, but rather to stagger helplessly into him. In the past, she'd seen a number of young women try collapsing at his feet at the shop, but he had offered them a quick glance and walked away. She suspected that his heart may be more receptive to a tired woman several decades his senior.

She was about to bump into him, when a tricky celestial elf decided to put a stone in her path, so when she fell, her cry was real, as was the impact of pain that followed.

The man was immediately by her side. "Mother," he said using a reverential term only pockets of their community used. "Are you all right?"

Bertha was still stunned by the authenticity of her fall, perhaps someone above knew better than she. "Yes, I think so. Oh, my bags." The contents had been scattered, mingling with the dirt and gravel.

"Gather those for me," he ordered a passing bystander. "Stay still for a moment, please." The 'please' was added for appearance since his words held enough of a command. He expertly felt all her limbs and studied her eyes. "Okay. Come on." He helped her to her feet then lifted her up and placed her on the back of his truck as if she were a child. "Thank you," he said to the man who handed him Bertha's bags. He glanced inside and frowned. "I'm afraid your purchases didn't survive the fall."

"Oh, that's all right—" she began, but the young man wasn't listening. He pulled out a handkerchief. "Use this to wipe the side of your face. I'll be right back," he said, then left carrying her two bags of squashed groceries.

He was gone before she could reply. Bertha wiped the side of her face, smiling to herself. Just what she had expected—he had a heart as soft as guava jelly so he kept it well guarded, except to seemingly feeble old women. She ran her hand over the rim of the truck. It was old but well-kept, that was a good sign. She stretched her back, wincing in pain. She had fallen harder than her old body was used to, and she would have to tend to her bruises once she got home. She slid down from the truck.

"Just where do you think you're going?" the man asked, returning with two brown bags.

"I've taken up enough of your time."

"Nonsense." He placed her bags in the truck. "Come on, Mother, I'll take you home. The people in the shop know you well and told me where you live."

"Yes, they know me, but I don't know you."

"True." He turned back to the store.

"Where are you going?" she asked him.

"To tell them who to blame if you go missing."

Bertha laughed. "Never mind. You can take me home," she said. She needed to know more about the man who'd caught Teresa's interest. Teresa was her heart and Bertha still remembered their first meeting more than twenty years ago. It had been a spring day and Bertha had been filling up her basket for a lunch with friends when she happened to look down and see a little girl with gentle brown eyes and a big grin. The little girl clasped her hands together and gazed up at her as if she'd just been given a pony for her birthday. "You look just like you did in my dream!" she said, then hugged her.

Bertha looked down at the child, not knowing what to do.

A well-dressed woman approached them. "I'm so sorry she—"

The girl looked to her. "Mummy, it's her. Isn't she beautiful?"

Bertha had never been called beautiful in her life, but knew that the child saw something no one else did. She was special, one who could see into the fourth-dimensional realm. They'd been friends ever since. Although Teresa herself was far from beautiful, she wasn't quite plain either. She had a gentle prettiness that most people overlooked, rarely seeing past her cocoa brown skin, full figure, large hoop earrings and bracelets to the gem she truly was. Teresa was a gem Bertha planned to protect. Teresa had skills, but Bertha knew she was still too young to depend solely on them. And when it came to men, she hadn't been tried yet.

Bertha allowed the stranger to help her into the passenger side of the truck and buckle her seat belt. When he got into the driver's seat he stared at her. "You look fine to me, but perhaps you should see a physician."

"Aren't I looking at one?"

There was the slight hint of a smile. "Perhaps you need a second opinion."

"Oh, no. I trust your judgment. Besides, a good soak will do me good."

He flashed her a surprisingly cynical grin then nodded.

He was a good driver. He handled the road and the truck in a masterful manner, but somehow his thoughts seemed somewhere else. She thought of asking him questions, but knew it was too soon to get the answers she wanted. She knew that she would have to prolong their visit together and if she read him correctly, he wouldn't mind.

"Here we are," he announced as he drove up to her house. She loved her green and white rambler. It was situated far enough away from her neighbors to avoid their gossiping and inquisitive eyes, but close enough to town. Its little shutters and door smiled at her every time she arrived home.

The young man helped her down.

"Would you mind putting my groceries away while I make tea?" she asked, as he retrieved her packages from the back.

He stared at the house a moment then turned to her with a wary expression, causing Bertha to wonder if he suspected what she was up to. He finally said, "I hope you don't make it a habit of inviting strange men into your home."

"I let them drive me home, don't I?"

He smiled. "Fair enough." He glanced at the house again and nodded. "I just hope this isn't common."

"I haven't lived this long without some common sense. Come on."

The swiftness with which he grabbed her bags hinted at an eagerness to help. She sensed it as both a strength and a weakness.

His mouth fell open when she walked to the front door and easily turned the knob.

"Don't you lock it?" he asked.

"Never had a need to."

He frowned but said no more.

He stepped through the door and glanced with appreciation at what he saw. His gaze briefly fell on a colorful array of plants, glass jars and quilted pillows. He didn't offer the obligatory compliment of her home, but kept his observations to himself. Bertha led him into the kitchen. She went to get the kettle and tripped over a loose tile. "I'm a klutz today," she muttered, embarrassed.

"It's not you. The tiles weren't put down properly. I'll come by one day and fix them for you. Sit down. I'll make the tea."

"I'll set the table," she said firmly. She would not allow him to order her about in her own home, no matter how kind his intentions.

He smiled indulgently. "Go ahead then."

She went to the hutch in her dining room and studied the array of tea sets. She decided to use her most delicate tea set— porcelain with twenty-four carat gold accents—just to test him. This set had put many people on edge with its tiny handles and petite elegance. She laid the setting out and waited. He didn't even blink at the elaborate tea setting. He poured her tea and milk and held the tea cup in his large hands as comfortably as he would a baseball, at times rubbing his fingers over the intricate designs as if trying to remember them by touch. There was no awkwardness in his movements. As their conversation progressed, she soon concluded that this was no ordinary man. He was well-mannered, educated, and kind. So what made him shun everyone's attention? She was thinking of how to broach the subject when he spoke.

"So who was that woman who was with you at the market?"

Bertha stared at him for a moment.

"The one who thinks she's a witch," he clarified.

She laughed at the description. "Oh, you noticed my little friend, did you?"

"Beautiful women are hard to miss," he said with casual boredom.

Bertha looked at him sharply. He thought Teresa was beautiful? Few men could see that. And he wasn't bad looking himself, she suspected he had plenty of female attention. "Why do you ask? Did she make you uncomfortable?"

"No, should she?"

"It was an innocent question."

A slight, hard smile touched his lips. "I don't think there's anything innocent about you, Mother."

"And yet you still came."

He nodded.

"Why?"

"Because I know what you are."

"And it doesn't frighten you?"

He poured more hot water into his tea cup. "I thought people like you had all the answers."

"Then you really don't know anything."

"I respect you, Mother, I'm just weary of your sort."

"Yet you have the gift to recognize me with just a touch. Few people do."

"Oh yes, 'the gift'." He took a sip of his tea then set it down. "It hasn't done me much good." He sat back. "Is she like you too?"

"Can't you tell?"

"No."

Bertha wasn't sure she believed him, but there was a note of uncertainty in his tone that hadn't been there before. Perhaps what Teresa had sensed he'd felt it too? "Again, you'll have to ask her."

"I don't want to."

"Afraid?"

He laughed without humor. "Terrified," he said, then stood. "I'd better go."

"If you're not careful, the darkness will kill you."

He held her gaze. "Is that a promise?"

Bertha shook her head. "You're too young to toy with such thoughts."

"But I feel as old as the beginning of time." He glanced at his watch. "I'd better be going," he said, clearing the table, then he grabbed a pen and paper and scribbled something down. "Here's my name and phone number. If you need help just ring. Night or day never hesitate to call."

For the sake of my loneliness or yours? she wanted to say, but knew better to keep her thoughts to herself. "Thank you."

"Goodbye Mother. Thanks for the tea."

He nodded and Bertha watched him leave with a smile until he was out of sight. Then she let her smile fall.

CHAPTER 4

Louisa set down the plate of roasted chicken and rice on the table and swallowed hard. The rice looked like soggy maggots swimming in slime. She swallowed again, feeling a wave of nausea sweep over her. She couldn't afford to be sick. She needed this job. At least for a couple more weeks. She gulped some air and forced a smile at the customer, a man with ruddy cheeks and beefy hands, letting him pinch her ass. It was normal, expected. Men wanted a good time at Hot Hannah's Sugar Shack, where the food was hot, but the ladies were hotter. It offered casual dining and was a place of tight T-shirts and short skirts, wooden floors and rocking music. She felt her stomach turn again and prayed it would settle. Hell, it was six in the evening, why did they call it morning sickness when she felt sick nearly all the time?

Thankfully, it wasn't a full night, so she left the table and went outside, grabbed a can of ginger ale and felt her stomach return to normal. She raced into one of the bathroom stalls, lifted up her shirt and pulled down her skirt to adjust her shape wear and the makeshift bandage to keep her changing figure in place.

Taping down her stomach wasn't going to be easy soon and damn it hurt. She let the bandage give, allowing herself to breathe without the restraint. Her figure was one of the things that helped her get the job, and once she lost it, she knew she'd lose the job too and she couldn't. Not yet. She rested her head against the wall of the stall and closed her eyes.

If things had turned out differently, she wouldn't even be in this mess. She'd had to lie at the hospital, remembering telling them that she'd just fallen on some rocks, and no, she hadn't tried to commit suicide. She didn't want to be monitored by the staff and she couldn't let her parents know. Part of her had hoped that the shock to her body would have gotten rid of the problem for her. But it hadn't. She had to think of something else. But right now she just had to get through the night.

Louisa left the stall and washed her hands then stared at herself in the mirror and fixed her makeup. She was a survivor and she'd survive this.

The bathroom door opened and a pretty redhead with enough curves to make the men drool sauntered in. "Thought I'd find you here," she said.

"Why?" Louisa asked, putting her lipstick away.

"Dave's looking for you."

Dave Pearsall looked like the kind of man better suited for Wall Street than as the manager of a greasy spoon in an overlooked county. Not that he looked rich, although his haircuts weren't done locally, he just carried himself like a man who knew more than most. He was of average height with polished shoes and dark hair slicked back over a bald spot no one dared look at or mention. Louisa sat in his office, which reflected the man, showing pictures of high rises and a quotation and photo of Donald Trump on the wall.

He fixed her with a hard stare, but she wasn't disturbed by it. He looked at everyone that way. She started to cross her legs then thought better of it and waited.

"You disappointed me, Louisa," he said, and to her surprise he sounded sincere.

Louisa blinked, feeling her heartbeat race. "What?"

"You got knocked up, didn't you?"

She froze. How could he know? She hadn't told anyone. She thought of lying, but she knew he was good at spotting girls when they were in that state. She had to think fast. "What do you want?"

"You know why I hired you."

"I still look good."

"Maybe, but I can't have your face turning green when a guy is smiling at you. He may take it personally and it's just bad for business. I made the rules clear. There's no maternity leave. You're out."

"I just need a couple more weeks."

"No."

"But I hardly show."

"You show enough. If men wanted to see the wide ass of a pregnant chick, they'd stay home with their wives."

"This isn't fair."

Dave's face spread into a cold smile. "What are you going to do? Sue me? Have you read your contract?" He pulled out his checkbook and filled one out. "I'll give you two weeks." He tore the check out and handed it to her. "And that's being generous."

She stared at it.

"Don't be too proud."

She inwardly swore, then took it.

"Does the father know?"

She tucked the check inside her pocket. "I didn't realize you cared."

"I don't, I'm just glad it's not mine."

She stood then blew him a kiss, flashing a rude gesture. "Me too."

Louisa left his office and got into her car, then rested her head on the steering wheel. It wasn't supposed to end up like this. She'd planned it all so carefully. She'd hoped she'd found the perfect reason to get him to finally leave his wife. She wouldn't have to share him anymore and he wouldn't have to feel trapped. She remembered the eagerness with which she'd shown him the sonogram.

"What's this?" he asked not out of ignorance, but curiosity. He was in a good mood after making love and held her close. They were in their regular hotel room.

"Our baby," she said.

He sat up. "Our what?"

"I'm pregnant."

"No, you're not."

"Yes, I am."

"How long have you known?"

"Long enough. This is the out you needed. So you can leave your wife and we can be together."

He slapped her hard across the face and looked at her in a way that he'd never looked at her before. As if she repulsed him. "You dumb bitch. You think I'd risk knocking up a piece of trash like you? How do I know it's mine?"

"Because I haven't been with anyone else. You'll have to take care of us or I'll make you pay."

But although her words were bold, the pain lingered, consumed her as she drove to Catlon Bay the next morning and as she looked at the waters and realized that he didn't love her. How could he not love her when she loved him so much? She remembered sinking into nothingness, then waking up in an ambulance. Part of her hoping he'd materialize by her bedside and tell her how sorry he was. Tell her that he didn't mean it and that he'd take care of her and their baby. Worship her for giving him the family he'd always wanted. Didn't he say that she was the only one who truly understood him? That his wife never made him feel the way she did? But he hadn't come and he hadn't returned any of her calls. There had to be another way to get him back. He did love her. She had to believe it or life truly wasn't worth living.

TERESA STARED at the report in shock. The supplements made by Valley Ray contained exactly what they claimed. She sat in the empty chemistry lab of her friend Dr. Wallace Knox at the local university.

"Nothing?" she asked, just to make sure.

"Nope. I think you're barking up the wrong tree."

"But I was certain."

"I could do another test if you want."

"No, you did enough. I'm sorry I wasted your time," Teresa said, suddenly feeling foolish about her suspicions. She'd befriended him while a student and had kept in touch after graduation. He had a trim goatee, lanky frame and large glasses. She always had to stop herself from asking if he'd eaten. But now she didn't care about food. She was wrong.

"Valley Ray is a solid company," he said, although those weren't the words she'd wanted to hear.

"I guess so."

"I thought you'd be pleased."

"I can't believe I was so wrong."

"It happens to the best of us."

She nodded and left.

Wallace wasn't surprised when his cell phone rang a few minutes later. "Well?" the female voice demanded on the other end.

"I did what you told me."

"I knew she wouldn't listen. At least she's predictable."

"I won't do this again. Next time I'll check for real."

The woman laughed. "You want to negotiate for more?"

"I mean it. I don't like faking tests, no matter how harmless."

"Don't start developing a conscience now, you already sold it to me."

CHAPTER 5

Nothing was wrong? She didn't want to believe it, but now she had to. That night sleep came slowly then when she did dream it was unsettling. She saw the stranger and the bay was a lake of amber.

"Who are you?" she asked him.

"You know who I am."

She shook her head. "I don't," she said then he seemed to fade away. She reached for him, but he disappeared. In an instant she found herself standing in a cemetery in front of her parents' resting place. She saw a tombstone next to them with no markings. Then she saw him again, except he sat on top of the headstone, gossamer and translucent as a ghost. "I like it here," he said.

"You're too young."

"I may be alive, but my heart is buried down there." He pointed to the ground. "So deep that no one can reach it."

"Why are you telling me this?"

"Because you can't save me any more than you could have saved them."

She saw a couple in the distance. She called out to them, but they kept their backs to her. Why wouldn't they look at her?

"I'm sorry!" she said. "Please forgive me. Just look at me once. Just once. Please!" but they kept walking away and no matter how much she ran she couldn't reach them.

Teresa woke up in tears. She'd been wrong about the supplements and she'd been wrong about Bess and her parents. Was she wrong about the stranger too? Had she imagined what she'd felt?

She went to Hollow Cove the next morning, telling herself that she wasn't looking for the mysterious stranger, that she was there to relax as always. However, she was disappointed when he didn't show up. The morning was warmer than last, but she still buttoned up her wool coat and tugged on her gloves. She went closer to the edge of the bank and gazed out at the water, almost willing him to appear as he had before. She watched the waves claw their way up the bank and kiss the toes of her shoe. She waited, but the man never showed. She sighed, staring up at the sky.

"Let me hazard a guess," a deep voice said behind her. "You're looking for me,"

Teresa spun around, and stared up into the face of the mysterious stranger. The light morning wind brushed the black curls from his forehead and he loomed over her like a willow tree. He was taller than she had remembered. Teresa found herself taking a step back to get a full view. His hand shot out and grabbed her arm, pulling her to him. She stiffened feeling a shock of awareness that was more potent than before. He hadn't even touched her skin; it didn't make sense. He immediately let go.

"I don't think you want to ruin another skirt," he said, gesturing to the waves.

"Oh." She glanced over her shoulder, seeing how close she had come to stepping in the water. Heat touched her cheeks. She usually wasn't so awkward and clearly he didn't feel anything. "Thanks."

He shrugged. She noticed that today he was not dressed to swim. He had on his same worn jeans and a bulky grey sweater that gave him the appearance of a fisherman.

"You haven't answered my question."

"Am I looking for you?"

He nodded.

There was no reason to lie. "Uh...yes."

He laughed briefly, not pleasantly. "At least you're honest, I didn't expect that. Come on then."

Teresa hesitated, staring at his back as he went up the incline. "You might as well come on," he called over his shoulder. "And satisfy your curiosity."

She wrapped her coat tighter around herself and followed, trying to keep her heart in check, although it felt as if it would beat out of her chest. He led her up the rocky path to a place that afforded them a beautiful view of the rising sun, peering over the bay. His cat was waiting for him. He gave it a quick pat, mumbling something under his breath. He spread out an old moth-eaten blanket and sat down, stretching out his long legs. He reached for a can of soda from a picnic basket he'd brought.

Teresa eyed the blanket, hoping that it wasn't crawling with insects she'd unsuspectingly take home with her. After a moment's hesitation, she finally decided to sit down. The cat stared at her for a few seconds with curious green eyes, then crawled into her lap.

"He likes you," the man said in a bored tone. "Unlike me, he seems to like people."

Teresa stroked the cat; it immediately began to purr. "What's his name?"

"Mist. He adopted me a couple of weeks ago. Just showed up on my doorstep."

"Oh." Teresa looked down at the contented cat, whose eyes were closed. The purring grew louder. "I've always wanted a cat."

"Hmm." He pushed the basket towards her. "Help yourself."

She took a can of soda and tried to pop the top, but it was difficult with her gloves on. She was about to take them off when the man took the can from her and opened it.

"Thanks," she said when he handed it back to her. She took a sip, then set it down. "Thanks for helping me the other day with Louisa."

He shrugged.

"I'm glad she's okay."

He shrugged again then looked away.

She took another sip, wondering what else to say. She knew what she wanted to say. *Are you seeing Louisa? Do you know what really happened? Do you feel this strange connection between us?* But she kept silent, searching her mind for something safe.

"What's your name, then?" he asked, watching her.

"Teresa. Teresa Clifton." She held out her hand to shake his.

He glanced at the hand then shook his head frowning. "I don't believe in shaking hands. It gives people a false sense of friendship."

Teresa withdrew her hand, embarrassed. "Oh." She cleared her throat. "So what's your name?"

"Sean Casey."

"Nice to meet you."

His eyes swept over her face in a hooded gaze, then he looked away. "We'll see about that." He took a gulp of his soda and set it down. "So, Teresa Clifton, why did you stand up for me the other day at the store when you don't even know me?"

Teresa was slow to reply, too caught up in his voice to pay attention. He had a surprisingly beautiful voice. A stark contrast to his rough appearance. She hadn't noticed it before. His voice was low, soft and lyrical with a Jamaican/Irish lilt. Teresa found herself straining, waiting to hear the musical cadence of his voice again, which seemed to wash over her like a morning hymn.

She took another small sip of her soda. "I beg your pardon?"

He repeated the question.

Because I think you're wonderful. "I don't know. It just seemed like the right thing to do."

He unwrapped a sandwich, quirking a questioning eyebrow at her.

She shook her head.

He nodded and finished the sandwich in four bites then grabbed an apple. He turned to rest on his side. "I'm not worth it."

"Not worth what?"

"Not worth getting in trouble over. It'd be best to try and keep your friends instead of standing up for strangers."

Teresa stared at her soda can. "They're not my friends," she said in a tight voice.

His mouth spread into a wide grin, displaying strong, white teeth. "Ah, I guess I did you a favor, then. You should thank me."

She sipped her drink, saying nothing, beginning to regret she had said anything. But she could feel his gaze and welcomed it. She'd taken care that morning and hoped he noticed her expensive wool coat, which complemented her brown skin, polished shoes and large gold hoop earrings. Her hair was pulled back in a ponytail and the wind toyed with the fringe on her forehead. "So you're the local witch, then?" he said. "I've never seen a witch up close before."

"I'm not a witch."

"You just like to pretend that you're one?"

She didn't reply. What's the use of explaining it to him? He wouldn't understand.

He bit into his apple and looked out at the bay. A few moments later he asked, "So why were you looking for me?"

"To thank you."

"And?"

"And?"

He kept his gaze averted. "I know you have another reason," he said in a low voice.

She swallowed. "Curiosity," she said, hoping the depth of her feelings for him didn't reflect in her voice.

"Yes, it seems I've raised the curiosity of a lot of people." His voice deepened with irritation. "Well, I'm harmless, I'm not here to rape any women, steal any children or rob any men. I just want to be left alone." He rested back on his elbows and stared at the sky. "I'll give you the chance to ask me three questions."

"Only three?"

He sent her a cool look. "I could make it two."

"Okay." She thought for a moment. "Where do you come from?"

"My mother."

She frowned. "That's no answer."

He slanted her a sly glance. "Next question."

She chewed her lower lip. "Why did you move here?"

"To live."

"Are you always so exasperating?"

"Yes." He abruptly stood. "Now with your curiosity satisfied, I suggest you leave me alone."

"No." She said the word quietly, but the reaction was the same.

Sean's eyebrows shot up in disbelief, giving her a good look at his eyes. They were undoubtedly his most compelling feature, hazel with a hint of innocence. It was then that Teresa knew she would never be afraid of him. He was the one. With every encounter it became more real to her. At first she had put his age as late forties, but seeing him now, she dropped his age considerably. She briefly wondered from what or whom he was hiding.

"What was that you said?" he asked.

She stared up at him. "I said no."

He folded his arms. "I'm being nice to you right now. Do you want that to change?"

"It won't."

"Why not?"

"Because I know why you don't like to shake hands."

A series of expressions crossed his face—surprise, fear then anger. "You don't know anything about me."

"I know you—"

He pointed at her in warning. "Say it just once and I'll make you regret it."

She stared, surprised by the vehemence of his tone. "But I'm—"

"Stay away from me."

He began to walk away.

"What about your things?" she asked, indicating the basket, blanket and sleeping cat.

"I'll come back and get them when you're gone," he called over his shoulder.

Teresa turned back to the items, sighing in defeat. She hadn't learned anything about him except that he had vulnerable eyes, denied his gift and was as irritating as a rash. It was her own fault for seeking him out, she reasoned. He didn't pretend to be anything he wasn't. She lifted Mist off her lap, placed him on the ground despite his protesting cry and then stood up, ready to leave as well. She folded the blanket and rested it against the basket. She was about to go when she noticed the picnic basket was open. Just what did a man like Sean Casey bring on a picnic? Mist watched her as if reading her thoughts.

"I'm just curious," she said. "I'm not going to steal anything."

Mist gave the best imitation of a cat's shrug and turned away.

Teresa knelt next to the basket and lifted the lid. There was nothing remarkable inside: three sandwiches, apples and oranges, crackers and cheese, and sodas. Either he ate a lot or he had suspected that he would meet her again. He knew. Why fight it? He was probably somewhere watching her right now like a scientist proving an experiment. She glanced over her shoulder, but didn't see anyone. She shrugged, it was too late to worry now. Underneath the food, she saw wood and carving tools. She took one small piece of wood out and saw that it was beginning to form the shape of a flute. So he liked to carve things and was perhaps musical. Hmmm....She closed the basket, feeling unfulfilled, instead of finding answers she only had more questions.

"You know who I am," he'd said in her dream.

"No, I don't," she said to herself as she stood.

Then she heard it before she saw it. The roar of an engine. She turned and saw a car weaving out of control and headed right for her.

CHAPTER 6

Teresa froze, then felt as if she'd been hit by a brick wall. She heard the sound of metal being crushed, the smell of burning rubber. It took her a moment to realize that she hadn't been hit by the car, but rather tackled by Sean.

"Are you all right?" he asked.

"Yes."

He quickly looked her over as if assessing to see if she was lying, then turned to the car, which was lodged against a tree it had struck. She followed him.

Sean grabbed the man out of the car, felt for a pulse, then pulled out his cell phone and dialed 911. She heard him relate the man's vitals to the woman over the phone, while she surveyed the situation. She didn't smell alcohol.

She touched the man's hand and sensed that the crash wasn't the problem. "He's suffering from an allergic reaction."

"What?"

"We have to do something or he won't make it by the time help arrives."

"Why do you—"

"Help me find an EpiPen!" she said in no mood to argue. She searched his pockets but came up empty. She raced over to the car and searched inside. She saw a bottle of water and a bag of trail mix, but nothing else. She opened the glove compartment and saw papers and a bottle of vitamin supplements from Valley Ray and then her gaze fell on what she was looking for. Before closing the glove compartment, she tucked the bottle away in her coat pocket, then returned to Sean with the EpiPen.

He unzipped the man's trousers and administered the EpiPen directly in the man's outer thigh. Slowly the man came to. Sean kept his voice calm and professional as he told the man to keep still while he asked him some questions.

Teresa noticed that Sean looked over the man with an expertise the average person didn't have. The quick questions, the detached assessment; she knew he was a doctor, but not a general practitioner. He had a specialty.

The sound of sirens soon pierced the air and she stepped back to let the medics take over.

"How did you know?" Sean asked her as the ambulance raced away.

"About what?"

"The reaction."

"Why aren't you practicing anymore?"

He just stared at her.

She nodded and smiled. "Right, you have your secrets and I have mine."

THE CRAMPED ROOM in the back of the police station smelled like cigarette smoke and dark fudge. She knew it was a smoke-free facility so she wondered if she'd caught Detective Hartnett after his break. Unfortunately, if he'd had a break, it hadn't improved his mood. He greeted her with polite disinterest as he sat behind his desk, dwarfing his chair. He was big, not fat, just large with a touch of silver at the temples of his short-cropped hairstyle. He stared at her with all the interest of a man forced to attend a knitting competition.

"It's very important that someone investigate what is going on there," Teresa said after she explained the situation about the two women at the nursing facility and the man at the bay. "This is the third person, I believe."

"You believe? You mean there's no proof."

She put the Valley Ray supplement bottles on the table. "People have gotten sick."

He glanced at the bottles, making no move to inspect them. "We haven't heard any complaints. It's flu season that's what happens. People take different remedies. Some work and others don't. They're not doing anything illegal."

"It's very important that the lab check to see the levels—"

"We'll look into it."

She knew he wouldn't and she couldn't force him. Perhaps she could persuade him with some sympathy. She saw a jar of aspirin on the side of his desk and could tell by his eyes and the absent rubbing of his temple what his current trouble was. "You can ease tension headaches with the essential oils of sweet marjoram. It's applied topically, so you won't have to worry about it upsetting your system."

She saw a hint of interest, then it quickly disappeared. "I'll remember that."

Teresa took a deep breath, she knew their meeting was over. "Thank you for your time."

He nodded. "Of course."

She sighed then left.

Detective Hartnett watched her go, wishing he had time for another cigarette. He left the room and went to the front desk. "Who the hell put her through to me?"

"She was insistent," the front clerk said.

"So what?"

That was the problem with some of the newbies. They didn't know how the office worked. They acted as if they served the public like some damn restaurant. Instead, they sent in people who just wasted his time. The police department had done a stupid campaign to polish their image with the community, and held diversity training so that the officers could better interact with the immigrant community. Of course, life would be a whole lot easier if the damn immigrant community understood how things worked in America instead of forcing his officers to change their ways to make the foreigners feel more comfortable. His family had been part of this soil for centuries. His ancestors had arrived by ship after being kidnapped then stacked in boats like sardines. There had been no special privileges for them and they had survived and thrived. He cared about law and order, he didn't care about creating good feelings and he wasn't interested in made up concerns when there were burglaries and murders that took up most of his time.

He'd had some of his men having to focus on stupid stuff like illegal rituals—hell if you're going to use a poor chicken as a sacrifice at least clean up the head after you finished using it—and he remembered a guy from another town having to educate some people about not killing chipmunks for consumption. Fortunately he didn't have to interact too much with those 'straight off the boat'. He knew immigrants' ways were strange and didn't want anything to do with them.

She was one of them. He could spot one a mile away, from the strange cadence of her speech to the way she talked about

herbs as if they were magical cures. If people didn't want to go to
a licensed doctor and wanted to take the risk with some quack,
that was their business. But he sensed her two little bottles had
trouble written all over them. It was part of his job to be suspicious of everything—especially big business. However, that didn't
mean he wanted to do anything about it. He didn't want to see
her again, she didn't know what she could be sniffing around and
he didn't want to educate her. "If she comes back here, come up
with an excuse."

He turned and pointed to another officer. "Follow me," he
said then walked back into his office and pointed to the bottles on
the table. "Get rid of these."

"Yes, sir."

"And make sure they disappear."

CHAPTER 7

"Do I look crazy to you?" Teresa asked her sister Michelle later that day. They still shared the same family house they'd grown up in.

"Of course not," Michelle said from the living room. She was still dressed for work, drinking coffee and looking over a new business venture.

"I know that police officer thinks I am. Nobody is taking me seriously. No, that's wrong. Dr. Knox said nothing was wrong, but it's still bothering me."

"What?"

"The Valley Ray supplements. I had him test them and he said they were fine. And then this man had an accident and I know it was an allergic reaction to something—"

"Actually, something, you're not certain. You can't make these kind of allegations without direct proof."

"You think I'm crazy."

Michelle nodded. "Yes, if you think you can convince people just because you 'sensed' something then you've lost your mind."

"Do you believe me?"

"What is there to believe? Yes, I know you have a gift, but that's not enough."

"You don't take me seriously. Nobody really does. Do you think I pushed Bess down the stairs too?"

"That's not fair."

"I know what I feel."

"So what? Being frustrated and angry about it will not change what people think."

Teresa rested her hands on her hips. "And people think I'm weak and simple and naïve."

"No, I don't—"

"I have to do something daring. I have to be strong. I have to do something really daring, at least for me."

Michelle put her papers in her briefcase. "Like what? Jumping in the bay like the man you think you'll one day marry to see what the experience is like?" Michelle paused as a light entered her sister's eyes. She grew nervous. Teresa only got that glint when she was up to something. "Wait, that was sarcasm."

"But it's a good idea. That's not something you'd ever think I'd do. It's something a daring woman would."

"It's stupid."

"No, it's not." Teresa stood up ready for action. "I'm tired of people like Helene and that police officer looking down their noses at me. I'm going to do this to prove to myself that I'm not afraid. That I can take chances. I'm not crazy. I know what I feel. Life is to be lived with courage and not fear," Teresa said, pacing back and forth as she thought about how she would pull it off.

"What?" Michelle asked, not understanding Teresa's train of thought.

Teresa stopped in the middle of the living room and stared at her sister. "Would you come with me?"

"Absolutely not."

"Fine, then I'll call, Jessie." She grabbed the phone. "I'm sure she'll understand."

Michelle frowned. "This is crazy. Jessie won't agree to trying to impress people who don't even matter. No one will see you."

Teresa grinned as she dialed. "I'll just tell her it's a bet. You know how Jessie feels about bets."

Michelle rested her coffee on the counter. Unfortunately, she did know. Jessie could never refuse a bet—the more daring the better. "Hopefully, she's learned her lesson."

Teresa shushed her. "Hello, Jess...? Hi...great. I was wondering if you could go to the bay with me tomorrow morning around five. I know it's early and cold, but I bet this guy I would jump in. Who? Uh...a police officer. Yea, a real jerk, macho type. What? Great...I'll see you around five. Bye."

Teresa hung up the phone and smiled with triumph. "It's all set."

"Yes, and you're crazy as a loon."

"I THINK you two have lost your minds," Michelle lamented as the three women drove to the bay the following morning as the sun was just about to rise.

"You've already said that ten times, Mich. You might as well recognize that we don't care," Teresa said.

"Yes," Jessie agreed already in a competitive mood. "Teresa has to show this police officer where to put his opinions."

"If he shows up," Michelle said.

Jessie turned to Michelle, who was sulking in the back seat. "What?"

"Teresa made him up."

Jessie turned to her. "What is she talking about? I thought you

said—"

"I just wanted your company," Teresa cut in. "And I wasn't sure you'd come otherwise."

"You don't have to lie."

"It's insane," Michelle said.

Jessie looked at Michelle through the rearview mirror. "Why are you coming with us when you're against this?"

"To keep you two out of trouble. Who knows what crazy scheme might enter your heads? You might convince her to run in naked just to prove a point."

Jessie waved the thought away. "This is harmless." She turned to Teresa, lowering her voice. "Besides, skinny dipping is best left for the summer months."

"You're not helping, Jessie."

She shrugged.

"She'll probably get pneumonia."

"No, I won't." Teresa parked the car. "Here we are."

Michelle frowned as she looked at the steep incline. "I thought you said it was off a hill, I could skydive off here."

"You don't have to come," Jessie said opening the door. "If you were really mature, you'd admit you're as curious as I am."

Michelle didn't reply as she shut the door.

However, once they reached the beach, Jessie became more cautious. "Are you sure you want to do this?" Jessie asked Teresa. She pulled on her gloves. It was a nippy morning. "You don't need to prove anything. I only came to support you, but you don't have to do it."

"I told you I'm doing this for myself. I want to be the kind of woman who does things like this. I just want to see what it's like."

"Then wait until summer," Michelle suggested, rubbing her hands together.

Teresa shook her head, taking off her jeans and top. She was already beginning to feel more alive. "No. I have to do it now." She pulled a green swimming cap over her head then jumped up and down to keep warm as she stared at the calm waters of the bay. She stopped and took a deep breath. "Well, here goes."

She ran and jumped in, a scream caught in her throat as the cold water assaulted her skin.

"Are you okay?" Jessie called.

Teresa only nodded, too shocked to speak. She slowly began to move her arms and legs and soon her body grew accustomed to the cold temperature. She quickly began to understand Sean's fascination with the morning swim—the quiet, the waves splashing her like kids in a pool; the sound of seagulls circling overhead. She did somersaults and spun around, closing her eyes.

She used her hands to direct her, trying to see the bay in a whole new way. She bumped into some rocks and let her hands trail over their furry smooth surface and curled her fingers into something that felt soft like seaweed. Oh, if only now, somehow, her world would fall into place, her destiny would take hold. Suddenly something encircled around her waist like an eel, it was solid and warm. She opened her eyes and screamed. Sean faced her with a smile on his lips, the hazel glint of his eyes spiked with wet, black lashes.

CHAPTER 8

"You're early!" she cried, backing away from his grasp.

"So are you."

She struck the water with the flat of her hand, splashing his face. "I can't believe you let me touch you like that without saying anything!"

He shrugged, wiping the water from his eyes. "You seemed to be enjoying yourself."

She covered her face with her hands. Just when she thought it couldn't get more awkward, it did. To think she had been touching him intimately and enjoying it! This had to be a nightmare, there was no other explanation. She would open her eyes and be in bed.

She peeked through her fingers and saw Sean arrogantly smiling at her. She groaned, she would just pretend it didn't happen. She let her hands fall to her side, lifted her chin and turned away; he grabbed her arm. "Why don't you finish what you started?" he challenged.

His eyes teased and baited her like a boy who'd asked his best friend to do something he was certain he wouldn't do; Teresa was up for the challenge, eager to remove that expression from his face. She narrowed her eyes in deliberation. "All right."

She didn't touch his chest first, she surprised him by curling her fingers over his left ear and massaging it. Sean took a deep breath, trying to combat the amazingly sensuous feel of her fingers there. Slowly her fingers left a caressing trail down his neck to the center of his chest. She watched him—his eyes darkened with fire as her hand continued their descent.

She smiled coyly. He captured her hand before it went too far.

"You don't want to do that," he warned in a gruff tone.

Her heart thumped uncomfortably. "I don't?"

"No."

"How about this?" She touched the curve of his neck.

"Only if I can do this." His hand rested in the space between her breasts and slowly drew little circles there.

Teresa caught her breath, heat emanating from where his fingers had been. "Fine, if I can do this." She wet her forefinger then let it trail the outside of his lips. He had beautiful lips, full and soft.

"You're in over your head," he grumbled, annoyed with the hoarse quality of his voice.

She tugged on one of the curls plastered against his forehead and twirled it around her finger. "No," she whispered. "You are."

She wrapped her arms around his neck and kissed him fully on the mouth. Since his mouth had been partly opened she delved into it completely, learning the intricacies of it from the moment of impact. She didn't know what she was doing, though it felt good and wanted to stop before she embarrassed herself, but Sean kept her in his arms, making this kiss his own—the captive became the captor. His kisses sent the pit of her stomach into a wild swirl. His hands held her close and she could feel his erection pressed against her like an uncoiled snake. She wrapped her legs around him; the movement pleased him and he emitted a low groan. They kissed until they had to pull away for air. They stared at each other—his hazel eyes clashing with her brown ones—full of a wonder and desire neither could fathom, trying to understand what had occurred, why their emotions had gotten the better of them and what it meant.

He turned and swam for the shore.

"You know what this means, don't you?" Teresa said, following him.

He ignored her and toweled himself dry.

"It means—"

"You know you're becoming a bleeding nuisance," he said.

She smiled, unbothered by his tone. "Oh my virgin ears, such language."

"How can a man enjoy his solitude with you crashing in it all the time?"

"I've been coming down here longer than you have," she said. "Besides I'm not bothering you."

"Your eyes bother me."

She shrugged. "Well, I can't help that."

He folded his arms, Teresa watched, fascinated, as his shoulders widened. He had a magnificent body that the chilly wind seemed to ignore. "Listen here, Trina."

She frowned, her good humor leaving her. "Teresa."

"Sorry—"

"That's all right Sam."

He flinched, but nodded. "I deserved that. Listen, I like to be left alone. What just happened was fun, but it didn't mean anything."

She lifted her chin. "Yes, it does."

He stared at her for a long moment. "What do you want?"

"A chance to get to know you better."

"That's not going to happen. What else?"

"I thought maybe you could use a friend."

"I'm fine," he said, turning.

"I know you're hurting. Give me a chance to help you."

His gaze sharpened. "What do you know? Are you trying to threaten me?"

"Threaten you?" she repeated alarmed by his assumption. "No. Why would I do that? I said I wanted to—"

He held up a finger. "I'm not letting you do this to me. I don't care how beautiful and tempting you are—stay away from me."

Beautiful? Tempting? No man had ever said that to her before and she knew they weren't true. And upon hearing those words a part of her died that day. His words shrouded her in a cloak of misery. She hadn't expected him to care or even like her, but his callous, sarcastic description ripped bare all her secret fears. That no man would want her, that she was too strange. He had said those words knowing she was the exact opposite.

Tears stung her eyes as she glared at him, but she wasn't ashamed of them. She didn't care if he knew how much he'd hurt her. "From the first moment I saw you, I wanted to be the salve that healed your pain. I know I'm not much to look at and I'm sure you have your pick of companions, but I just wanted to be your friend. I thought you were different." She glanced at the necklace on his chest. "I was fooled. Thank you for proving me wrong. I will leave you alone and let you have your precious peace and I hope you drown in it." She turned and walked to where her sisters were waiting for her.

Teresa glared at them. "You could have warned me he was here," she said, as she snatched a towel out of Jessie's grasp.

"We didn't even see him," Jessie said, defensive. "You know we would have warned you."

Her teeth began to chatter, she wasn't sure if it was the cold or because she was so angry. "You didn't see him at all? He just magically appeared in the water?"

"We were too busy watching you," Michelle said. "You looked like you were having a lot of fun."

"Were you really kissing him or was that our imagination?" Jessie asked.

Teresa wiped her legs dry. "It was nothing."

Michelle glanced at her watch. "It was about five minutes of nothing."

She stopped and stared. "You're joking."

Both sisters shook their heads.

Teresa placed a hand against her forehead. "I don't know what came over me." She bunched up her towel. "He just made me so angry."

"Then I hope he doesn't make you furious," Michelle said. "You could get into a lot of trouble."

"Don't worry, I've satisfied my curiosity. I'll never come back here, especially knowing that he might show up."

Jessie stared out at him, he was contently swimming and quickly becoming a dot on the horizon. "It was sort of odd how he just appeared though," she said. "Like a ghost."

"Don't you start," Michelle ordered. She handed Teresa her clothes. "Come on, let's go. This fantasy is over."

Sean watched the three women leave, anger heavy on his chest, for a moment wondering what had just happened. He felt as though he had stepped out into a drizzling rainfall only to find out that it was actually a hurricane. She had aptly cut him down to size, for a moment making him feel as big as a beetle and he hadn't even done anything!

He just wanted to be left alone, but she'd attacked his character, scratching at the hard surface he'd carefully surrounded himself with.

He could feel hot blood rushing through his veins. Odd, that hadn't happened in a long time, he hadn't felt a strong emotion like anger since Renee.

Was it wrong to be honest? He hadn't expected her to be the kind of woman who got angry at not making a conquest. But he'd been wrong about beautiful women before.

He shouldn't have kissed her. What had come over him? Why had he kissed her? It was fun at first, but then his hands started to take over and he couldn't pull away. He was attracted to her like a magnet.

He turned towards the water, a strange emptiness touching his heart. It was a new emotion so he didn't analyze it much. Teresa Clifton was a nuisance. He didn't want to think about her, he didn't want to care about her or feel anything, but her tears surprised him. She genuinely looked hurt. He'd just meant to tease her.

When he saw her spinning around in the water like a mermaid, his plan was to come up behind her and scare her, making her feel flustered and awkward as he had in the past. He didn't know what made him stand still, what made him watch her like a scientist would a rare fish—with intent, admiration and studied detachment. When she bumped into him, he meant to speak but he didn't—couldn't somehow. Then she began to touch him, awakening feelings he had kept hidden for a long time. Her fingers weren't soft as he had expected, she had working hands, which made him wonder more about her. What woman, who wore expensive coats, had such rough hands?

Surprisingly, the calluses felt good against his skin. They were both rough and gentle at the same time. Unexpectedly, his hands seemed to work on their own, circling her waist as if they were always meant to be there. She was round, with enough solid curves to make a man thank God. He was about to get himself into serious trouble when she opened her eyes. It was evident that she was not happy to see him and that had delighted him.

He'd challenged her again, expecting her to give him one of her passionate lectures, but again she surprised him. When her eyes narrowed, his pulse quickened like a boxer preparing for a fight. He knew he was in danger when she began to touch him again. It took all his effort not to pull her to him and raise the ante of their little game. Then she kissed him—a simple drug-inducing kiss that surprised them both with its potency. He licked his lips as if remembering a fine meal. She tasted good. No, more than good. Right...perfect.

He swore and jumped back into the water, splashed his face, shaking his head. What was wrong with him? He wasn't interested in her. He wasn't interested in anyone. He didn't have the luxury.

He came out of the water, sat on a rock and toweled himself dry. Mist came up to greet him, meowing, her green eyes bright with intelligence.

"It wasn't what it looked like," he muttered.

Mist sat on her hind legs looking smug.

"All right, it was, but that doesn't mean anything."

The cat continued to look smug and all-knowing.

He turned away, frustration gnawing at him. Why would the woman give him no peace? Even though sleep eluded him most nights, when he did sleep, she'd followed him into his dreams. She reached out to him, her bright light making the shadows around him recoil, but he did his best to stay out of reach.

"Why won't you leave me alone?" he remembered telling her in one dream as they stood among a sea of lavender, the sky overhead dark with rainy clouds.

"Do you really want that?" she had asked him.

"I don't want you here." He gripped his hands into fists and the clouds darkened above them. "I could hurt and destroy you if I wanted to."

"Perhaps," she said as if the thought didn't bother her and then she smiled. It was the smile that enraged him. He grabbed her arm and held her until he'd enveloped her into his darkness, a fierce wind wiping away the lavender field and leaving only cracked, barren soil. And as all the light around her faded, he looked at her face and expected to see fear or anger, but instead he saw sadness before all her light was gone.

Sean reached down and stroked Mist. Teresa was no match for him. No woman was. He would not be any woman's conquest again. And he'd never let anyone shatter his heart again. He liked living alone, being ignored. He didn't know why his honesty had brought her to tears, but it was the price he had to pay for his solitude.

CHAPTER 9

Teresa had become aware of Second Chances used bookstore by accident. Her car had broken down and she had wandered into the bookstore while she waited for the tow truck to come. She knew it was just the place she needed to forget about him. She would bury herself in a stack of books and she'd never think about him again.

She was looking through the shelves when Pernelle, the new bookstore assistant, approached her. She was new to the area and had come to town several months ago.

"I haven't seen you here in a while," Pernelle said.

Pernelle was a remarkable-looking woman with a glowing quality not even a Hollywood studio could imitate. She wore stylish clothes that hinted of New York elegance, her hair was luminous and cascaded like a black waterfall down her back; her eyes were a dark purplish brown. She reminded Teresa of her cousin Olivia, except Olivia never glowed unless she was given something expensive. Teresa was shocked when the stunning woman had made it her mission to befriend her, but always enjoyed discussing books and Pernelle had told her about JS Braden.

"I've been busy," Teresa said, wanting to be polite, although she wanted to be left alone too.

"I've got another book you're going to adore. A classic romance, where the heroine suffers tremendously but triumphs in the end, and another JS Braden book you're going to stay up all night reading."

Teresa smiled. "You need to have a long talk with my sister Michelle. She thinks my book reading habits are a problem."

Pernelle dismissed the thought with a wave of her hand. "She just doesn't understand." She leaned on the bookshelf, her eyes sparkling. "So have you got any news?"

"No," Teresa replied, confused. She never had any news to share. Her life was as exciting as mayonnaise.

Pernelle rested her chin in her hands. "What I mean to say is have you met him yet? The mysterious stranger," she added when Teresa continued to look blank.

Teresa lifted a book and gazed at the cover, trying to cool her temper. The last person she wanted to talk about was Sean Casey. "As a matter of fact I have," she said in a low voice, hoping her disinterest would stop the conversation.

Pernelle rubbed her hands together. "Go on. Tell me."

"There's nothing really exciting to tell," Teresa said, replacing the book. Had Sean seen Pernelle, he probably wouldn't have dismissed her so readily. "I saw him down at the bay, he told me to leave him alone."

Pernelle laughed. "He hasn't changed."

Teresa turned to her. "You know him?"

She lifted a perfectly arched eyebrow. "Very well, I'm afraid."

"How do you know him?" she asked, then regretted it when Pernelle turned and motioned for her to follow.

"Come to the back and I'll tell you."

Teresa shook her head. "I really don't think..."

"I know you're dying of curiosity."

"I don't like him."

Pernelle laughed. "Welcome to the club," she said, then opened the door marked Employees Only.

Teresa sighed and followed.

They settled in the storage room; it smelled of musty old books and papers. Teresa moved some books off a chair and set them on the ground, then sat and waited.

"He was a family friend," Pernelle said. "My husband knew his wife."

"You're married?"

"Was dear." She held up her bare finger. "You notice the ring is missing."

"What happened?" She couldn't imagine anyone divorcing such a fun, vibrant woman.

"I drove him crazy. Not literally, so you can relax, we just weren't well suited."

"Oh." Teresa thought for a moment, trying to process the information. "I haven't seen his wife."

"You won't. They're not together either."

She'd sensed a loss. Had it been the loss of his marriage that haunted him? Teresa mentally shook her head. It didn't matter. "So you've both come here to mend a broken heart," she said. "Perhaps you should go to Hollow Cove and see him again."

Pernelle vigorously shook her head. "I don't purposely go running into my past, I prefer to look ahead. Besides, I don't plan on seeing him again, not until I'm ready."

"But do you miss your husband?" she asked, thinking of her sister Michelle's failed marriage. "What was he like?"

Pernelle crossed her leg and swung her foot looking a little smug. "Probably not as much as he misses me."

Teresa stared stunned. "Why?"

Pernelle shrugged and continued to swing her foot. "Because I didn't want him focused on anyone but me and now he can't."

She shook her head. "I'm sure no man could ever forget you."

Pernelle laughed. "I like to make sure of that. I can't help it."

Teresa was silent for a moment, unable to comprehend what she'd heard.

"I bet you're wondering what this has to do with Sean?"

"No, really I—"

"He'd already left his wife by then. Although that's not the story he'd tell you. He'd say that she left him."

Teresa nodded ready to leave. "I'm glad you've both moved on."

Pernelle took out a compact from her pocket and checked her makeup. "She was a lot like me. Attractive, intelligent, wealthy. She was a savvy and brilliant newscaster."

Teresa fought to keep her expression neutral as she remembered his cruel words. Was he thinking of his wife when he said those words to her? Was he laughing at her now? Had he wiped her kiss from his lips? "I wonder why she married *him*," she said, not understanding how such a cultured woman would end up with such a rugged, offensive man. Perhaps it was all about opposites attract.

"He was different back then. We all were." She laughed. "Don't look so upset," she said misinterpreting the slight scowl on Teresa's face. Pernelle patted her knee. "I don't know about Sean, but I never loved my husband. And some would say he's better off without me. So are you going to see him again?"

Teresa started. "Me? Never. I'm going to stay as far away from him as possible."

"I've never heard a woman say that about him before. I think you should go after him. You're the kind of change that he needs."

Because I'm not attractive, intelligent and wealthy? Teresa wanted to say, but kept her thoughts to herself. Perhaps if Sean knew she had money, he wouldn't have discarded her offer of friendship so coldly. "Unfortunately, he's not the change I'm looking for." Teresa took the two books Pernelle had selected for her, then left.

SHE DECIDED to stop by Bertha's after leaving the bookstore. She loved Bertha's house, which was located on the tip of South Bank, situated on an acre of land. Teresa walked inside since Bertha always left the door open. The house smelled like strawberry candles.

"What's wrong?" Bertha asked, removing a kettle from the stove.

Teresa was not startled when she did not turn around. Bertha could hear a feather move. "Nothing."

Bertha sighed. "You've started to lie to me now?"

Teresa sat on one of the chrome seats, watching Bertha in her flowing red dress and matching turban, looking out of place in her modern steel kitchen. "I just don't want to talk about it."

"What do you have there?" she asked, looking at Teresa's bag.

"Two books Pernelle suggested."

Bertha sniffed.

"I don't know why you don't like her. She talks too much but she's always been nice to me."

"She's frivolous."

"When you're that pretty you're allowed to be frivolous."

"I don't mean in looks, but in manner. Be careful there. Besides, you're prettier than her in the way that counts."

"Spoken like a true friend."

Bertha settled into a chair and studied her for a moment. "Did you want to know more about Sean?"

Teresa briefly covered her ears. "Why does everyone seem to think I have an interest in knowing about him?"

"When did I become 'everyone'?"

She let her hands fall to the table. "I'm sorry, I didn't mean to exaggerate, it's just that I had to endure twenty minutes of Pernelle telling me about Sean and his former beautiful wife."

"How did she know that?"

"She knew his wife. She said it wasn't a good marriage." She held up her hand. "Not that I care in the least."

"That's a change. What happened?"

Teresa swallowed feeling her hurt resurface. "I knew that he wouldn't fall into my arms, but I thought there was a connection. I didn't think he'd make fun of me. I know that his unruly hair doesn't hide how good looking he is, but I thought...I didn't think he'd be cruel."

"He's not cruel. You once told me he had the hands of a healer. Well, he has the hands of a handler too."

Teresa gasped knowing the significance. She remembered as a young woman on spring break from college, overhearing her parents speaking in the living room when they thought she was asleep in bed.

"Finding a man for her won't be easy," her mother said.

"We don't have to find him, he'll find her. Relax, my darling. All our daughters are safe."

"But how will she know him?"

Teresa leaned in closer.

"Come in, Teresa," her father said with a smile in his voice. "You'll need to hear this."

She walked into the room with a sheepish grin. "I was just getting something from the kitchen."

Her father motioned to a chair. "Sit down." Once she did he said, "You know I consider my daughters my most precious gems. But every stone needs a different setting. You'll need a man who's strong enough to hold you and brave enough to protect you. You'll know him by his touch." Her father lifted up his hands. "He'll have the hands of a handler."

Her mother shook her head in dismay. "But men like that are rare."

"But they do exist."

Teresa frowned. "I don't know what you're talking about."

"Handlers are a very special breed," her father said. "They are usually women, but some men have the gift too. They handle things with care. Not everyone can do that, but they do so naturally. They rarely break things, their fingers always bring a sense of order and women like you need their touch because they know how to keep you safe..."

Her father's words lingered in her mind as she stared at Bertha now. "Then my father lied to me because he's not safe at all." She tapped her chest and spoke before her friend could. "I know how people see me. I know they think I'm odd, strange, maybe a little crazy. I can take that, but when they make fun of my looks..." She shook her head as if searching for words. "I know I'm not fashionable or slim, but I'm a good person."

"Of course you are," Bertha said, taking Teresa's hand, her face perplexed. "What did he say to you?"

"I can't say it without getting angry." She took a deep breath. "You're right that he has dark shadows and he can keep them. I know when to stay away and I will." She held up a hand. "That's all I want to say about it."

Instead she told Bertha about Dr. Knox's report and her meeting with Detective Hartnett. Sensing her restlessness, Bertha told her about a small beauty shop whose owner was thinking about going out of business, knowing Teresa liked finding nice deals. The shop was hosting a sale today on bath salts and other select items. Teresa drove to the location.

When she approached the building, she was surprised it was still in business. It was a small house with a wraparound porch and crooked sign saying "Beautiful You", hidden on one of South Bank's quiet side streets. Inside was quaint with antique furniture and rows of beauty products, bath items and jewelry. The owner greeted her looking sad and worn. She was a heavyset woman, whose shoulders slumped with considerable effort. Her eyes were deep-set and half closed. She began showing Teresa around with the slow movements of a lugubrious bloodhound.

"It's just too much work," the woman said when Teresa asked her why she was closing. "Business is good, but I just don't care anymore. I'm overwhelmed with handling inventory and online orders picking up..."

The woman rattled on, but Teresa barely listened, looking at the potential. The business wasn't failing, it was doing well, probably not as well if it had been located in Bedford, but she clearly had a clientele from the look of the other customers. If she added herbs to the selection of offerings, she could expand it. This place was her chance for a new start. She now knew how she could use the money Bess had given her. She would help people be beautiful on the inside and out.

"Never underestimate the power of the right cream," her mother told her one day after a spa treatment her daughter had given her. She'd indulged in all the skin creams and gels Teresa would create—whether the experiment worked or not, patiently giving her suggestions to improve them. Of the three sisters, Teresa spent the most time with her mother because they both loved gardening, body lotions and dining. Her mother had a keen taste and hosted elaborate dinners. Teresa remembered how she'd beamed with excitement the day when she was allowed to help her.

She was not an easy woman to know, however. She spoke in a clipped manner, reminiscent of her nanny and the strict English headmasters she'd studied under and at times she cared more about decorum than her children's feelings. But Teresa saw past the hard demeanor and sensed her mother's softer side. Teresa could always tease out a grin even when her mother meant to scold her.

Teresa looked around the store, knowing she could turn it into a store her mother would love.

"Are you willing to sell it?" Teresa asked her once the woman had finished speaking.

"You'd want this place?"

"Depends on the price."

The woman gave a tired sigh as if it took all the breath in her body to reply and gave her an amount.

"I'll buy it," Teresa said.

Her eyes widened a fraction then quickly dropped. "I'll get the papers."

A week later, Teresa sat and stared at the signed documents wondering how she would tell her sisters.

She sat at the kitchen table contemplating her options when the phone rang. She picked it up and answered.

"Oh Teresa, thank God you're there," her Aunt Margaret said. "I hate to bother you, but I didn't know who else to call and you were so kind at the hospital."

"What is it?"

"Louisa's been sick all day and we can't afford to take her to the hospital again. And we don't have a doctor—"

"I'll be right there," Teresa said, then hid her contract and left with her bag of remedies.

CHAPTER 10

Unfortunately, getting to her aunt's house was easier said than done. Since it was a long drive through one lane back roads, twice she had been caught behind a slow-moving tractor and was forced to go twenty-five miles an hour. When she finally turned onto her aunt's property and drove up the dirt drive to the house, her fears heightened. Her aunt's house was worse than she expected.

The house looked out at her like a tired old woman waiting to meet her maker. The garden, if it could be called such, was choking to death under vicious weeds, paint peeled off the sides like a skin disease, and the front porch had a broken swing and crooked steps. Teresa gasped at the site of the outhouse, but breathed a sigh of relief when she noted that it was boarded up.

She parked her car and grabbed her bag from the trunk, then made her way to the front door, moving around an old tire and bathroom sink that lay in the front like lawn ornaments. She took a deep breath and lifted the knocker, but it fell off right into her hands. She used her knuckles instead.

Margaret's husband, Darren, answered the door, with a cigar

sticking out of his mouth and worry etched on his face. He was a long, slim man who had been handsome in his younger days, his hair was silver grey and his skin the color of a rubber band. "She's over there. We weren't sure you'd show up." He opened the door wider, allowing her access inside.

The interior was no better than the outside. The living room doubled as a dining room, and the kitchen looked like it was better suited for an efficiency apartment. The floor was dirty and the air musty. An old upright piano, covered with a tablecloth and overflowing with a hodgepodge of old reference manuals, stood near the wall. They led her to Louisa's bedroom. It was a cramped space about the size of a walk-in closet.

Teresa's eyes finally rested on a figure lying on the bed. Even ill she was beautiful, with liquid brown eyes and elegant features although her dark brown hair cascaded over her shoulders like a limp mop. She had a thick yellow blanket pulled up to her chest, making her look as helpless as a toddler. She lay on the bed with a bucket near her head.

Teresa's apprehensions grew.

"I don't think it's food poisoning because no one else has gotten sick," Aunt Margaret said.

Teresa sat beside Louisa and looked her over. Her brown skin was pale and she was clearly in pain. Cramping and nausea did sound like food poisoning, but she had to make sure. She wanted to keep Louisa's privacy, clearly feeling her aunt and uncle's gaze on the back of her neck so she slipped her hands under the sheet and felt with her hands. The moment she felt Louisa's abdomen, she knew. She lifted her gaze to meet her cousin's and saw fear in her eyes.

"Um...Aunt Margaret could I talk to Louisa alone? It's very important so that I can concentrate."

"But—"

"Please."

She waited until they were out of the room then lowered her voice because she knew the walls were thin. "What did you take?" she demanded.

"It's nothing."

"Louisa, I need you to be honest with me, if you want me to help you."

"What do you think? Something to take care of the problem." She gripped her hands into fists as another cramp seized her.

"This isn't the way to do it."

"She said it would be quick and fast."

"Who?"

Louisa's eyes flashed with anger. "Does it matter now?"

Teresa tenderly touched Louisa's abdomen again. "You're too far gone to try something like this."

"Shit, you think I don't know that?"

"What did you take?"

"Why won't you just leave me alone?"

"I want to help you."

"I don't want your help," she said, then turned a sickly shade and bent over the bucket. When she was through, she moaned.

Teresa looked around the room. "Where is it?"

"Just let me die. Why do you always have to show up?"

"Fine then I'll tell—"

She grabbed her arm. "I hate you."

"Where is it?"

"In my drawer," she said in a weary voice.

Teresa retrieved the plastic bag and looked at the selection of herbs. She recognized them. There would be no label to see who put them together. She softly swore. The concoction would give Louisa the symptoms she had, but nothing more and it could damage them both. Fortunately, she knew how to remedy it. She went to the kitchen and made a mixture—keeping her aunt and uncle's questions at bay—then forced Louisa to drink it.

"I doubt I'll be able to keep it down," Louisa said.

"You will."

And she did. The cramping and nausea eased almost immediately. Once Teresa felt the crisis had been averted she said, "You have to tell them."

"I can't. You do it."

"But—"

"If you hadn't interfered I wouldn't have to," Louisa said in an ugly whisper. "Why are you so determined to save a life that isn't worth saving?"

"I'm not the only one who cares. Sean saved you too," she said, although saying his name still hurt. She stopped herself from asking if he was the father. She didn't want to know.

Louisa turned away.

"You can't keep this a secret forever. Your parents will be angry and shocked, but they love you and—"

She turned to Teresa. "What do you know about love?"

"I know a lot and—"

"My parents aren't like yours."

"My parents are dead," Teresa said in a soft voice.

"Yes, exactly. Lucky you."

Teresa gritted her teeth, remembering why their families had never been close. But she knew frightened animals tended to bite the very people who tried to help them. "Louisa, just—"

"Either you tell them or get out. I don't need your self-righteous preaching."

Teresa opened her bag and pulled out a small bottle of oil. "Close your eyes for a minute."

"What?"

"Do you want to be bent over a bucket again? You're not completely healed yet."

She widened her eyes. "I'm not?"

"No," Teresa lied. "Now close your eyes."

Louisa dutifully did. Teresa put some oil on her hands then lathered it on Louisa's arms.

"Hmmm...that feels good."

"That's the point," Teresa said, but knew it wasn't. She wanted to sense what was really going on. Why had her cousin wanted to kill herself and why had she gone to such dangerous lengths to end her pregnancy? She took a deep breath and opened up her senses; not every person was easy to read, but she didn't have time.

Fortunately, Louisa responded to her touch and soon Teresa felt Louisa's deep longing and hunger for love. Then she felt her rage and despair and she saw a little girl being led to a man's bedroom.

She snatched her hands away not wanting to see anymore, but she knew Louisa's childhood hadn't been as happy and care-free as hers. She didn't know what love was. She didn't know true happiness and the thought brought tears to Teresa's eyes that a young woman so beautiful could have been discarded. She remembered one of the brief visits they'd had with them years ago when she was about six and Louisa was just a pretty eighteen month old who giggled at the sight of bubbles and clapped at the sights and sounds of firecrackers that would have other babies in tears.

Teresa looked down at the woman that child had become and her heart filled with pity. Perhaps if she were offered some compassion she wouldn't hate the world the way she did.

"Okay, I'll tell your parents," Teresa said.

But when Teresa called her aunt and uncle into the bedroom

and told them Louisa's secret, their reactions were nothing she'd ever seen before. Uncle Darren looked at Louisa, then laughed, though Teresa could not see the humor.

Aunt Margaret folded her arms, her face unreadable. "Are you feeling better now?"

Louisa nodded.

"Then stand up."

"Mom, please."

"Get your body up."

Louisa pushed away the covers and stood.

Aunt Margaret looked her up and down then punched her in the stomach. Louisa doubled over in pain. Teresa gasped in shock at her aunt—whose ageless beauty belied her violent streak—and put a protective arm around Louisa then pinned her aunt with a hard look. "What is wrong with you?"

Aunt Margaret kept her gaze on her daughter. "Hopefully you'll start bleeding by this evening."

"Aunt Margaret!"

"What?" she said, looking at Teresa with cold, dark eyes. "Did you expect mi fi cheer?" she said dropping her proper dialect. "As hard as we work, this is the kind of foolishness she gets up to?"

"Unexpected things happen and—"

"Where's the *fadda* then?" she said dipping into the dialect of her youth. "Bet you can't even name him. You're—"

"That's enough," Teresa said trying her best to be respectful although she found her aunt's behavior appalling.

Aunt Margaret fixed her with a gaze now shining with tears. "What do you know about enough? Just like your fadda you think you're betta than everyone. That you know everything, but life hasn't even touched you yet." She pounded her chest with her fist. "All my children—every last one—has squeezed the life out of my heart. All so pretty and useless. I wish every last one was as dark, fat and plain as you."

"Margaret," Darren said in warning.

She looked past Teresa and glared at Louisa. "And what about your job, you expect to live off of us now?"

"She can work for me," Teresa said. "I bought a shop. And if I could stay for a couple weeks while I get things renovated I could pay you rent and that could help," Teresa added thinking up a quick lie that would convince her aunt to let her stay. She didn't trust leaving Louisa alone with them.

Aunt Margaret sniffed. "You wouldn't last here a day, but we'll take your money anyway."

CHAPTER 11

"Let me get this straight," Michelle said as she sat behind her imposing office desk and looked over the paper Teresa had given her. "You just bought a beauty store that you want to extend into a natural health store that doesn't sell Valley Ray supplements?"

Teresa nodded, her gaze briefly dropping to the peach carpeting. "I've already spoken to another supplier so that shouldn't be a problem."

"That *is* a problem because Valley Ray is very popular here."

"And people can find it somewhere else."

"Why didn't you consult me first?"

"Because I wanted it."

"If you'd wanted a business, I could have—"

"I want this one," she said, shifting her gaze to the large window that afforded her sister a gorgeous view of the downtown area. "It's established. There's a great manager, clerks, the hours are good and it's doing well."

"But it's in South Bank."

Teresa looked at her sister. "The location is suitable. It's not stylish, but I don't need it to be."

Michelle shook her head and sighed. "It won't be that easy." She sighed again. "And signing without negotiating or a lawyer representing your interests is just—"

"I can make this work."

"And the commute—"

"I'm staying at Aunt Margaret's for a while."

Michelle's head shot up. "Aunt Margaret?" she said then started to grin and looked at her calendar. "Is it April Fool's Day?"

"I'm not joking."

Her smile fell. "But that woman is awful and her family—"

Teresa shivered remembering her aunt's outburst. "I know."

"You can't be serious."

Teresa crossed her legs. "I need to do this to help Louisa."

"Why?"

"She's pregnant."

Michelle folded her arms. "And this concerns you because—?"

"She needs someone. Her mother is...well..."

"A monster?"

"I wouldn't go that far," Teresa said, remembering her aunt's tears.

"Coarse, loud, crude?"

"She's a woman who's been disappointed by life," Teresa said gently.

Michelle briefly closed her eyes and groaned. "You're always so understanding."

"I have you and Jessie, but Louisa doesn't have anyone." Teresa lifted her hand and stared at it. "I felt her suffering and I feel I can help. She needs a job."

"But you don't need her help. You already have a manager and two clerks."

"I'll find something for her to do."

"You don't have to live there to do it," Michelle said. "That area isn't safe. People try to move out, not move in."

"Bertha lives near there and she's fine."

"She lives near there, that's the difference and it helps that people think she might turn them into frogs."

"That's not true."

"We all know nobody messes with Bertha."

"I'm not staying long. Louisa needs someone to take care of her and I know Aunt Margaret and Uncle Darren need the money."

"Money?"

Teresa cleared her throat then said, "I offered to pay rent."

"For what? A space next to one of the rat holes?"

"You're being a snob," Teresa said.

"Of course I am," Michelle agreed, nodding her head for emphasis. "There's nothing there." Michelle looked down at the papers again. "Have you told Jessie?"

"No, you're the first person."

"And I can't change your mind?"

"No."

She shrugged, resigned, then sighed. "So you'll continue to play Catherine of Siena?"

"Who?"

"A twelfth century nun who cared for the sick and dying during the plague."

"That's not fair."

Michelle rested her chin in her hands. "Since you're obviously not here for advice, what do you want?"

"I just need some contacts to do some minor renovations on the store. Will you help me or not?"

Michelle glanced out the window. "Are you doing this because of a man?"

Only partly. "No."

Michelle shifted her gaze to her. "Promise," Michelle said, knowing a Clifton's word was golden.

Teresa tugged on one of her bracelets. "This is important to me."

"That isn't a promise. Are you still thinking about that stranger?"

"No. I'm not doing this because of him."

"Okay," Michelle said with an air or resignation. "I'll make some calls and then let me see what we have to work with."

KENNETH PRESTON LOOKED over the papers Michelle had handed him to review then set them down and swore.

The three of them sat in Kenneth and Jessie's living room. They could hear a video game being played in the next room by their adopted daughter Syrah. Jessie and Kenneth sat together while Michelle faced him. Her brother-in-law was, at times, an unnervingly handsome man with chestnut skin and brown eyes. He and her sister had settled well into married life —as if they'd always been together. But what surprised her more was how well he fit into all their lives. She trusted him and that was rare.

At times seeing them together briefly reminded Michelle of being in love, but she always brushed the thought away. Her life was settled now and so was Jessie's. Her youngest sister had always given her cause for concern with her reckless behavior and quick temper. Now it seemed that Teresa had taken her place.

Michelle nodded at Kenneth's words. "My thoughts exactly. What do I do?"

Kenneth frowned. "Nothing. It's lucrative. Actually considering the location, it's making more money than I thought it would be."

Michelle stared at him surprised. "But Teresa doesn't know anything about running a store and—"

"We have to support her," Jessie said.

"And watch her fail?" Michelle said.

"She might not fail."

"She doesn't want to sell Valley Ray products. That's going to hurt her."

"Have you seen the place?" Kenneth asked.

"I'm afraid to," Michelle said with a shiver. "She hasn't been acting like herself recently and this," she pointed to the papers, "has me worried. She's being reckless and ridiculous."

Kenneth shook his head. "I disagree. I don't see what the problem is."

"Aside from buying a store she's moving in with Aunt Margaret's family...Mum would have a fit."

"Mum's not here," Jessie said. "And Teresa's a grown woman."

"Don't tell me this doesn't bother you."

Jessie shifted in her seat looking conflicted. "Teresa has a right to live her own life. To make choices we may not understand. You got separated and we still don't—"

"We're not talking about me," Michelle said in a tight voice.

"That's right. We're never talking about you because your life is so perfect."

"That's not—"

"Why we're here," Kenneth said resting a hand on his wife's knee to stop any further protests.

Michelle turned to him. "Teresa trusts you, couldn't you have a word with her?"

"And say what?"

"I don't want Kenneth involved with this," Jessie said.

"He's family, he's already involved."

Kenneth squeezed Jessie's knee, stopping her from saying her next words. "I think Jasmine's right," he said, using her given name. "We have to let Teresa do what she wants."

Michelle nodded, grim. "Of course, you're a united front. A happy wife is a happy life, right?" She stood.

He stood also, his cutting gaze holding her still and instantly making her regret her words. He spoke in a soft tone of warning, "Don't play dirty, Michelle. You know I can beat you."

She sighed. He was right, she was being petty. "I just have a bad feeling about all this." She turned to Jessie. "Read her stones or something and convince her—"

"I don't like doing readings for family," Jessie said. "You know that."

"Right," Michelle said, gathering up her things. She walked to her car and was about to open the door when Kenneth called out her name.

She turned to him, curious at the seriousness of his tone.

"I know," he said, once he reached her, the understanding and compassion in his gaze nearly brought her to tears. He understood her worry; he had a complicated relationship with his younger brother who he'd worried over all his life. She took a deep breath, taking comfort in the fact that she wasn't alone.

"Thanks," she said gathering herself. "It's just...she talked about some guy—"

Kenneth's gaze sharpened. "Did you get a name? Want me to look into it?"

Michelle shook her head. "No, I'm sure it's nothing."

Kenneth nodded, but his serious gaze remained. "If you change your mind, you let me know."

"You will not stay with your Aunt Margaret's family," Bertha said when Teresa told her about her plans. The two women sat in Bertha's living room with an afternoon sun touching the leaves on a bouquet of violets on the coffee table.

Teresa blinked, shocked by her friend's outright opposition to the idea. She figured she would be the only one who truly understood. "Bertha, they need me, especially Louisa. What I sensed from her was a desperate unhappiness and in a vision I saw—"

"I know what you saw," Bertha said in a soft voice. "And it's tragic, but that doesn't mean you can save her."

"I'm not trying to save anyone, I just want to help her. Louisa needs me."

Bertha kissed her teeth in annoyance. "And you need to be needed. Your father did you a big disservice by making your heart so big."

"That means I have a lot to give."

Bertha frowned. "Right, and a lot for others to take." She adjusted the colorful scarf she had wrapped around her shoulders. "I don't like this at all. That girl is trouble. Your father helped bring his sister and her family over here and likely regretted it. They should have stayed in Jamaica. The entire family has made their bed and now they must lie in it."

"Nobody chooses to be poor."

"They're not just poor in money." She touched her chest. "But poor in heart and spirit."

"I can change the heaviness in that house and fill it with the joy they desperately need. And with the store I can prove—"

Bertha sent Teresa a sharp look. "You have nothing to prove. You have done nothing wrong, you've prosecuted yourself needlessly."

"I think Bess would have wanted this," Teresa said. "And I want this."

"Are you ready to tell me what Sean said?"

"There's no need," Teresa said with a bright smile. "I've pushed him out of my heart and mind completely."

Bertha nodded, but didn't believe a word.

CHAPTER 12

"Is it as ugly to you as it is to me?" Michelle whispered to Jessie as they stood outside the "Beautiful You" store. Teresa had closed the store for a few days so that they could make changes.

"Yes."

Teresa beamed at her sisters. "Isn't this great!"

Michelle and Jessie pasted on smiles.

"I know the outside needs some work," she continued.

"That a bulldozer could fix," Michelle mumbled. Jessie nudged her.

"But the inside has lots of potential," Teresa finished, not hearing her.

The sisters set out to make that happen. Both Michelle and Jessie took time off work—cleaning the windows and floor while Teresa set out to clean up the weedy bushes. Inside, Teresa put her design skills to work and created an environment to encourage customers to linger by using different levels for display, installing adequate lighting and mirrors and painting the walls a warm cream-yellow. They also provided a coat rack, a place for a bag check and an umbrella stand so that customers could roam unencumbered. By the end of a few days, even the two shop clerks were amazed.

Teresa spent two days discussing the various products with the store manager, a stocky man with a shifting toupee, and the clerks, instructing them on how they were to interact and advise customers. On the day of the grand re-opening she hosted a special sale that gained some local news coverage, but not the kind she'd hoped for. Instead of focusing on her expanded product line, the reporter only focused on the fact that she wasn't selling any Valley Ray supplements. Unfortunately, neither of her sisters could be there. Michelle had to travel out of town and Jessie had a pressing former engagement. But they had a bouquet of flowers delivered, which Teresa displayed in the center of the store.

"Is there a reason you're not supporting one of the largest employers in the area?" the reporter asked.

"I am a small, independent shop giving other companies a chance. I have nothing against Valley Ray."

But the press hurt some early sales. Feeling a little defeated at the end of her first week, as she saw her hopes for instant success fade, Teresa packed up some rolls from the local bakery and decided to go visit Bertha. She stopped and stared when she saw a suspiciously familiar truck parked in the driveway. She marched up to the door and turned the handle—it was locked. When did Bertha start locking doors? She pounded on the door. Sean answered.

Teresa stumbled back in shock. He wasn't supposed to be here. Bertha's place was hers. He had the bay, but this little place was her true sanctuary and he acted as if he were at home. She felt violated, as if he'd stolen something precious from her.

"What are you doing here?" Teresa demanded. "And where's Bertha?"

Sean flashed a slow smile. "Relax, Mother is—"

Mother? Teresa waved her hands. "Never mind, you're busy. I'll come back later."

His smile fell. "Wait. Let me go get her and—"

She took another step back. "No."

"Teresa, at least let me—"

"I'm sorry I bothered you," she said, hurrying to her car, hot tears stinging her eyes. First he'd ruined her mornings at the bay and now she couldn't even visit Bertha without him popping up. He even knew her cousin Louisa. What if he stopped by the store to visit her? Teresa shook her head and took a deep breath. That was okay. She had to get over him and if Bertha wasn't free, she had to depend on herself.

SEAN WATCHED Teresa speed down the drive, pensive.

"What is wrong with her?" he said to himself.

"Who was that?" Bertha asked, appearing by his side.

He turned to her. "Teresa."

"And she just left without coming in? What did you say to her?"

"Nothing."

"What did you say to her before?"

His brows shot up. "Did she tell you about that? I didn't mean to upset her, but I meant what I said and I'd say it again." Sean groaned deep in his throat, then pounded the frame of the door with his fist. "I don't want this." He pointed out into the distance. "I don't want her. She's driving me crazy." He tapped the side of his head. "But for some reason she's stuck up here and

I don't like it. I don't want to care. I want my space and I want my peace, don't I deserve it?"

"What did you say?" Bertha asked.

He paused. "She didn't tell you?"

"No."

He walked back into the house and sat in the living room. "I said I wouldn't let her beauty tempt me and...what's so funny?"

"Poor thing," Bertha said taking a seat in front of him. "She doesn't know you mean it."

"What?"

"Teresa doesn't know how beautiful she is. She thought you were insulting her."

Sean looked at her for a long moment then shook his head. "No, that's not it. She's just annoyed I didn't fall for her."

"Sean—"

"And she's trying to manipulate me," he said, warming to his subject. "She even used tears. And she's good, she almost got me."

"Teresa has no guile, she wouldn't try to manipulate you. Your honesty hurt her because she didn't believe you."

He shook his head and pulled on his beard, annoyed. "That doesn't make sense."

"Teresa isn't like most women. Around here she's just dark, fat and plain."

His eyes flashed fire. "She's what?" He held up a hand and flashed a cynical smile. "Good one. You nearly got me." He stood and opened the door. He pointed to his truck. "You know the things I love? My truck and my cat and that's it." He folded his arms. "I didn't come here to get myself involved with—" He shook his head. "Never mind."

"You both know something is there. You should stop fighting it."

Sean looked away, staring down at the driveway. He absently

pounded the door frame with his fist. "No. I can't," he said, his voice cracking on the last word.

"Tell her about your wife, she might be able to help you."

He turned sharply. "I don't talk about things like that with anyone and I only told you—"

"Because you trust me," Bertha said sensing his fear. "And you can keep on doing so. Your secrets are safe with me." She gently covered his fist. "But Teresa has a few secrets of her own that may help you one day."

"I'm fine. Besides, she doesn't go to the bay anymore..." he said, letting his words trail off, knowing he'd revealed too much.

"No, but she's staying with Louisa. When's the last time you visited them?"

CHAPTER 13

Teresa didn't expect a warm welcome when she arrived at her aunt and uncle's place. Twice her sister Michelle had tried to talk her out of moving out, but the news her Uncle Darren gave her was still a shock.

"Margaret's gone," Uncle Darren said to Teresa as he opened the door. "Went to stay with a sister of hers for a while. So it's just us," he said, tugging on his Valley Ray T-shirt in an uncharacteristically nervous gesture. He turned to Louisa. "Show her where to put her things."

Teresa followed Louisa to the small room she'd use. It had a bed that looked no better than a cot that was set up in the corner for her and an old pink blanket was neatly folded at the foot of the bed. Fortunately, there was a window, although it was so filthy no light was allowed through. Teresa looked at her blanket, it had holes that she knew wouldn't keep the winter chill out, she'd have to get a replacement. She put it back on the bed.

Louisa sat on the bed. "Bet you wish you didn't come, huh?"

"No," Teresa said with a smile. She opened a dresser drawer

that looked as if they'd picked it up off the side of the road, hoping nothing would come crawling out.

"I heard your sister Jessie got married," Louisa said, crossing her legs. "Heard it was beautiful."

"Yes, it was."

"Sorry we couldn't make it."

"Yes." Teresa didn't admit that with the crowd of people in attendance nobody noticed their absence.

"I really didn't think you'd come back."

Teresa began to unpack. "I said I would."

She sniffed. "People always say things they don't mean." She watched Teresa put an expensive nightgown into one of the drawers. "So your boyfriend won't mind you being here?"

"You don't have to pretend, you think I have one."

"I'm not pretending, I'm curious. Isn't there a special someone out there?"

"What do you really want to know?"

"Why someone like you would want to end up in a dump like this. We both know you don't belong here. Growing up, all I'd hear about the Cliftons was how 'special' they were, but I never could figure it out. We got the looks and you got the money. I bet you went to the prom in some fancy limousine and—"

"I never dated."

Louisa stared surprised. "Not once?"

"Nope."

Louisa looked her up and down. "Even at your age? Not one man?"

Teresa grinned at Louisa's horrified expression. "Nope. Not once."

"That means you've never been with a man?"

"Nope."

"I can't believe you've lasted so long. I had needs that had to be met. Is it some religious—"

"I just haven't met the right guy. "

"No wonder! You can't wait around for that or you'll be a virgin forever." Louisa patted her cousin's knee in reassurance. "Stop thinking that way and you'll get your chance."

Teresa toyed with her bracelet, choosing her words carefully. "I know that this may sound strange, but I've given up on that."

Louisa tilted her head to the side. "You're right. It does sound strange. Why give up? You're not even thirty yet."

"It's just not in the cards for me. I fell in love with a man who doesn't care I exist."

Louisa felt her pity subside and a feeling of understanding took over that surprised her. She'd wanted to hate Teresa, but her sincerity reluctantly drew her in, even though they had little in common. By age seven, she knew what boys were best for and liked getting their attention. She knew the power of her looks. Plain girls like Teresa stayed home writing poetry on Friday nights and lived boring lives. She never thought they could feel the same way she did. "It's better than him rejecting you," Louisa said.

"Give him time," Teresa said, hearing the words Louisa didn't say. "He might come around."

Louisa absently rubbed her stomach. "I know I'll get him back somehow."

"And if you don't, I'm here."

Louisa shrugged, feeling sorry for her. Teresa was too simple to understand that she was a poor substitution for a man. But since she'd never had one, she wouldn't know. Louisa still didn't understand why Teresa felt the need to move in to help her. Although they were family, they were still strangers.

"Hungry?" Teresa asked.

"Starving." And she was, but by the time dinner was ready, she wasn't sure she could get near it. Curry spiced the air and the sight of black beans on a bed of rice, a meal that used to be one of her favorites, made her stomach lurch. Louisa took a deep breath, grabbing the back of the chair hoping her stomach would settle.

This baby was supposed to be the start of a new life for her, but all it did was take. It was taking her figure, it had taken her job away, the man she loved and now her appetite. She turned and stormed out of the house, wanting to scream at the sky. It wasn't fair. She didn't want her life to be like this. She didn't want to work in her cousin's shop, let alone share her place with her. She didn't want to be in this ugly house. She wanted to escape. She wanted to be with him. In his arms, hear his voice.

"Louisa, are you okay?"

She turned and saw Teresa's concerned expression. She couldn't understand. She had so many things she wanted to say, but only one she could give voice to. "I hate this."

"This?"

"Being pregnant. I hate feeling sick nearly all the time."

"I have something that can help. It's a special ginger mix that will make the rest of your pregnancy feel like a breeze."

"Really?"

"I helped you before, right? You'll be eating curry in no time."

Louisa felt her hopes lift, if she could go a day without bending over a toilet she'd be grateful. "Thanks," she said and for the first time in a long while, meant it.

YOU WOULDN'T LAST A DAY. Teresa lay in bed and stared up at the ceiling knowing her Aunt's words were right. She wanted to go home. She wanted to be in her own bed again. She missed the grey country-style house she shared with her sister Michelle. The beautiful house she'd grown up in. But she was determined she would stay a while so that she could help them. But she couldn't stay with things this filthy. She had to do something.

"Uncle Darren, do you mind if I make a few changes?" she asked her uncle one morning as he headed out to work.

"Sure. I don't care."

His words were music to her ears and she immediately went to work. She cleaned all the windows and mopped the floors, then painted. Painting filled up three days. With Darren's help and four of his friends, they painted Louisa's room a soft pink, Teresa's a warm blue, Darren's master bedroom and the living room an off white. She shopped at Hartland's Warehouse, a place that had been turned into a large thrift store where many vendors showed up on weekends to sell a variety of items. She purchased new beds, a couch and tables and chairs and had them delivered.

"I can't believe I'm in the same house," Darren said one evening as he sat on his new burgundy couch and watched Teresa place a plant on a windowsill.

"I'm glad you like it."

"Must have cost you more than the rent."

"Oh, I had some paints and things leftover from renovating the shop so it wasn't much." That was only partly true. She didn't want to tell him that she would have spent a lot more if she'd had to because she couldn't have stayed there as it was.

But now the house felt fresher and happier. She'd gotten her second chance and so had the house.

The following day, Teresa spent time at the store. But it was a slow day, so she let Louisa go home early since she didn't have much for her to do. Once again the store manager, whose toupee lay low on his forehead today, asked her to consider carrying

Valley Ray supplements, but she sidestepped the issue, telling him she had something else in mind.

That evening she returned home and saw Louisa raiding the cupboards, a bag of chips and a half eaten cookie in her mouth.

"Someone's gotten their appetite back," Teresa said with a smile, glad that her remedy had worked.

"You don't know how hungry I am," Louisa said. "Now that I can eat without feeling sick, I feel like I can't stop."

"I'll make dinner soon."

"There's not much here."

When Teresa checked what was in the kitchen, she announced she would make red beans and rice and ginger spiced chicken, Uncle Darren sat back with a sigh. "I haven't had that in years."

"Just a few more minutes and you'll be in heaven," Teresa promised.

"How are things at the shop?"

"Early days yet, but I'm seeing progress." She saw Louisa grab another cookie. "Leave room for dinner."

"I have plenty," Louisa said. "I used to worry about my weight all the time. Now I say 'screw it'."

"You still want to be healthy."

Louisa lifted a brow. "If I start looking like you, I'll stop."

"Louisa," Darren said in warning.

"Mom's gone. I don't need another one," Louisa said then left the room.

"Ignore her."

"I know she's just angry about a lot of things and wants to take it out on me," Teresa said, determined not to take offense.

"Do you still play the piano?" Darren asked. "I remember Margaret said you could play."

"Yes, would you like me to play something?"

He nodded.

She took the cover off the piano and sat down, hoping the piano was in tune. She hit a few keys and ascertained that it was.

"Do you have a request?" she asked, flexing her fingers.

"Something fun."

"I'm afraid I only know classics."

"That's okay."

She chose a song by Chopin, running her fingers lightly over the keys like a humming bird. The dull little house filled with a melodious sound, changing the atmosphere to one of enchantment. This was what Teresa loved most about music, that it belonged to all people.

Teresa could imagine people dancing at a ball as their expensive jewelry glittered in the light or campers out on a mountain, watching a sunset. Her uncle began to hum along. He stopped when he heard a knock on the door. "I wonder who that could be?" he said then opened the front door, welcoming a cold March wind. A tall stranger, with bags underneath his arms, stood in the entrance like a dark messenger.

CHAPTER 14

"There's nothing that warms a man's heart more than to be greeted by the soothing voice of music," the man said.

Darren jumped back, eager to welcome his friend. "Oh, Sean. Come in, come in." He took one of the bags from him and pushed him in a chair. "You have to meet my niece who's staying with us for a while, Teresa. She's the new owner of the store down the street."

"We've already met," Teresa said coolly, measuring Sean with her eyes. She began to play a more somber piece.

"Good God, what's happened to this place?" Sean said, looking around.

"Teresa's magic touch," Darren said.

Sean looked over at her. "I thought you said you weren't a witch."

"So what did you bring us?" Louisa asked, coming into the room before Teresa could reply.

He kept his gaze on Teresa a second longer, then turned to Louisa. "Nothing much, see for yourself." He stood and placed the other bag on the couch. She delved in and pulled out oranges, bread, matches, ham and a blanket. Louisa turned from the items she'd set on the table. "Sean Casey," she said in a low purr, running her hand through his hair before giving him a sound kiss on the mouth. "You're the best."

Darren grinned, waving his package of cigars. "Very wonderful. You and Teresa are the best things to happen to us." He put the food back in the bag. "You're just in time for dinner." He headed for the kitchen. "Let me put these away."

Sean sat down on the piano bench next to Teresa. "Next time I'll bring something for you," he said, his voice deepening to an intimate level.

"Don't waste your time." She wished he wasn't so big, he took up most of the seat and smelled like a cold night, wood and fresh soap.

"We need to talk."

She stopped playing and started to stand. "No, we don't."

He grabbed her wrist and forced her back down. "Yes, we do."

She nodded. "Okay."

He eased his grip.

She quickly stood and moved away.

"What are you doing?" he asked, surprised by the sudden distance.

"I'm giving you the space and peace you first asked me for. You don't have to worry, I'll stay away so you can have your time with Uncle Darren and Louisa," she said, then marched to the kitchen.

SEAN SCRATCHED his beard and watched her. She was slowly driving him insane. The woman bugged him and he didn't know why. She gnawed at his mind like a termite—he couldn't understand why she had captured such prominence in his thoughts. Many people annoyed him and he brushed them aside, but something about her lingered. Dammit, why did she have to be so lovely with her beautiful cocoa skin and soft, gentle brown eyes?

Why did she have to carry herself with such soft elegance? Her gauzy red top and flowing blue skirt stood out in the dull little kitchen like a rose peeking out of the cracks of a sidewalk, hinting of an outer gentleness, but an inner strength, an inner resolve. Plus, she stirred up questions within him: how had she known the diagnosis for the man? Who was she really? He knew his secrets, but what secrets did she keep?

When he had driven up to the house, hearing the music echoing in the wind, he felt like he'd come home. Come to a place for his weary soul to rest. He knew Teresa would be there, but when he'd opened the door, he hadn't expected to see the one woman who'd haunted his mind, sitting like a mythical Muse creating melodies that stirred the sleeping man inside him. Something strange, yet wondrous, touched his heart, a pleasurable pain he couldn't comprehend. It couldn't have been that he was happy to see her again, that would be crazy. Yet the entire evening he hadn't been able to keep his eyes off her as she served them a delicious meal of red beans and rice and ginger spiced chicken, and even now he continued to stare at her while she washed the dishes at the sink.

"That meal was everything you promised, Teresa," Darren called over his shoulder as he stretched out in his chair.

"It was my pleasure," Teresa said, turning on the water to rinse the dishes.

"I guess I should come over more often," Sean added.

Teresa didn't respond. Her rebuff was as tangible as a slap.

Sean reached in his front shirt pocket for a cigarette, then remembered that he'd given up smoking nine years ago. He softly swore.

"She doesn't seem to like you for some reason," Darren said, eyeing his friend.

He rested his forearms on the table. "No."

"Some men just don't have the ability to charm like others."

Sean laughed bitterly. "Yeah, I suppose so." He quieted into a melancholy silence. He should leave, but he had no desire to return to his large solitary house. At times he wondered if Teresa had put a curse on him, for as she had hoped, he was drowning in his solitude—peace hammered at him on all sides and an aching loneliness began to creep into his evenings, which was why he'd come visiting.

"Sean, come over here and talk to me," Louisa ordered from the couch. Glad for the release of his confusing, tormenting thoughts, Sean joined her. She was always a nice distraction. She knew how to be with a man, how to touch him and make him feel good. But for some reason he'd been avoiding her most of the evening, but maybe that had been a mistake.

"What do you want to talk about?"

She patted a space closer to her. Sean scooted over, used to Louisa's flirtatious ways and not surprised when she rested her hand on his thigh. "Tell me about your day."

"Today was pretty boring, but...first I found a diamond bracelet, which I later discovered belonged to Lady Winterthorn who's vacationing here with her Italian prince."

Louisa grinned, enjoying their childish game of make-believe. "Can I see it?"

"No," he shook his head, keeping his expression serious. "I had to give it back. She'd tossed it after having an argument with her lover. She thanked me by taking me on her yacht and serving me caviar."

Louisa's smile grew. "Is that all she served you?"

Sean grinned. "Let's just say that I made her forget about the prince for a few hours before he decided to return and I had to escape undetected."

"Which of course you did."

He nodded. "And when I came back to shore, I did my grocery shopping, then came here."

"You're right," Teresa said, overhearing their talk as she picked up three empty soda cans that Louisa had left lying near the couch. "That was a rather boring day."

He captured her with his eyes. "Give me a chance, I'm usually better the second time."

Teresa didn't misunderstand his reference to their kiss. "It's a shame you even need a second time," she said then went to the kitchen.

Louisa laughed. "Did you piss in her punch or something?"

"Or something." Sean rubbed his nose trying not to appear too interested. "So...why is Teresa staying here?"

Louisa stared at him for a long moment then swore. "Are you interested?"

"Hell no, I was just curious."

"You've never been this curious about me."

He let his gaze slid down the length of her. "I've never had to be curious about you."

Louisa licked her bottom lip and crossed her legs so they pressed against his. "Maybe, I should change that."

"And maybe you don't have to," he said, but as he said the words he couldn't help wondering why Teresa was still mad at him and wondering if she was watching him with Louisa now. And why the hell did he care if she was? He stood.

Louisa stared up at him disappointed. "You're leaving already?"

"No, I just have some personal business," he said then went to the bathroom. When he was through, he didn't return to the living room. Instead he headed to the kitchen where he found Teresa scrubbing a pot with such vigor her entire body shook. He snuck up behind her and whispered in her ear, "You should use gloves."

Her response was even better than he could have predicted. In surprise, she dropped the pot in the water splashing herself. Water soaked her shirt and dripped from her hair.

Sean burst into laughter. Teresa took the hose and squirted him in the face. His shocked expression was priceless. She couldn't help herself, she doubled over in laughter.

Sean brushed wet hair from his forehead. "You think that's funny?"

"Yes, and if you take one step closer, I'll do it again," she warned when his eyes narrowed.

"I'll risk it." She squirted him as he grabbed for the hose. It continued to soak them as they fought to possess it.

"I hope with all the fun you're having you two will be willing to pay my water bill," Darren said, casually getting a beer from the fridge.

They immediately broke away from each other, the hose slithered back into its place like a lizard.

"Sorry, Uncle," Teresa said.

"Why don't you both dry off?" He looked at Sean. "You can borrow a shirt from my closet."

"THIS IS ALL YOUR FAULT," Teresa said under her breath as they walked down the hall.

"What are you so worried about? Nothing happened."

"I was suppose to be washing dishes not—"

"Having some fun?"

She went into her room. "No, seeking revenge."

"Prude."

Teresa closed the door in his face.

She opened a drawer, then slammed it closed. How could she have let him get to her? How could she have gotten so carried away? He wasn't supposed to matter and she didn't like him. At least she didn't want to. She knew she had to keep her distance. He wanted his space and she wasn't the woman to help him heal from a marriage to a woman who looked like the beautiful Pernelle.

A part of her had started to hope that maybe he was a little curious about her when he'd sat down and talked to her at the piano. And her heart had betrayed her by beating a little faster, but Louisa's kiss and seeing them together and flirting, replaced her quickening pulse with pangs of jealous.

There was definitely something between them. He never smiled at her like that, but of course a man like him wouldn't. She had heard the rumors. For all she knew, Louisa's baby could be his. Keeping her distance was the best way to keep herself safe. Running the store and helping Louisa was all that mattered. It had been a risk to stay here even for a brief while, but she didn't regret it. Seeing him with Louisa would be a sobering reminder of her foolish heart.

Teresa quickly changed her shirt and fixed her hair. She took a deep breath and opened the door.

Sean stood there wearing one of Darren's old shirts—the sleeves were too short and with each breath the buttons threatened to pop. Teresa covered her mouth to stop herself from laughing.

"As you can see, this will not work," Sean said dryly.

Teresa bit her lip and nodded, fighting to keep her gaze on his face and not his chest.

"I was wondering if you had something I could borrow."

Her humor fell. "What are you implying?"

He came into the room. "Relax, I'm not making any insulting references to your healthy, womanly figure. I just notice that you like baggy clothes."

"And why should I help you?"

"Because I'm asking you nicely." He placed his hands on his hips, the movement was followed by a loud rip. The shirt split in two and fell down his arms. Sean glanced down. "I was afraid that would happen."

Teresa fell into helpless laughter.

Sean tore the shirt off. "Yea, go ahead and laugh."

Teresa fell on her bed and laughed harder.

Sean tossed the ruined shirt on the floor.

"It's like a scene from The Incredible Hulk," Teresa said between breaths.

He turned to her with interest. "You watch superhero movies?"

She just wiped tears from her eyes and grinned at him, making no move to answer.

He shrugged. "Fine, don't tell me. So where are your clothes?"

She pointed to the dresser drawers. "In there."

He opened the drawer and pulled out a pair of panties. "Just what I thought, knickers as white as a christening gown."

She snatched the item out of his grasp. "Pervert." She pushed him out of the way and searched for a shirt.

"Here's one."

He didn't respond.

When she turned to him she saw him surveying the room.

She in turn watched the muscles play in his back. His presence made the space even smaller. He began to flex his muscles. Teresa closed the drawer. "Show off."

"Hey, you're willing to watch. I'm willing to perform."

"I wasn't watching you."

"Good, then you didn't notice the small birthmark on my shoulder."

"You don't have a small birthmark on your shoulder."

His whole face spread into a smile. "I know."

She threw the shirt at him. "There."

"Thank you." He slipped into the shirt.

Teresa reluctantly acknowledged that it fit him perfectly. While it hung on her, it fell on him as smoothly as an oiled glove. The truth was, he could probably make a potato sack look good—the bastard.

"Is this where you sleep then?" he asked, pointing to the tiny bed.

She clasped her hands together and fluttered her lashes. "Your powers of deduction astound me."

"What are you doing in a place you don't belong?"

"That's none of your business."

He took a step towards her and lowered his voice. "I'm making it my business, planning to stop me?"

"I want you out of my room."

"Why?"

"Because I don't like you."

His gaze held hers. "Yes, you do."

She chose not to respond, although her breathing turned shallow and her mouth dry.

"You know you have nothing to be angry about."

She turned, pointing a finger at him. "I don't like men who maul me like a—"

He took another step forward. "Maul *you?* Talk about having an overactive imagination. You came at me like a swarm of bees."

"Just to shock you." She folded her arms. "But you turned it into something else."

His mouth curved into a smug grin. "What? Scared because you liked it?"

She returned the expression. "Why, because you are?"

His smiled dropped. "What?"

"You're scared because in spite of everything, you can't believe that chubby plain old me, actually was exciting and tasted good."

"P-plain?" Sean said, stumbling over the word. "Did you just say plain?"

"You hate how much you liked it, don't you?"

She was taunting him. She had no right to have that kind of control. He was suppose to be the one to make her feel uncomfortable. He was supposed to make her admit that the kiss was good. That *he* was good. He wasn't the one who was supposed to feel this bare and vulnerable. Bertha said Teresa had no guile, but he didn't believe that. She flaunted her beauty at him.

"Don't flatter yourself, I've been with better and far more beautiful." As soon as the words left his mouth, he regretted them. Behind her bright brown eyes was a flicker of hurt he knew he'd inflicted. His chest tightened as he realized that Bertha had been right. Teresa didn't know she was beautiful. But how could that be? He was so used to playing hardball with cold sophisticated women with ice for blood, that he'd become cold as well. He was too proud to apologize, too proud to show that she had hit upon one of his weaknesses, so he'd shot back like a wounded dog, lashing out with fury and spite.

He turned away from her, regret making his heart pound with an aching strength, knowing that distance was the best thing right now. He headed for the door, then stopped. Only a coward would leave like this, leave her alone in this little room after stomping on her feelings. He turned. "I'm sorry. I didn't mean that."

"Don't apologize for being honest," she said, her eyes bright with tears she didn't let fall.

He stopped her before she could reach the door. He grabbed her arms and stared down at her, amazed that a woman nearly half his size could hold a strange power over him. "You don't know how dangerous you are to me," he said in a hoarse whisper. He took a deep steadying breath. "I don't want to like you. I don't want to feel anything for you or for *anyone*. I don't want to feel anything when you look at me like that." His grip tightened. "I don't want to think about you or hold you close or imagine the smell of your skin, the feel of your lips, the touch of your hands," he said, letting his gaze fall down to her hands as if willing them to do the very thing he didn't want them to.

Teresa sensed his conflicting need, the strange sense of awareness seizing her again as it had the first day she saw him. She said his name in a soft whisper and when he lifted his eyes to meet hers, she felt for a moment as if they were one soul in two bodies. And that all the pain and confusion she felt, he felt it too.

"I don't know what this is," he said. "Or who you are."

"But you feel like you know me?" she asked, eager to hear him say what she felt. "I'm sorry. I realize now that you weren't making fun of me that day. You just hadn't known the right words to use. I understand that."

His gaze swept over her face in wonder and he lifted his hand to touch her cheek. "The right words? How can you not know how

beaut—" He released her and stepped back. "I can't do this," he said in a raw whisper.

"You once asked me how I knew about that man's allergic reaction. I could sense it."

"What?"

She bit her lip, holding his gaze, feeling that she could trust him. "I could just sense it. I know it sounds crazy but—"

He shook his head. "No, it's not crazy. I can sense your power." He cupped her face in his hands.

She closed her eyes and smiled. "And I can feel yours. You always make me feel calm."

"Is that why you won't leave me alone to dance with my shadows?"

Teresa opened her eyes. "No, it's because you deserve to feel alive again."

He let his hands fall. "But I can't—"

Louisa came into the room, interrupting him. "What's taking you two so long?"

Teresa knew the mood had been broken and stepped away from him. "Nothing," she said ducking past them.

CHAPTER 15

That night, as the stars twinkled high above the house, Teresa replayed Sean's words in her mind, the feel of his hands on her arms and face and the look in his eyes. He didn't want to like her, but did that mean that he did? Did he want her to stay away or was he telling her not to? She couldn't understand him even though she felt as if she knew him. Out of the corner of her eye, as he held her, she saw the tiny stones of his necklace and they seemed to twinkle at her, but she didn't know what that meant. Jessie knew more about stones than she did. As Sean held her she wanted to feel angry, but instead, she felt as if her heart would burst.

Several days later, she felt more herself. Sean hadn't stop by and she was relieved, although her heart still longed to know what he was thinking. She was fixing a sign on the front porch of her store before it opened when she heard Sean's rusty truck drive up. It made a ghastly sound, then quieted.

She was so stunned by the sight of him that when she gave the sign one last whack, she missed the target and hit her thumb. She gasped then bit her lip to keep from screaming as tears filled her eyes. Vulgar epitaphs circled in her head at a dizzying pace. She paced back and forth holding her thumb, willing the pain to go away and cursing herself for being so stupid. She blinked back her tears and cradled her hand when she heard him slam his door closed. By the time he approached her, she looked calm. She kept her face averted and pretended to be busy.

"Need a hand?"

She turned to him to say no but the word died on her lips. "What happened to your hair?" she cried. In the sun the black curls had been tinted a distinctive dark green.

He ran a self-conscious hand through his hair. "St. Patrick's Day at Preek's Bar...I thought I'd do my share."

"Couldn't you have just gotten drunk?"

He grinned. "And who's to say I didn't?"

She folded her arms, believing him because his eyes were a little red. "Did you enjoy yourself?"

"Yes."

"How long is it going to stay that way?"

"A couple of washes."

"Why didn't you dye your beard as well so that you could look completely ridiculous?"

"Someone has sharpened her tongue today."

"Louisa's not here."

"I came here to see you."

"Oh..." she said, surprised by his honesty. She turned back to the sign, not wanting him to see the joy on her face. "Go on inside. I'll be with you in a minute." But she didn't hear him move and turned back to him and saw that he was gone, although his truck remained. She sighed, not knowing what to think and straightened the sign, then glanced down at her thumb.

"Psst."

She turned around to see where the sound was coming from

and looked down. On the porch railing she saw a little, wooden grey cat with big green eyes. Suddenly a dark curly head and laughing eyes appeared next to it. "Do you like it?"

Teresa walked over to the carving amazed by the sight of his joy. "Is it for me?"

Sean straightened to his full height looking irritated. "Do you see

anyone else hanging about?"

"No, but why?"

He frowned. "Stop asking silly questions. Do you like it or not?"

She touched the object briefly, then pushed her hands into her pockets. She wanted to be happy but she wasn't sure. She didn't know men the way Louisa did and wasn't sure how she should react. Should she pretend that it didn't matter? Or tell him how beautiful she thought it was? She didn't want to push him away, but she didn't know how to play games either. "Does this mean...that we're friends now?"

Sean scratched his beard and turned away. "Do you like it or not?"

"How come you never bring Mist with you?" Teresa asked, not ready to answer his question.

"I only take him with me to the bay." He looked at her and suddenly grinned. "And you're getting as good as me at not answering questions."

"I do like it. Thanks."

He raised his eyebrows affronted. "Thanks? That's it?"

She leaned on the railing to ask him what more he expected, not quite sure if he was flirting with her or not, but without warning she heard a loud crack, like a gunshot, pierce through the air and she and the railing fell on top of him.

She quickly rolled off him. "Oh, no. Are you okay?"

He took a deep breath then pushed off the railing. "I suggest you get that fixed," he said in a hoarse voice.

She touched his arm. "I am so sorry. Where are you hurt?"

He stared up at the sky. "Everywhere and then some."

"I'm sorry." She saw blood seeping through his shirt, a piece of wood had punctured his skin.

"I think I just saved you from a lawsuit," he said with a painful chuckle.

"It's not funny."

He slowly sat up and was about to say something—when his statement was cut off by an exclamation.

Teresa looked at him alarmed. "Are you hurt somewhere else?"

He grasped her wrist and pulled her hand towards him. "What happened to your thumb?"

She glanced down and saw it was swelling and turning blue. "I hit it with a hammer."

"What for?"

She glared at him. "I didn't do it on purpose."

"Sure," he said with teasing doubt. He took out a handkerchief from his back pocket. "Don't worry it's clean," he said as he gently wrapped the handkerchief around the finger and tied it together. "Now we're both the walking wounded."

"Come on inside. I'll have to close the store today and see about getting the railing fixed, but we have to look at you first." She made a quick call to the store manager to notify the clerks that they wouldn't need to come in, then turned to Sean.

"I'm fine," he said.

But she didn't believe him until she had him in the back kitchen area. She grabbed some fresh herbs and quickly chopped them.

Sean looked at her, curious. "What are you doing?"

"Making a poultice to draw out any hidden splinters, don't worry it won't take long," she said, efficiently moving through the kitchen. She blended the herbs with some water until it was a mushy consistency then spread it on muslin with a spoon. "This is so it won't stick to the wound," Teresa explained when she rubbed some body oil on the affected area, aware of his nearness, the warmth of his skin and his steady gaze on her. She then placed the poultice on him, moving fast so that her hands wouldn't tremble, then she applied a bandage to hold it in place. "Keep it on overnight and come back tomorrow so that I can check it."

"Yes, doctor," he said with such solemnity that she couldn't help a smile. She turned to the fridge and poured him something to drink.

"Hmm," he said after a long swallow and holding his glass out for more. "This is delicious."

"Mint lemonade always refreshes," Teresa said, refilling his glass.

"I can get that railing fixed for you by tomorrow. I know a guy who's helped us with repairs at the clinic who's reliable."

"You work at a clinic?" she asked, unable to mask her surprise.

"I volunteer there."

"Why?"

The corners of his mouth kicked up in a grin. "Because they wouldn't be able to afford me."

"That's not what I was asking."

His grin widened. "I know." He studied her for a moment. "I used to be a surgeon and that's all I'm going to say."

"Somehow I'm not surprised."

He looked around at the bowls, oils and herb mixtures on the counter. "What were you up to before you hammered your hand?"

"Making some peppermint gel for the women at the local garden society."

"You're making a lot. How much do you charge them?"

Teresa blinked. "Charge them?"

He nodded.

"Oh, it's just something I've always made," she said with a dismissive wave of her hand. "When I was a piano teacher, one of the ladies complimented me on my hands and I told her my secret for keeping the fingers limber. It's nothing special."

"But isn't the time, effort and materials worth something?" he said lifting up one of the jars and sniffing it. "How does it work?"

"Oh, it's just a simple gel." She took his hand and smoothed some gel over it, only realizing too late how bold her action had been. She could have just told him, instead of holding his large hand in her own and massaging the gel over his beautiful brown skin. She kept her gaze lowered, hoping in the quiet of the room, he couldn't hear her pounding heart. "It has a wonderful restorative effect on dry, working hands."

Sean touched his hands impressed. "You should make this available in your store and see if it sells."

"But the clientele around here doesn't have time to work in gardens and play piano."

"But the clinic sees a lot of women who work hard all day. Not just pampered women want to feel and look good."

"I wouldn't know how much to charge."

Sean asked her a few more questions then came up with an amount that hit the right price point for their target audience. He then helped her come up with a product description for the jar and to put on the store's website.

Teresa bit her lip. "Do you really think this will work?"

"It's worth a try."

To her shock, the gel was an instant hit. Soon "Beautiful You" was buzzing with new customers and the sales receipts reflected their success. Louisa rang up five customers in a row, already feeling tired, even though the day had barely started. Her mood lifted when she saw Sean enter.

"Is Teresa around?" he asked.

"No, but you can keep me company."

"Another time." He winked at her then looked around the busy shop. "Don't want to get in the way."

Louisa watched him leave, with a frown. Flirting with him wasn't half as much fun as it used to be. He used to be more attentive, but now he seemed distracted, as if he wanted to be somewhere else. No, with *someone* else. That bothered her the most. He was an attractive man and always made her feel beautiful and now things weren't the same. Of course she could blame her expanding waistline, but she still had a pretty good figure and could definitely turn heads and she was definitely smaller than Teresa. Though a baby hippo was smaller than Teresa. Teresa. She couldn't believe she was a little jealous of that plain little goody-two shoes. People liked her. Sean especially, not that Louisa thought much of it.

She doubted he wanted to get in her jeans. Who would? The girl was probably as dry as the Sahara—no action there. But something about him was different whenever Teresa was around. Once she'd caught him staring at Teresa as she washed the dinner dishes, but couldn't figure out why. Even her father seemed to be under Teresa's spell, always asking her to play a tune or praising her cooking. Like that was all a woman was good for? Who cared about cooking nowadays? It wasn't like she was amazing at it.

But she knew part of her jealousy wasn't Teresa's fault. She missed her lover. She even went to town to follow his daily route just to be with him in spirit. Then she went to the shop he owned with his wife. She'd never been inside before. Never been interested, but now she was curious. An attractive woman approached her. "Can I help you?"

"I'm just looking." She saw a corner where there were a number of sale items. She knew they were poor sellers since Teresa had gotten rid of the same items when she had taken over the beauty shop. She had a sense about things like that.

Louisa's heart started to race as an idea came to her. She knew of a way she could get him back. It would fix everything and he would need her this time and wouldn't be able to toss her aside. Then he'd realize how much he loved her and would leave his wife.

She went to his private practice. He kept his expression fixed when he saw her, although there was an edge of tension she chose to ignore. She smiled at him. "I may have a way to help you with business."

CHAPTER 16

Helene kept her gaze on the television screen when she heard her husband come through the door. She briefly let her gaze glance at the wall clock. The living room was designed more for style than function and they both liked it that way. The sparse furniture and minimal accents suited them. She smiled at the portrait of a little Siamese. Precious had been a darling cat, too bad they'd had to get rid of her because she clashed with the furniture. Fortunately, the aquarium was a better fit. She liked the life she'd created with her husband and she wouldn't let anything change that.

She still couldn't believe Teresa had taken over a store. She'd carefully damaged her reputation after her aunt Bess's death and didn't think Teresa would ever have the gumption to use the money that she knew should have stayed in the family. It just proved that Teresa wasn't the sweet innocent everyone thought she was. Her aunt had been so besotted with her. She always pretended that she didn't know how much people liked her, acting as if she didn't know how much older people and children loved her company.

But Helene knew Teresa was a threat. She remembered the first time she'd heard about her aunt's new piano teacher. From her aunt's description, Teresa Clifton was an accomplished woman who had traveled extensively as a young pianist and had gotten a degree in Music. She only had a select number of students. Helene had been delighted for her aunt, who seemed excited that she'd been chosen, but when she met Teresa, that joy died. First, Teresa was a lot younger than she'd expected—about six years younger than herself—and she was not only an accomplished musician, but she knew about herbs at a level that stunned her. She'd studied for hours to gain the information that had easily rolled off Teresa's tongue. Teresa made her feel like a fraud. She didn't act impressed by the fact that Helene was a Master Herbalist and that her husband was a doctor.

Teresa had a special way of assessing people's needs. Any time she and Aunt Bess visited the store, people would ask her questions and Teresa would smile and patiently answer their questions. Teresa always smiled a lot, but her smiles were superior and smug. Aunt Bess's death had put an end to that.

But now Teresa's shop was a rival. She couldn't believe it was actually doing well without Valley Ray products. Its success threatened them and had come as a surprise. They dominated the market in their county and she planned to keep it that way. She just had to figure out how.

Thomas came into the room and bent over to place a light kiss on her cheek. An unfamiliar whiff of perfume lingered when he stood.

She sighed annoyed. "Must you smell like one of your whores when you come home?"

"I think I found a solution to our problem."

She turned to him, eager, remembering why she ignored his infidelities. "What?"

"I have someone working at Teresa's store willing to give us some valuable information."

CHAPTER 17

Spring with its promises of everything new and fresh gave Teresa the courage to believe that she could make all her dreams come true. Her store was flourishing and her relationship with Sean, although still nebulous, gave her hope that she could turn his feelings towards her into something more. She worked in the garden she'd started at the side of the store to let visitors see what they could grow and use themselves. She hoped to eventually hold classes or workshops and educate the community about the use of herbs in cooking and healing. She was glad for the spring rain. It made the ground soft and easier to weed.

Teresa was doing just that when she heard Sean's truck roar in. It coughed and groaned then quieted.

"When are you going to put that thing out to pasture?" she asked him without looking up.

"Priscilla? Never. I saved her from the scrap heap and she's served me well ever since."

"I see," she said, wrestling with a nasty looking weed when two large boots stopped in front of her. She paused and stared up at him. His face looked tired and his eyes a little red, making her wonder how much—and often—he enjoyed going to Preek's Bar.

"I never knew the depths of masochistic pleasure 'til I met you," Sean said. He grinned and squatted down in front of her. He handed her a package wrapped in a brown paper bag. "Here."

"Why do you always come around bearing gifts?"

He smiled. "There's no crime in it. Take the bag."

"What is it for?"

"Do I really need a reason?" He shoved the package into her hand.

With a show of great reluctance, just to tease him, Teresa opened the package. It was a limited edition, fully illustrated JS Braden book. She gave a little squeal. "Where did you get this?" she asked, hugging it to her chest.

"Do you like it?"

"You really have to ask me that?" she said in surprise, then impulsively hugged him. "I know it's expensive and I probably should say 'no you shouldn't have', but I won't. Thank you!"

He held her snugly, letting out a relaxed breath. "I'm glad you like it, Sweets."

Teresa smiled, her cheeks warming at the nickname he'd given her. "I love it."

He continued to hold her then drew away. "I'm glad."

She laughed, running her hand over the embossed cover. "It's beautiful. But you don't have to keep giving me gifts."

He tossed her gloves aside, wiping his hands together. "I know."

"Have you read her work?"

"No, I don't read."

Teresa stared at him appalled. "You don't read?"

"I like to live life, not read about it."

"Then you're missing out on a lot."

He shrugged, unconcerned. "Maybe, maybe not. Books just sprout the ideas of their creators. I prefer to create my own ideas."

"And have no one dispute them?"

"JS Braden's books are just children's fantasies."

"JS Braden's books aren't just fantasies. They're new ways to look at life. I love to put myself into the world of magic and dreams."

Sean lightly touched a flower petal. "Do you believe in magic?"

"No."

He lifted an eyebrow in disbelief. "A witch that doesn't believe in magic, that's strange."

"I'm not a witch."

"I have yet to figure that out. For the past couple of weeks I've wondered if you've put me under a spell."

"Well, if I had, you've awakened from it."

"I'll decide that."

"I already know."

"And how would you know that?"

"Because if I truly had you under a spell you would..." *be in love with me* she silently finished.

"I would what?" he pressed.

She turned away no longer able to face him. "Not be driving a truck that's about to die on the side of the road and I'd know why a former high-priced doctor was volunteering at a clinic."

"I'll tell you one day."

"But not today?" she asked, looking at him.

He shook his head.

"See? I have no power over you so you have nothing to worry about."

He playfully tweaked her cheek. "How wrong you are. Sometimes I wonder if you're as naïve as you look."

"I'm not naïve, although my sisters would say so," Teresa said, wishing her racing heart would return to normal. Just the touch of his hand made it flutter. "I don't believe in magic, but I believe in dreams. Every single one. Even the wild ones that dart out of your grasp like dragonflies." She turned back to him, ready to meet his stare. "All dreams must be handled with care."

"But I, being poor, have only my dreams; I have spread my dreams under your feet; Tread softly, for you tread on my dreams."

She grabbed his sleeve, her eyes wide. "You know Yeats?"

"Not personally." He grinned. "Was that a little too learned for you?"

Her eyes suddenly narrowed. "I thought you didn't read."

"I don't read generally, but I'm not completely aliterate."

"I didn't say you were. Do you believe in dreams?"

Sean shook his head and turned away to watch an ant try to carry a large leaf. "I believe that dreams are what makes life tolerable," he explained. He met her eyes. "However, I do believe in magic. The daily elves who toil to show us the wonders of what is usually hidden from view."

"Like what?"

Like the fact that right now, right at this moment in her muddy jeans and lopsided ponytail with her fresh plain face, she was beautiful to him. Beautiful like dewdrops on a spider web, a robin's redbreast against a tall tree, a calm ocean reflecting the rays of the setting sun. There definitely had to be magic that day, in this muddy weedy garden, that had been sprinkled in his eyes. God how he wanted her. He inwardly groaned, he knew he was treading on dangerous territory. He was on the edge of falling in love.

But Teresa was too gentle for the passion that consumed him, his wild ways. The ones he was careful to keep hidden. She needed guidance, not someone who would overwhelm her, not someone who would take as much as he could. He could never offer her what she needed.

He glanced down at his boots, trying to clear his roaming thoughts. "Like...like friendship."

"Or love?" Teresa said in an eager voice. "The ability to be able to look at someone for years then suddenly see them in a new and transformed way, I believe in that kind of magic too."

He sighed. "And it's a magic I can't offer you, but—"

"That's okay."

His head shot up and he looked at her, amazed by her simple acceptance. She didn't know how much power she already had over him. She truly was innocent; he could use that to his advantage. He wouldn't let himself fall in love with her, but he wouldn't deny how much he wanted her. "Teresa. Let's go out tomorrow."

Louisa's voice cut through Teresa's reply. "She can't. She's going to a party with me."

"With you?" Sean looked at Teresa then back at her cousin.

"Yes, isn't that right, Teresa?"

For a moment Teresa looked torn then said, "Yes."

Sean nodded. "Okay, then we'll do it another time."

He stood and left.

Teresa stood too and turned to her cousin. "Why did you say that?"

"Because I'm saving you from making a big mistake. If you're too eager, you'll just be a 'man bag'. You know, something a guy carries around because he has too, but not something he shows off to the guys. Some people call it friends with benefits. I call it being a loser."

"But I don't think—"

"I know men more than you do. Trust me, let me show you some tricks that we'll try at the party to help make Sean yours."

Teresa regretted going to Louisa's party the moment she stepped into the place.

"This is not like those fancy parties you're probably used to," Louisa had warned as they got into the car. "But it'll be worth it."

Teresa wasn't sure of that. But she did know she was wearing too much makeup, too tight clothes, and she was out of her element. She'd let her younger cousin take the lead because it made her happy and Teresa didn't see the harm in it until it was too late to change her mind.

The party was held at Preek's Bar, a rundown pool hall that had a crooked roof, but solid wood flooring and drinks that flowed freely. When Louisa and Teresa entered, eyes turned to them, though Teresa didn't see it through the haze of smoke. Louisa deposited her at a table, then immediately disappeared. The music was a mixture of calypso, jazz and salsa.

Abandoned and not knowing what to do, Teresa rested her arms on the wooden table and listened to the exploding drumbeat that deafened most of the dance song's melody. She felt calm, smelling the pungent odor of cigar smoke and weed. The dancing couples appeared as dark shadows swinging to and fro in the warm, sweat-soaked room.

A few men came up to her, but after saying yes to one man with hands like an octopus, she declined other requests. The crowd quickly changed from civil to rowdy once one o'clock rolled around.

Teresa was crushed against the wall, holding her beer like a can of mace, when a man swaying on his feet came up to her.

"Would ya like to dance?" he asked. The last word came out in a drunken hiss as 'danshhh.'

She offered him a polite smile and tried not to wrinkle her

nose at the smell of beer and sweat clinging to his Hawaiian shirt. "No, thank you."

He grabbed her arms, roughly pulling her away from the wall. "That's not the kind of answer I'm looking for right now. We've seen you turn down our best men. You're not even that pretty, think you're too good for us?"

"No, I just don't feel like dancing," she said, trying to free herself from his grasp, but his hands were clammy, sticking to her skin like masking tape.

"Fine, then we can do something else." He brought her close and opened his mouth to kiss her. She saw his tongue come towards her like a pink snake and knew she had to do something. She bit down on his bottom lip so hard his entire body shook in pain. He let out a loud curse as she pushed him away and wiped her mouth of the taste of his lips. He cursed, covering his bleeding lip. He grabbed the back of her hair, bending her head back until she thought her neck would crack. His dark grey eyes were mirrors of hate.

"Somebody needs to teach you some manners." He was now completely sober and his tone held a promise of revenge.

She refused to be afraid. "How can you when you don't have any?"

"That's just fine, 'cause I'll leave it up to them." He gestured to two men who stood up behind him. A shiver of panic shot up her back. She grabbed a fork off a nearby table and stabbed him in the side. The man screamed and released her.

Teresa ducked into the crowd and disappeared before the other men could get her. The harmless crowd of shadows now felt like a maze of seaweed. She couldn't find the exit and people were unwilling to let her pass. She could feel the two goons fast approaching like bloodhounds on a scent.

A man pulled her into a dance pose. "Don't look up, just bury your head in my chest and move with me," he ordered.

She did exactly as instructed, pressing her head against him. She held onto him as if she could melt into his body and completely disappear.

"Not so tight, Sweets."

"Oh sorry." She loosened her grip, but something made her pause. It could have been the smell of wood that clung to his shirt or the way he said 'sweets', but in a moment she knew whose arms she was in. She looked up at him. "What are you—"

Sean pushed her head back down. "Keep your head down." He spun her around just as the two men pushed past. She could hear Sean's heart beat beneath her; it beat as fast as her own.

He slid his keys into her pocket and began to speak rapidly. "On the count of three. I want you to be ready."

"Ready for what?"

"One...two...three..." He picked her up and tossed her out the window. She landed on a bush. "Drive Priscilla around the back," he ordered, then ducked his head back inside.

Teresa stood up and went to the parking lot. Her heart stopped when she stared at over twenty similar trucks.

CHAPTER 18

It was only a flash of luck or a kind ghost that positioned the moonlight to shine on Sean's rusty truck. She opened it, jumped inside and had to stand on her toes so that she could reach the pedals and sped it around the back. She arrived just as Sean exited the bar. She slid to the passenger's seat as he leaped in. He slammed the door shut just as one of the men lunged for him. He shifted into gear and sped off.

They didn't speak until the lights of the bar were a distant memory.

"Louisa's still back there."

"Louisa can take care of herself," he said in a grim tone. "She shouldn't have taken you there in the first place."

"She was trying to help me."

"Help you?"

Teresa shook her head. "Never mind."

"What did you do to that guy's mouth?"

"I bit him."

He gave a low whistle. "Glad you never minded me kissing you."

She fell silent.

"If you're mad at me just say so, but don't pull another stunt like this."

"I'm not mad at you and it wasn't a stunt. Louisa—"

"If I hadn't come along do you know what those men would have done to you?"

Heat warmed her cheeks. "And you'd feel responsible?"

"Yes," he said in a quiet tone. "Because then I'd have to kill them."

"Don't talk nonsense."

"You really don't know me well, do you?"

"You're a doctor. You're meant to heal."

"I used to believe that too once."

"Why did you stop?"

He pulled on his beard and swore. "I never thought Louisa would stoop so low. She should know better."

"Louisa didn't do anything, she just—"

"She should have stayed with you."

"I can take care—"

"You're as naïve as a two year old and you don't read people well."

"I...wait. Why are you stopping?"

Sean turned the car off and opened the door. "Because we're going to eat."

"Okay," Teresa said, then tried to unlatch her seat belt.

"Sometimes it sticks," Sean said, unlatching it for her then unlatching his.

They both got out of the truck and Teresa looked up at the friendly little restaurant where he'd parked. She wondered how she had ended up here when her evening had taken such a dangerous turn. She shivered at the thought of the man's mouth coming close to hers.

Sean looked at her. "Cold?"

"No." She shivered again.

He reached in his truck and grabbed a jacket from under the seat. "Stubborn witch," he muttered, putting her arms in the jacket as if he were dressing a doll.

She tried to fix his torn sleeve. "Arrogant wizard."

He put a hand under her arm and laughed. "Come on. Let's go."

The place was a squat, rundown building with a crooked sign and wobbly front steps. When they entered, a jukebox played and people chatted amongst themselves while sitting on wooden benches, and in the far corner was an upright piano with a picture of ships overhead. There were round wooden tables with glowing red candles. Sean grabbed a menu from near the door, then they seated themselves.

He handed her one. "This place doesn't look like much, but the food is terrific. The soups are the best."

The tables were so small that their knees touched. Sean didn't seem to notice.

Teresa glanced at the menu, surprised. She had expected to see hamburgers and hot dogs, but instead she saw a list of exotic appetizers. "These are real meals. What would a chef of this caliber be doing here?"

"She likes it," the waitress said overhearing the conversation. "Said that people here really appreciate her food."

Teresa looked around the sparse crowd. "But she doesn't appear to be getting many customers."

"She gets enough," the waitress replied. "Have you two decided what to order?"

"I'll have the crab soup," Sean said.

Teresa handed her the menu. "And I'll have the vegetable soup with pesto."

"Good choice," she said and walked away.

Teresa looked around the room, thinking of changes. Perhaps if more people in the neighboring county knew about the restaurant, it would get more business.

Sean watched her under half closed lids. "Whatever you're thinking, cut it out."

"Why?"

"Because the place is fine the way it is."

"I know it's fine, but don't you ever look at a place and think how it could be better?"

He shook his head. "Never."

"You're lying."

He grinned. "I know." He stretched out his legs, letting one rest between hers.

"Cut it out," Teresa warned, feeling warm.

"What?"

"Stop acting innocent."

"Sweets, I've got long legs."

"Do they make up for a short—"

He narrowed his eyes. "Watch yourself."

"See?" she said with a smug grin. "I'm not as naïve as you think."

"You think it's wise to tease a man like that?"

"No, not any man, just you."

"Why me?"

"Now who's being naïve?"

A basket of warm rolls arrived. Sean broke one in half, buttered both sides and handed one to her; the simple gesture had an intimate feel to it. It felt right that they were breaking bread. A companionable silence descended. Sean seemed lost in thought and Teresa didn't want to tread on them.

The waitress came back with their food.

"You know, I couldn't help noticing how beautiful your hair is," she said, staring at Sean's curls.

He slanted her a cold stare. "Try."

She looked blank.

Teresa smiled. "Ever since he witnessed the murder of Jingo Biggs, the smuggler from Texas, he's been in hiding. The wig is part of his disguise," she said.

"Wig? But it looks so real," the waitress said, cautiously reaching to touch a silky black curl.

"Don't touch my hair," he warned. She snatched her hand back and scurried away.

Teresa shook her head. "Stop scowling, she's gone."

"It's ridiculous, women's attraction to my hair."

"It's not just the hair of course. It's those piercing hazel eyes which you hide pretty well."

His scowl increased.

"Just be happy you're not an animal. You'd probably end up being someone's coat."

The corner of his mouth lifted. "They wouldn't be able to catch me."

They were quiet as they ate. On the jukebox, Patsy Cline's lyrical whine came on singing 'Crazy'. Perhaps it was the song and the mood, but something made her want to be honest with him. "I really appreciate you helping me tonight."

"You're welcome."

"And I know how hard it is to be with someone since your wife..."

He sent her a sharp look. "Mother promised—"

"Bertha didn't tell me anything. I just...sensed you suffered a heartbreak," she finished, not wanting to tell him about Pernelle. Perhaps that would make him shut down even more and Pernelle didn't seem eager to have him know about her. "Did she leave you?"

He sniffed. "That's one way of looking at it."

"And you can't get over her."

He shook his head. "I don't think I ever will. Sometimes I even think I still see her."

Teresa's heart constricted, feeling the pain and loss that echoed in his voice. She envied his love for his wife. "And I know she was beautiful."

"Exquisite." His intelligent eyes studied her face, then he lowered his gaze and mumbled. "Seems to be a damn weakness of mine."

"Loving someone isn't a weakness."

He lifted his gaze. "That's not what I mean and...you don't need to hear about that."

"Yes, I do. As your friend—"

"Teresa, haven't you figured out by now that I don't want to be your friend?"

Teresa reached across the table and held his hand. It was a brazen move for her but she couldn't stop herself. She didn't want him to push her away, she didn't want to lose the fragile bond they'd created. She couldn't imagine him not being in her life even though it hurt that he didn't feel for her the same way she felt for him. His pain was all that mattered. "I know," she said gently. "I know you miss her and that you loved her so much that you've buried your heart. No, please don't look at me like that," she said when a look of surprise and anguish crossed his face. "You can trust me." She looked at their interlocked hands. "I can truly feel your pain. Just like I know why you don't like to shake hands, because you calm people and then people are drawn to you. Usually you're okay, but lately your defenses have been down and you're not sure you can absorb anyone else's hurt." She felt his hand tremble, but she didn't release her hold. "I know your love for her frightened you and the loss sometimes hurts so much that you feel as if you can't breathe. That your arms ache from her absence."

"Yes," Sean said, knowing how much that admission cost him. He took a deep shuddering breath, feeling as if a mist had been swept from his mind. And although the dark shadows that loomed around him didn't lighten, their pull did not feel as strong. He held her grasp as though she were a lifeboat that could save him from a raging sea. He'd never wanted to be saved before, he didn't want to live before and now he saw her true danger. He hadn't only been afraid of loving her, but that she'd make him want to live again. To be truly alive and not just a shadow of himself.

He'd grown used to his misery and reveled in his isolation. But she'd shone her light of truth on his solitude and saw the loneliness there and he didn't have his anger to keep him safe. He couldn't block her out and realized that he didn't want to. He didn't want to be alone anymore. He'd never felt at one with anyone else and for the first time he'd met someone who could clearly say all that he felt, without judgment.

"Yes," he said, again feeling strong enough to admit the truth. "I buried my heart the moment I buried my daughter."

CHAPTER 19

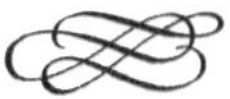

Teresa nearly released his hand. His revelation stunned her. She thought all his pain and love had been metaphorical. That the demise of his marriage had been like a death to him, she hadn't sensed that it was literal. She didn't know what to think and thought of Bertha's warning about the shadows around him. Had the death of their child led to the end of their marriage? If she helped him heal, would he return to his wife?

For a moment, she selfishly thought of pulling away. She didn't want to heal him and help him resurrect his heart only to see him turn to another woman. She didn't want to be just an itch he'd scratch and then discard like Louisa suggested. Louisa, who still refused to tell her who the father of her baby was. Louisa, who probably knew more about seducing a man like Sean than Teresa ever could. She knew it would take a lot more than a pretty dress and makeup to get him to see her in a new way.

He was wonderful and she loved him. She loved everything about him, from his unruly hair, his sharp hazel gaze, his old truck and his teasing humor. But he didn't see her as a possible replacement for the woman he'd married, the mother of his child. Teresa swallowed her bitter jealousy and cast any hope aside that their friendship could be anything more.

"What was her name?" she asked with a tender smile.

"Chloe. She died at four from cystic fibrosis. And after she died, I just worked. I worked to save as many people as I could and it made me feel good. It made me feel alive. It made me feel useful when for so many years I'd felt helpless." He stared down at his soup. "I never thought I'd be able to talk about this again, but it feels good. It actually feels good to say her name. Chloe. I remember her tiny hand against my lips telling me to stop when I made funny faces at her. I took a picture of her in a little white coat and plastic stethoscope because she wanted to be a doctor just like me." His eyes shone with unshed tears. "And I remember her telling me not to be sad when she lay sick in her hospital bed."

"Because she loved her daddy so much."

Sean blinked back his tears and sighed. "And her daddy loved her."

Teresa released his hand. "And that love made you strong, not weak."

Sean pushed back his chair and motioned to the waitress. "I want to go home."

"Yes, of course," Teresa said, taking his abrupt action in stride. He probably felt he'd revealed too much and wanted to be alone. They were silent as the waitress put the food in a takeaway bag and he paid.

"Thank you for everything," Teresa said, climbing into the truck and closing the door.

Sean groaned and rested his head on the steering wheel. "Please don't do this to me." He sat up and pierced her with a hard look. "I want you. I want you in my bed and I want you by my side and I want to get you out of my system."

"I know you're being honest, but—"

He effectively kissed the reply from her lips. His tongue tasted the sweetness of her mouth, then his hot lips burned their way to the side of her face and neck.

"Sean."

"Please don't say no to this," he breathed.

"I wasn't, I just—"

"Then don't say anything at all," he said, efficiently removing his jacket and her top. With one expert tug on her bra, the latch unhooked and her full breasts spilled out into his waiting hands. Like a man who had happened upon the lost city of Atlantis, he merely stared, holding and stroking them.

"What are you doing?" Teresa asked when he continued to stare, making her embarrassed.

"You just turned me into a breasts man." He brought one luscious hanging fruit to his lips and sucked like he would a ripe mango. "Had I known what was waiting for me, I wouldn't have been so patient." He watched a nipple harden under his touch then skimmed his hands down her side. "You're so round, full, soft," he said each word as he planted a kiss on her shoulder, stomach and chest. "So much to explore."

"It's called the fat girl advantage," Teresa said a little embarrassed.

He didn't hear her. He was too busy unzipping her jeans.

"Sean, wait. You don't even have your shirt off."

He quickly shed his shirt and pulled her close. Teresa never realized flesh could feel so fiery; his soft curling chest hair rubbed against her breasts, sending electrical shocks through her body.

Sean suddenly swore. "We can't do this here."

"Why not?"

He smiled at her irritation. "It's too awkward. The gear shift nearly turned me into a woman."

She sat up, her face flushed. "And you want to go home," she reminded him as she quickly latched her bra and pulled on her top.

He groaned. "I hope I can make it there."

She glanced at her watch. "Want me to call a taxi?"

He turned sharply to her. "What are you talking about?"

"You want to be alone."

"What gave you that idea?"

Teresa hesitated, surprised by the question. "You said you wanted to go home."

Sean rested his head on the steering wheel and shook his head. "I keep forgetting it's you."

"What?"

He sat up. "Yes, I want to go home and I want to take you with me."

"Take me with you?" Teresa repeated, not sure she'd heard him correctly.

"That's right, Sweets," he said with a soft smile, his voice deepening into huskiness. "I want you to stay with me tonight."

CHAPTER 20

Teresa stared at him, seeing the hunger and desire in his gaze, not knowing what to say. He wanted her and that made her feel gorgeous and desirable. Then she caught a glimpse of herself in the rearview mirror. Her makeup and tight clothes reflected a false image of her. Was this what Louisa had been trying to help her achieve?

And did he feel true desire or did he only want her because he wanted to forget his pain? Was his hunger a primal desire for any kind of solace? Would he look at her this way if she looked like herself and he hadn't told her about his daughter? He didn't share her feelings. Maybe if she waited longer, he'd see her for more than just a good time. After tonight would she lose what little power she had over him? Would the novelty end?

But as Teresa looked into his smoldering gaze, she couldn't pretend that he was the only one interested. She wanted it too. Just as much. Maybe more. Teresa clicked on her seat belt, coming to a decision. "Let's go."

But when she got to his house, some of her courage failed her. Teresa inwardly grimaced as they drove up to his house, the moon touching it with a faint light. It was a great monstrous insult to architecture. A Gothic mausoleum with turrets, and arched windows melded with contemporary lines. It looked like the designer was on LSD at the time and unsure of what style the house should be. One side was handled with care while the other looked like the builders had gotten tired and given up. Yet the location was spectacular. Suddenly a deep mist came in from the bay cloaking the house in a haze.

"Ugly, isn't it?" he said proudly.

"Terribly."

"However, it has character."

"It looks like it has a nasty temper. I bet the floors creak and the windows rattle."

He laughed. "You get used to it."

Teresa was pleasantly surprised when she entered the foyer. The outside was imposing but the inside was welcoming, if not stark. When she glanced at the living room, she saw the dark panel flooring covered by a red area rug, a big grand piano, and a large stone fireplace faced an overstuffed maroon couch and ottoman. Large windows faced the water.

Mist came up to greet her. Teresa patted the cat on the head. "Hello."

Sean took her hand. "You can talk to her later," he said, then led her up the squeaky stairs. They passed four closed bedrooms before reaching the master suite. It was a man's room with dark wood flooring and dresser, a metal standing lamp, a woven blue rug on the floor and a large picture of a castle over the bed. A beautiful tan spread covered the bed, but she noticed only one pillow.

Sean saw her look and said, "I never expected company."

She nodded. The room was neat and clean, just what she expected from him. She went to the window and saw it afforded a view of the bay. She turned to Sean, who was watching her with a guarded expression.

"It's lovely," she said, swinging her arms a little, not knowing what else to say or do.

He took a step forward, his gaze never leaving her face. "No, you're spectacular."

Teresa shook her head and smiled. "But I wasn't talking about me."

"I know," he said, then made her forget her surroundings. He captured her mouth with his own and the impact was like hot wax poured over ice; the same rush of pleasure and surprise raced through their veins. Sean couldn't get enough of her. She was a cool spring to a parched man, a shower of rain to a man who was burning. With her he felt something completely unfamiliar. His hands cupped her breasts, enjoying their fullness. He held them like he would any new object that held a fascination.

He'd never felt such a desire before and he couldn't understand what it meant. Everything about her held him captive—that had never happened before. He'd never been a patient lover before, so it took some effort to restrain himself. Her pleasure mattered to him. He never again wanted to be the man he'd once been. And for a moment, he felt the weight of her innocence, he knew she'd never been with a man before, and the selfish part of him took it as a burden as he rolled on a condom, but the other half took it as a gift.

And in his life he'd been given many gifts—his brilliance, his wealth—which he'd taken for granted, until he'd lost Chloe and the ability to care about anything. But Teresa had changed all that. In her arms he found redemption. She was genuine and without guile and a place for his battered and tired soul to find solace.

Teresa felt the soft sheets on her back as she sank deeper into the bed and inhaled the scent of him. He had hands that roamed and smoothed her body until she felt like a perfect gem cradled in the hands of a jeweler. In the unfamiliar wave of emotion she felt safe with him, following his lead, unashamed of her inexperience, eager to learn. He was a master teacher—attentive and tender—arousing in her such sweet delight that any slight pain quickly turned into pleasure.

She welcomed him inside her with no inhibition, surrendering completely to him.

And with her simple action she caused some stones around his heart to fall and though Sean knew his vulnerability, he had no way to stop and soon didn't want to. Although he knew she was surrendering her body to him, he also knew she was dangerously close to capturing his heart and forcing his own surrender. She knew how to touch him just the way he liked it. He moaned deep in his throat. She was so soft and smelled so sweet. He moaned again.

She giggled.

"What?" he asked.

"You sound like a purring panther."

"I can't help it," he murmured. She was what he wanted. Needed. His hands, mouth and body sought every inch of her with a greediness he did not try to abate and as a conclave blanket of stars hung overhead he let himself lose control.

Afterwards, Teresa slipped into a deep, satisfied sleep only to be abruptly awaken when something warm and hairy touched her leg—she screamed and leaped out of bed. Sean did the same grabbing a knife from under his pillow.

"What happened? What's wrong?" he demanded, turning on the lights.

"Nothing." She felt embarrassed realizing it was only his leg touching hers. It had all felt so much like a dream, she'd forgotten it was true. She wasn't alone in her bed at Louisa's house, but with Sean.

He ran a hand through his hair, exhaling with annoyance. "*Nothing* made you scream and jump out of bed?"

"Yes. Put the knife away." She got back under the covers. "Sorry, I've never slept with a man before."

He got back under the covers as well, but looked at her, his eyes bright with amusement. "Afraid I was going to maul you again?" he asked, pulling her to him.

She relaxed, resting her head on his chest, listening to his heartbeat. She remembered when her father would hold her on his lap and tell her stories and when her mother would lie in her bed and stay up with her after a nightmare. She could feel the weight of his tiredness that she knew had nothing to do with sleep, but she wouldn't ask him about it. "No."

He closed his eyes. "Good."

She took the opportunity to study his face, what she could see of it. She pushed some hair from his forehead, then from the side of his face.

"Hmm, that feels good."

She stopped. "I was just checking to see if you have pointy ears."

He laughed. "No, I didn't inherit those."

She touched the necklace on his chest. "And where did you get this?"

"Don't remember. Want one?"

"No."

"I can get one made for you in the shape of a butterfly. Would you like that?"

She toyed with his hair again, to give her nervous fingers something to do. He wanted to give her another gift? "No, I don't like butterflies."

"Why not?"

"When I was little, I prayed and waited for the day I would come out of my cocoon and have beautiful skin, exquisite features and a shapely body." She laughed at her childish hopes. "I never even made it to the cocoon stage. My Aunt Yvette—the most obnoxious British Caribbean immigrant to touch American soil as my sisters like to say—always hoped I'd grow into my looks. I know she means well. The Amarids, my mother's people, have excellent genes. Every time she came over to our house her poor face would fall in disappointment. All of us, my sisters and I, are considered plain, you see. She actually considered paying for plastic surgery, we have a reputation to uphold, she likes to say."

Sean looked at her for a long moment then frowned. "That's a dumb story. Tell me another one."

Teresa widened her eyes. "It's the truth."

He shook his head. "I don't believe you."

"If you think Louisa has looks, just you wait until you meet Olivia."

"So you're calling me a liar, then?"

"I never said that."

"I say you're beautiful and you don't believe me. Maybe you have a hard time believing an ugly man like me?" he said stroking his beard.

"You're not ugly."

He ran a hand through his hair. "I don't know if you've noticed, but I have a mess of curls."

"Actually, I hadn't noticed," Teresa said with mock innocence.

"Well, at school the girls loved to pull my hair."

"Why?"

He stared up at her. "To make sure I wasn't wearing a wig. Another girl said she loved to see how my hair bounced back. So one day I shaved it all off. Do you know what my mother did?"

"She cried."

"No, she laughed so hard she hiccupped. When my dad saw me he laughed 'til tears streamed down his face. Only my little sister cried. I never did it again."

"When did you grow the beard?"

"When I got tired of shaving. Now tell me something else about you. When did you know you had a gift?"

"You'll think it's silly."

"No, I won't."

"I first heard about the gift from the stories my father used to tell us about our ancestors. It's believed that we descended from people who came fully formed from the insides of a petrified tree when the God of Whispers cried because no one could hear his voice.

"So our lineage always had a special connection to nature, destined to use our talents to honor him. My sister Jessie and cousin BJ have an affinity with stones, while from an early age I knew that herbs and healing was my calling. Sensing people's pain and visions came in my teens. But I can't read minds or anything," she quickly added, not wanting to worry him. "It's just that, at times, I can sense a person's greatest pain and I might see a vision. But I have to be on the right energy wavelength and it doesn't work with everyone and—"

He placed a finger against her lips. "Relax, your gift doesn't scare me."

Teresa smiled feeling a warm glow fill her. "I'm glad and your gift doesn't scare me either."

He stiffened. "My gift couldn't save Chloe."

"And I couldn't save my parents or my friend Bess," Teresa said with feeling. "Some people think I murdered her," she said, then her mouth went dry as fear and despair swirled inside her. She hadn't meant to share that and didn't want to ruin the connection they had. What would he think of her now? "I mean—"

Sean cupped her cheek, his fingers warm and strong against her skin, and she felt her anxiety ebb, as her fear and despair disappeared. "I know," he said, smoothing back her hair. He held her gaze. "Okay?"

She nodded, amazed by how much his touch calmed her. How safe she felt when only seconds ago she felt frightened. He had the handler's gift; he'd never let her fall apart. She knew he was the man for her even if he didn't know it yet.

"Are you tired?" he asked.

"No."

He pushed back the sheets and grabbed a robe from his closet. "I want to show you something. Wait here," he said, then disappeared. He came back moments later, sat on her side of the bed and held a picture out to her. His hand shook, but Teresa pretended not to notice. She took the photograph from him and stared down at a little girl, sitting in a wheelchair outside of a hospital holding a large brown teddy bear and wearing a big smile.

"She died a week after this picture," Sean said.

"And lived every day with joy." Teresa waved at the picture. "Hi, Chloe. It's nice to meet you. I'm a friend of your daddy. What was that?" She brought the picture close to her ear then shook her head. "I don't know." She looked at Sean. "She wants to know if you're going to keep being sad?"

He rested his hands on his knees and hung his head. He didn't move, but she saw a tear fall. She touched his arm.

"She was my life, my heart, my everything," he said quietly.

Tears welled in her eyes as she felt his pain and remembered burying her parents and Bess. "And that's too much for a little girl to bear."

"I know."

Teresa gently rested the photo on his lap. "Is Daddy ready to be happy now?"

Sean lifted the photo and traced a finger over the little girl's face. He took a deep breath then nodded and Teresa felt the weight of his sorrow dissipate, replaced with memories of love.

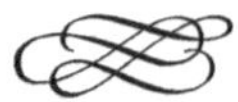

CHAPTER 21

"What should I tell them?" Teresa asked as she sat in Sean's truck outside of her Uncle's house.

Sean frowned at the house. "How much longer are you planning to stay here?"

His question surprised her and reminded her of a similar conversation she'd had with Michelle. Her sister had lost her temper when Teresa finally admitted that Aunt Margaret had disappeared, and then threatened to pull up the garden Teresa used to tend. They reached a compromise when Teresa agreed to come over every other weekend, but hadn't agreed to anything more.

"Uncle Darren told me that some of the guys at the Valley Ray factory have been giving him a hard time because I don't sell their products."

He shook his head. "That wasn't my question."

"And he told me how much the rent I give him has helped them

and—"

Sean shook his head again. "Still not my question."

"Another couple of weeks."

"Make sure it's no more than that."

"I thought you liked them."

"I do, but that doesn't mean I'd live with them," he said, getting out of the truck.

Teresa followed him. "What are you doing?" she asked, hurrying after him as he marched to the door.

"Making sure you get home safely," he said, then pounded on the door.

Teresa grabbed his arm, frantic. "What are you doing? Are you trying to wake the whole house? Uncle Darren sleeps late on the weekends and Louisa—"

"I know," he said in a tight voice, then pounded harder.

"Wait," Teresa said, looking through her mini handbag. "I have a key."

Louisa swung the door open before she could reach it. She squinted at them and swore. "What the hell is your problem?"

Darren came up behind her, holding his head. "Sean, what brings you here?"

Sean motioned to Teresa. "I'm bringing her home. I know how worried you two were."

Darren had the grace to look a little embarrassed. "I knew she'd be okay. She's a big girl."

"Everyone knows that," Louisa said then laughed as if she'd made a clever joke and expected everyone to join in.

But Sean didn't laugh, he didn't smile, he didn't even move. He fixed Louisa with a look of such icy contempt, Teresa inwardly shivered. "You think what you did last night was funny?" he said.

Louisa's smile slipped. "I just—"

He narrowed his eyes. "Did that sound like a question I expected you to answer?"

She closed her mouth.

He held up a finger. "Just once. I'm going to let this pass just once, but if you do something like this again you won't be the one laughing."

He shifted his gaze to Darren. "I'll talk to you later," he said then squeezed Teresa's arm before he turned and left.

To Teresa's relief, Louisa didn't ask her any questions about where she'd disappeared to after the party. Neither did Uncle Darren, who spoke to her a couple days later only to tell her one thing.

"You're going with us to church this Sunday."

"But I'm not Catholic."

"It's Easter, God will forgive you."

TERESA ENDED up at church that Easter Sunday and fought desperately to keep her eyes open. Twice she had to nudge Darren to keep him awake because he began to snore. Asking her to attend church with them was only one of the strange changes he'd developed over the past couple of days. He'd also dropped her rent considerably and told her that Aunt Margaret would be returning soon, although she wasn't sure she believed him.

She nearly burst into tears of joy when the ceremony was over. She was heading eagerly towards the exit when someone familiar caught her eye. She'd never seen Sean in a suit and the sight surprised her, as did the dark sunglasses.

"Sean," she called out to him.

He spun around and waited for her to catch up to him, but he had a guarded expression. She hesitated, wondering how to approach him. Did he regret the other night? Should she mention their time together or pretend that it hadn't happened? Her weary expression stared back at her in the reflection of his dark lens. "Would you like to come over for dinner?" she asked, feeling that was a safe topic.

"I can't." He took off his glasses and rubbed his eyes.

She could see that they were red. "Are you okay?"

He shoved his sunglasses back on. "I just need a couple of days, okay?"

She swallowed her disappointment. He wanted to be alone again. "Okay."

He shoved his hands into his pockets and shook his head. "No, it's not," he said, then bent down and kissed her. "But I'll make it up to you," he whispered against her lips before he turned and got in his truck.

"Wow, I didn't expect to see him here," Darren said, watching Sean's truck drive away.

"I'm sure he could say the same about you," Teresa said.

"No, I show my face at the appropriate times. But Sean hasn't entered a church since his wife died."

Teresa turned to him stunned. "She died? I thought she left him."

"No, he won't talk about it so I don't suggest you bring it up. It still hurts him. But he's getting better. When I met him he was a mess."

"He still drinks," Teresa said softly, imagining him trying to drown the pain of losing both his wife and daughter.

"Of course he drinks. Any healthy man drinks."

"I mean heavily."

"Sean? No."

"Then why the hangovers?"

Darren frowned. "He doesn't suffer from hangovers."

She wondered if he was being purposefully dense. "At times his eyes give him away."

"Oh that."

"Yes, that."

Darren seemed to hesitate. "He's a private man. I don't think it's my place to give out a man's secrets."

"Fine." She'd wiggle that bit of information out of Bertha.

Unfortunately, Bertha proved to be just as tough to persuade.

"If he hasn't told you, then it's none of your business," she said clearing up the tea cups.

Teresa followed her into the kitchen. "I just want to know."

Bertha sent her a long, measuring look. "Why?"

"You know why."

Bertha released a heavy sigh and returned to the dining table and sat down. "He worries me," she said running her finger over the sparkling sheen of the recently polished table. "I'm not sure you're strong enough to help him carry the weight of his sorrow. He may never recover fully from it."

"I am. He told me about his daughter."

"But not his wife."

"Telling me about his daughter was hard enough." Teresa gripped her hands together. "You should have seen him."

"You're making excuses."

Teresa's gaze flashed with warning of the temper she kept in control. "I'm telling you what I know," she said in a curt tone.

"Because you slept with him? You think being in his arms means you know him?"

She spun away.

"Don't you turn your back to me," Bertha demanded.

Teresa took a deep, calming breath and turned. "I'm sorry, I just—"

"Have the Clifton temper," Bertha finished with a smile. "You think I don't know that?"

Teresa folded her arms. "I love him."

"I know that. I also know he's awakened something inside you and I'm glad. But what do you know about him?"

"Are you warning me away from him?"

"No, I'm asking you to mind the arrogance of your words. I'll tell you what you know. You know how *you feel* about him, you know *your desire*, but do you really know his? Do you know what you're up against?"

Teresa let her hands fall. "You're right. He doesn't feel the same way about me as I do him, but given time that can change and..." She let her words trail off when Bertha shook her head.

"That's not what I'm saying. Let me tell you what I know. If you really want him, you'll be fighting a strong force that may be more powerful than you are."

"You mean his love for her?"

"Perhaps something even bigger than that. You have to decide if this is a battle worth fighting."

"Battle?"

"Yes," Bertha said her voice grim. "For something even more precious than his heart."

SEAN DIDN'T KNOW what had possessed him to go to church that Sunday. He yanked off his tie as if it were strangling him and threw it on the bed. The closure he had expected, had prayed for hadn't come yet. He'd grown arrogant. He should have known it wouldn't be easy. Remembering Chloe was one thing, but forgetting his wife was something else entirely. He'd briefly thought of having a future with Teresa. He wanted a second chance.

But what if he truly opened himself to her? Let her meet the real Sean Casey, instead of the mirage he'd created? What would happen if instead of seeing him as a grieving father, she saw the unrelenting, ruthless man who had made money without thinking of others? The surgeon who'd thought he was God?

He still saw his wife's face and feelings of guilt, failure and rage always followed the sight of her. What would Teresa think of a man like that?

And yet, he wanted her to know the truth, at least part of it, so that she wouldn't romanticize him. So that there could be someone else he felt safe with. He craved her acceptance, hungered for it, as dangerous as that was. Sleeping with her was one thing, but he was getting greedy and knew it, but couldn't stop. Somehow he had to take a risk to be honest with her and let her choose.

"I NEED TO TALK TO YOU," Sean said a few days later as Teresa opened her car door ready to drive to her sister's house. He noticed she was dressed in a loose fitting blue knit top and flowing chiffon skirt. He wouldn't admit that he'd missed her.

"I can't."

He wasn't sure if it was the look or the tone, but something about her alerted him that she knew more about him than she had before. He squeezed his eyes shut and rested his head against the truck, heat stealing into his face. "Oh shit, she told you about Renee."

"No, Uncle Darren."

He merely shook his head, muttering things under his breath.

"And Bertha didn't tell me anything."

"Just enough to make you feel sorry for me?"

"I don't feel sorry for you."

"So she didn't tell you that sometimes I can't sleep for three days because I think of her? That sometimes I smell her exact perfume?"

"No, you just did," she said, glad she now knew why his eyes were sometimes red.

He turned to her; Teresa caught her lip in her lower teeth.

"Oh, you don't pity me, you find me amusing instead?"

"No, I just never imagined you as a blusher."

"Get in the truck. I'll drive you where you need to go."

Teresa looked at his truck doubtful it could make the journey. "I'm going to my sister's. She's hosting a small party. She lives in Bedford."

"Priscilla can make it," he assured her, helping her inside.

"You know you're incredibly sexy when you're embarrassed."

"Shut up." He closed the door. She grinned.

He didn't speak until about ten minutes into the drive, and Teresa remained silent too.

"I understand that she'll be a ghost between us," she finally said. "But I'm glad you're giving me a chance."

Sean adjusted the rearview mirror. "I didn't love her as much as you think, and you're the one taking a chance on me." He reached over and took her hand. "I'm working hard to deserve you."

Teresa laughed. "You don't have to do that."

He shifted gears.

Her heart sank as they drove up to the house. Cars poured out of the drive onto the street.

"Is this what your sister calls a small party?" Sean asked parking.

"No, but her husband does." She opened the door then hesitated. She turned to him. "How about you join me?"

He drummed his fingers on the steering wheel. "Why?"

"Because I'd like you to meet my sisters."

He hesitated and she understood why. Meeting family was a big step and their relationship wasn't settled yet. She was probably asking too much. "Never mind, I—"

He glanced down at his clothes. "You don't mind them seeing me like this?"

"No."

He grinned. "You want to give them a shock, don't you?"

She returned the expression. "Maybe."

"Will there be plenty of food?"

"Yes, and I won't stay more than an hour and there's no reason to be nervous."

He turned off the car. "I'm never nervous. Is your sister a good cook?"

"No, but fortunately they have caterers."

"All right, let's go."

The house was filled with well-dressed guests and for a moment Teresa wondered at her reckless decision. Sean looked completely out of place. He looked like a lumberjack on the run in his jeans and flannel shirt, his hair windblown. Although he received a number of surreptitious glances, he seemed unbothered and grabbed a biscuit from a tray. At least he was comfortable.

"These are good," he mumbled, taking another.

"Save your appetite," she warned, grabbing his hand. She spotted Kenneth's best friend Nathan Philips, a handsome man who liked to wear bold colors. Today he wore a crushed purple velvet jacket as he stood in the dining room talking to his colleague, Stephanie Radson and Jessie's best friend Wendy.

They both talked to Clayton Ross, a man who owned property in the South Bank. Michelle had helped him start two successful businesses and from what Teresa had heard, other businesses were starting to consider South Bank as well, which would revitalize the county and be great for "Beautiful You".

"New money is rolling in from somewhere," she overheard Mr. Ross say.

"That place needs it," Stephanie said. "Although Valley Ray has helped."

Mr. Ross cleared his throat. "I don't trust one factory towns. Factories come and go, but someone's getting the interest of people like me and that's a good thing."

"Where's my sister?" Teresa asked Nathan.

They all stopped talking and stared at her—or rather past her to the man who was munching on one of the hors d'oeuvres and softly humming to himself while looking around.

Teresa waved her hand in front of his face. "Nathan?"

He shook his head. "Uh, sorry. She's in the kitchen."

"God, he's gorgeous," Wendy whispered.

"How can you tell?" Stephanie asked.

"Just look at the way he stands. He's straight off a movie screen. Who is he?"

Teresa motioned Sean over and introduced him. "He's my...uh—"

"Lover," he said.

"Close friend," Teresa corrected, then grabbed Sean's arm and headed towards the kitchen. "Why did you say that?"

"Because it's true. I thought that's why you wanted me here. You wanted me to shock people."

"Not that much. I wanted you here as a *boyfriend*."

He winked at her. "I was just waiting for you to say it first."

Teresa stopped just outside the kitchen. "Just wait here for a minute. Don't move." When he nodded, she went inside.

Teresa spotted Jessie arranging food on a tray, and her housekeeper Freda was arranging glasses. "I thought you said this was going to be a small get together," she said.

Jessie groaned, looking more like a caterer than hostess in black pants and a crisp orange blouse. "It was supposed to be, until Kenneth got hold of the guest list. I have to get rid of Kenneth's unhealthy enjoyment of company."

Freda laughed. "That's like asking a leopard to change his spots."

Unexpectedly, two kids burst into the kitchen, then ran squealing outside again.

Jessie handed a waiter a tray and sat down in a chair. "I wish these people would at least watch their kids or leave them at home. You'd think we were running a daycare."

"Never mind," Freda said. "Ace will keep them in line," she said, using Syrah's nickname.

Jessie shook her head then took Teresa's hand. "I'm glad to see you could make it."

"Oh yes, I brought someone to meet you." She pulled Sean inside the kitchen before he walked off after a tray of hot current raisin rolls. "This is Sean."

Jessie leaped to her feet, failing to mask her surprise. "Oh, right, Sean...well...Nice to meet you."

"He doesn't shake hands," Teresa said in order to prevent an awkward moment.

"Okay." Jessie measured Sean from his boots to the top of his unruly hair. She sighed. Of all the men her sister had to fall for he looked like a perfect suspect for America's Most Wanted.

Freda came up to him and grabbed his hand. "Well, I'm a hand-shaker and I must say you're very welcomed here. Nice to see Teresa with new friends."

The corners of his mouth lifted. "It's a pleasure to be here."

"I hope you eat to your heart's content," Jessie said.

He turned to her and smiled. "Thanks. It's a nice place you have here," he said, running his hands along the counter.

Jessie paused for a moment, as if coming out of a dream. Did that beautiful voice really come from this man?

Freda thought the same, and of course felt the need to express herself. "Did you make a pack with the devil to get a voice like that?"

"No, I sold my soul for a lot worse," he said.

The women stared at him not knowing what else to say. Freda spoke first. "Well, enjoy yourself."

"Thank you." Teresa and Sean left the kitchen, stopping briefly at a large banquet table, filled their plates then walked over to a corner.

"Isn't there anyone else you want to introduce me to?" Sean asked.

"In a minute, I won't have to," Teresa said, spotting her eldest sister. "She'll introduce herself."

Michelle approached them. She looked like an intimidating warrior princess, sporting a cool grey suit and dangling silver earrings that shone like tiny daggers in the light. She blocked their path, placing one foot in front of the other and resting a hand on her hip. She stared at Sean with unabashed curiosity and distrust.

"You must be Sean," she said, her cool brown eyes taking in his attire. "I won't shake hands to introduce myself since I've heard you don't believe in it." She folded her arms. "My name is Michelle. What brings you here?"

"I invited him," Teresa said.

Michelle's eyes didn't leave his face. "I didn't ask you."

"It's as she says," Sean agreed.

"And you're seeing each other?"

He smiled. "Are you worried about my intentions?"

Michelle narrowed her eyes. "I know your intentions. That wasn't my question."

His smile remained, but developed a hard edge. "Yes."

"How long have you been in this country?"

"Since I was sixteen."

"And how long have you been seeing my sister?"

"Not long."

Michelle tilted her head to the side. "Is it wrong to hope that it will stay that way?"

"Yes, because you might be disappointed."

Michelle glanced at Teresa, then returned her gaze to his face. "Somehow I doubt it." She offered him one last look then walked away.

"She doesn't like me," Sean said, watching Michelle disappear in the crowd.

"No," Teresa agreed.

"And the feeling is mutual."

"She takes some getting used to." She took his hand. "Come on, let me show you the woods in the back."

Sean followed her then abruptly paused. Teresa turned to see what he was staring at and saw her cousin Olivia standing by the fireplace looking like a model out of a catalog. Her dark hair was piled high on her head with ringlets falling around her face. She wore a slim, yellow blouse, cream trousers, and heels that could double as lethal weapons. Teresa felt her heart fall. She couldn't blame him; he was like any other man in the presence of a beautiful woman—gawking, awestruck. Then she remembered how beautiful his first wife had been and how much she paled in comparison. She let his hand go and swallowed, although she felt a lump forming in her throat.

"That's my cousin Olivia," she said, fighting to keep her voice neutral. "Would you like to meet her?"

He suddenly seemed to remember himself. "Uh, no. She's your cousin?"

"Yes, can't you see the family resemblance?" she said with a note of sarcasm.

He stared at her for a moment, dazed. "No."

"It was meant as a joke."

"Oh," he said absently, glancing back at Olivia.

Although she understood his fascination, his unabashed gawking still hurt and made her sister Michelle's prediction seem more evident. They wouldn't last long together. Sean didn't love her and maybe never would, she had to accept that reality.

Teresa turned in disgust. If he preferred Olivia's company, he could have her. They'd had fun and now it was over. She had no one else to blame but herself, she was the one who'd brought him. However, if Teresa hadn't been so lost in thought and had been paying attention, she might have been able to prevent what happened next.

Sean got his foot caught on the strap of a woman's purse and tripped. His food flew through the air and landed on Olivia's blouse; her drink leaped out of her hands and splashed him. She glanced down and screamed in horror at the yellow stain on her blouse—curried chicken, a deadly mix on any material.

"My new blouse is ruined!" Olivia screeched. "You horrible, clumsy oaf!"

"It was an accident, Olivia, you left your purse in the way," Teresa said, lifting the cause of the accident off the floor.

"That's no excuse. It's been there all this time and nobody else has been so awkward and boorish to trip on it. That's what you get for inviting someone like *him* to a party like this. I don't know what you're trying to prove by bringing him here."

"Now listen—"

"Quiet," Sean ordered in a low voice instantly commanding

obedience, lightly touching her arm. Olivia shut her pretty mouth and stared at him amazed. "I apologize for ruining your blouse. I assure you it was an accident. There is no need to insult your cousin."

Olivia quickly relented under his dark gaze and tender touch. His deep voice cascaded around her like a waterfall and she suddenly felt warm. Never had she seen eyes so beautiful or felt so serene. "I'm sorry. I don't know what came over me." She placed her hand on her chest, resting her fingers right in the crevice of her breasts. Sean's eyes followed. "Please forgive me, I was overcome by shock."

"Close your mouth, Teresa." Michelle nudged her as they both watched the pair.

She did but couldn't believe what she was seeing. She'd seen him flirting with Louisa, and endearing himself to her, but she'd never seen this side to him before. This powerful, sexy charmer. "What's going on here?"

"You just lost your boyfriend," Michelle said.

Teresa gripped her hands into fists. "He's not like that."

"How do you know? Right now I'm seeing one of those fairy tales you like to read. And in this version Olivia is the big bad wolf and Sean is grandma." She saw Teresa's face fall and hated Sean for hurting her sister like that. She walked up to the pair who were still trying to outstare each other and said in a voice only they could hear, "Go find a room."

Sean shot Michelle a look, releasing his hold on Olivia. Olivia gasped in outrage and again wailed about her ruined top and demanded Michelle offer her an apology, Michelle ignored her and asked Sean to leave, two guests whispered about Sean possibly being an escaped convict, while Teresa tried to get them all to calm down.

"What's going on in here?" Kenneth asked, entering the

room. The sight of Olivia's soiled blouse and Sean's wet shirt explained only a part of what had happened. He couldn't understand why others looked frightened or why the room had suddenly fallen silent.

"I think we'd better go," Sean said, taking Teresa's plate.

"No, I think *you* should go," Michelle said. "I'll take Teresa home."

"Nobody should go," Jessie interrupted, appearing behind them. She glanced at her husband and sent him a private smile. "Brings back memories, doesn't it?"

He winked. "More than you know."

She grabbed Sean's sleeve like she would a school child. She looked at Kenneth. "Do something about Olivia. If she squeals one more time I may have to belt her."

Kenneth nodded and went to soothe Olivia, who had just realized her trousers were ruined as well.

"Michelle, stop frowning and get someone to clean up this mess," Jessie ordered. "And don't say another word. Teresa, continue to eat and relax, he's in good hands."

CHAPTER 22

Jessie led Sean upstairs, still holding onto his sleeve in case he decided to run. "You sure know how to make your presence known," she said opening the door to the master bedroom. The room was enormous with the sun coming in, polishing the large oak bed, and a marble chess set sat on one of the side tables. He didn't reply. "I was in your shoes once." She laughed. "I can tell you don't believe me. But it's true. I used to waitress and I once broke an entire tray of glasses."

He lifted an eyebrow.

"Yep, I was pretty embarrassed, but I survived. You, however, are something else. My cousin has never been calmed like that before. Well done."

"That was—"

"Never mind. Sit down."

She opened a closet and began shuffling through Kenneth's shirts.

He glanced at the marble chess set and basketball hoop attached to the door. "I don't want to take your husband's clothes," Sean protested when she held a shirt out to him.

"That's too bad. It's a hostess's duty to take care of her guests. Besides, it gives me an excuse to disappear."

"You're not a people person, then?"

"Is it that obvious?" She sighed. "And I try so hard. Go on and change." She studied him for a moment. "Now I know why my sister liked to watch you swim."

She saw the red on his cheeks surprised by how easily embarrassed he could be. She hadn't expected that then she noticed the necklace around his neck. "Hmm, that looks familiar. I wonder why."

He shrugged.

She decided to drop the subject and focus on what was important. "Why are you really seeing my sister?"

He stuffed the shirt in his pants. "Why do you think?"

"That you may give me an answer that will make me angry."

His head snapped up at her tone. "You approve of me as much as your sister Michelle does."

"Not quite. I don't trust you. Michelle plain doesn't like you. And your reaction to Olivia was—"

"No, let me explain—"

"No need to explain to me." She shook her head. "I hope you don't plan on going out looking like that."

"What?" he asked, having a hard time following the conversation.

She pointed to his shirt.

He looked down and noticed that he had buttoned it wrong. "It looks expensive," he commented, unbuttoning it.

"It's his favorite, just joking," she hurriedly added, when his eyes widened. "Damn, you're taking forever. Let me do it." She straightened his shirt and quickly buttoned it. "Who are you really, Sean Casey?"

"I like your sister and that's the truth."

Jessie sent him a hard look. "The only truth you're willing to share?" She held up a hand before he could reply, then looked around and lowered her voice like a child ready to do mischief. "I probably shouldn't do this, but I can't help myself." She pulled out a wooden box from one of the side tables. "I'm going to do a reading. It won't take long. Okay?"

He nodded and sat. "Okay."

Moments later Jessie stared down at the black velvet cloth where the nine stones Sean had selected lay, feeling a tinge of unease. She knew the stones—from the cool clear aquamarine to the golden look of the iron pyrite—had no power of their own, that they were just a vehicle for her intuition, but she didn't like what she saw. The size and positioning of the stones puzzled her. She saw rage and a soul in conflict, deception, and death. She didn't know if the death was in the past or future, but she sensed a man suffering. They sat facing each other, but she couldn't raise her gaze to see his face. She didn't know what to tell him and regretted her rash action.

She started to bite her nails then rested her hand on the table. "You've been through a lot—"

"Your sister means a lot to me and I'd never hurt her," Sean said, covering Jessie's hand.

Her mind told her the action was incredibly bold, but her body couldn't move. Soon all her apprehension seemed to fade away and as she looked into his eyes, she felt as if everything would be okay, that Teresa was safe with him. She looked down at his hand and remembered her father's stories about the 'handler's gift' and recalled how Sean had handled the stones in a way —with an easy reverence and sensual beauty— she'd never seen a man do before.

"I believe you."

The hint of a smile touched his mouth and she felt her pulse quicken. She was happily married, but still a woman who could be affected by a handsome man's gaze. "Good," he said.

"But you have to be careful," she said, knowing he knew more than she did about what he was up against.

He nodded. "I will."

Jessie stiffened when she heard footsteps and swiftly removed evidence of her reading just as the door opened.

"Hey what's going on in here?" Kenneth demanded, coming into the room.

Sean immediately pulled away from Jessie and stood. "Nothing," he said.

Jessie sent her husband a sly glance. "What do you think is going on?"

Kenneth rested against the wall, shoving his hands in his pockets, a lazy smile teasing his lips. "Why don't you tell me?"

Jessie stood next to Sean and looped her arm through his. He failed to discreetly pull away, not wanting to be the puck in their dangerous game. "I've decided you're too perfect. I want a man with some flaws."

"Thank goodness," he said, pushing away from the wall. "I was running out of ways to get rid of you." He grabbed his wife's arm and gently tossed her out the door. "Now go take care of the guests." He shut the door before she could argue. He turned to Sean, who was deciding whether to fight or flee. It wasn't that he was afraid, just that he had caused enough trouble and Kenneth would be a tough opponent. Although he had an easygoing appearance, he had a strong presence and dangerous eyes.

"Take a seat for a minute," Kenneth suggested, staring at the carpet.

"We weren't doing anything."

Kenneth glanced up surprised by the man's vehemence. "I know. Jessie likes to tease."

Sean still looked uneasy. Kenneth sighed, pulled out a chair and sat down. "Relax. I want to talk to you."

Sean hesitated, briefly wondering if he'd ever get a chance to leave, then eventually sat.

Kenneth rubbed his chin. "Looking at other women is an art form. No secure woman minds a quick glance, but gawking like a prepubescent teenager is offensive." He leaned forward, resting his elbows on his knees. "And as a man who respects women, I find it offensive too."

Sean ran a hand through his hair in frustration. "I wasn't staring. I mean, I was, but not for the reasons you think. " He rubbed his beard, and looked away, letting his voice drop. "She reminded me of someone." He hesitated. "Your wife wouldn't let me explain."

"Yes, it's her way of making you feel more guilty."

"It worked. When I—"

His statement was cut off when Kenneth softly swore under his breath.

"Give me a minute," he said, standing up. He waited by the door then suddenly opened it. Jessie fell into the room. He stared down at her with a smug grin. "May I help you?"

Jessie scowled at him. She stood up, brushing off her trousers. "I just wanted to make sure everything's all right."

Kenneth gestured to Sean who was watching the interaction with apparent amusement. "As you can see, everything's fine."

She lowered her voice. "You'll behave yourself, right? It wasn't a big deal."

"Now why wouldn't I behave myself?"

"Don't hurt—"

His tone hardened. "Go downstairs, Jas."

She held up her hands in surrender. "I'm going, I'm going."

He waited until she was at the top of the stairs before he shut the door, shaking his head.

Sean stared amazed. "How did you know she was there?"

"Because I know her." He resumed his seat. "She's afraid I might do something I'll regret, like break your face for insulting my sister-in-law in front of family and friends, but I wouldn't do that." He smiled, softening the veiled threat. "You wouldn't give me a reason to."

"I'd never hurt Teresa."

"That's good to know."

"But I—she wants something I can never give her."

"Such as?"

The guy was too damn easy to talk to. He couldn't believe he'd already revealed this much. But as Kenneth stared at him waiting for a response, Sean found no reason to retreat. Part of him was glad Teresa had family who knew her value and wanted to protect her, the other part wanted them to leave him alone. There was still so much he hadn't told her and he wasn't going to tell them. But he'd pretend to be as honest as they needed him to be. "I've been married before," he admitted.

"Okay."

Sean thought that was explanation enough, but Kenneth stared at him, obviously expecting more. "And it was...hard."

He nodded, his eyebrows furrowed. "What does that have to do with Teresa?"

Sean hesitated knowing he couldn't reveal too much. He sensed Kenneth was a man of strategy and he had to use the right one. "I'm just not marriage material. I mean, your wife seems nice enough, but I couldn't take a woman hovering and fussing over me."

Kenneth rubbed his chin for a moment, trying to soothe his temper. Jasmine was a soft spot with him; he didn't like anyone, especially strangers, criticizing her. He knew to others their relationship seemed strange, but it worked beautifully. However, he knew what Sean was saying. In the beginning, Jasmine's involvement in his life seemed burdensome and nagging. But it had ultimately been his salvation.

"You're right. Fortunately, Jas is perfect for me. Personally, I couldn't fall for a semi-witch who spends a great deal of time either daydreaming or making potions."

Sean's eyes flashed. "Teresa's not a witch and she doesn't make potions."

Kenneth shrugged, beginning to grin. "To each his own."

Sean recognized the smirk and sighed. "All right. I admit it. She means more to me than I want her to. But that doesn't change anything."

Kenneth nodded then said, "I just wanted to get you talking for another reason. I recognize a man with secrets."

Sean froze, realizing he'd underestimated him. "So?" he said with a nonchalance he didn't feel.

"Are you running from your secrets or protecting them?"

Sean stood. "I don't—"

Kenneth kept his voice soft. "Sit down."

Sean rested his hands on his hips. "We're through here unless you have something else you want to say."

Kenneth slowly rose to his feet and pinned him with a hard look. "Your secrets better be worth the consequences."

Sean sniffed. "Consequences?"

"If your secrets hurt Teresa in any way—"

"You'll make me pay?" Sean said unmoved by the threat.

"No." Kenneth lowered his gaze and lightly smoothed down Sean's collar. "I'll make you suffer," he said and his lethal gaze made his words a promise.

CHAPTER 23

"How is he?" Teresa asked, meeting Jessie at the bottom of the stairs. Thankfully Freda had helped Olivia find something to wear.

"I checked his pulse and his heartbeat seems to be fine." She paused. "However, I don't know what Kenneth is doing to him right now. Hopefully, his body parts are still attached."

"Jessie, be serious."

"He's okay, relax," she said, taking her sister's arm and heading for the kitchen.

They found Michelle organizing dishes. "You shouldn't have brought him in the first place," she said.

Teresa rolled her eyes. "It was an accident."

"How can you bring a man to a party by accident?"

"I meant the incident with Olivia."

"It wouldn't have happened if he hadn't been staring at Olivia like a salivating dog. Everyone saw it." Michelle shook her head, disgusted. "So tasteless."

"I'm sure he had a reason," Jessie said. "He wanted to explain, but I wouldn't let him."

Michelle rested her hip on the counter and adjusted her earring. "Yes, he has an excellent reason. He's a man."

"Just give him a chance," Teresa pleaded.

"And he's no ordinary man. He's a handler," Jessie said.

Teresa turned to her surprised. "How did you know?"

Jessie hesitated, not wanting to tell her sister about the reading. "Dad taught me how to spot them."

"It doesn't change anything," Michelle said. "He's not to be trusted."

Suddenly a boy came running through the kitchen and darted into the other room. Jessie's daughter, Syrah, soon followed, her face red with anger, her baseball cap sitting precariously on her head. "I'm going to get you, Marvin!"

Jessie grabbed her collar, halting the tirade. "Syrah, no running in the house," she ordered.

The girl wiggled free. "I promise I'll stop running, once I catch him." She raced into the other room.

Immediately after, her best friend, Daniel, entered the kitchen, holding up his hands to assure them. "Don't worry, Mrs. Preston, everything is under control," he said, then followed the other two children.

"Looks like Syrah's got your temper," Michelle said amused.

Jessie didn't disagree. "Fortunately, Daniel keeps her out of trouble most of the times."

Kenneth came into the kitchen, playfully wrapping an arm around Jessie's neck, pretending to strangle her. "I wish you would tell me when you invite live entertainment. People are still talking about Sean and Olivia."

Jessie pinched him on the arm. He flinched and let go. "This coming from someone who added twenty-five people to my list of seven," she said.

"The more the merrier." He turned to Teresa. "I had a nice chat with your new friend. He's a good guy."

Michelle folded her arms and tapped her foot. "Don't you dare encourage her, Kenneth."

"Why not? He seems like a decent guy."

She shot him a look. "What did he say to you?"

"We came to an understanding." He smiled at Teresa. "You have nothing to worry about."

Michelle threw up her hands. "You're not giving me any specifics. How can you tell he's not trouble?"

"I just can. I like him."

Jessie patted his cheek. "Kenneth, you're so nice, you'd befriend a rat if it smiled at you."

He ruffled her hair. "True, I fell in love with you, didn't I?"

He ducked when she tried to hit him and backed out of the kitchen blowing her a kiss.

"Do you two ever arm wrestle?" Michelle asked, always amazed at the physical nature of her sister's relationship.

"Sometimes. I usually let him win."

Michelle shook her head with an affectionate grin. "Kids."

"Speaking of kids," Teresa said. "You know it's oddly quiet."

Everyone paused. There wasn't a child's voice to be heard anywhere. When they left the kitchen they looked around and didn't see a child in sight.

"Now don't panic," Michelle demanded. "They have to be somewhere."

"Wait, listen," Teresa said.

Under the hum of adult voices, they heard a faint tune on a flute. The women stared at each other then followed the sound out into the wooded backyard. There they found Sean sitting under a tree surrounded by children, scattered about like fallen leaves, listening to him play his flute. Some rested against his legs, others played with twigs on the ground while the rest sat and stared, captivated.

He abruptly stopped playing. "Then what do you think happened?" he asked the group.

"A dragon comes down and eats them," Marvin said.

Syrah hit the boy in the arm. "There are no dragons in this story, silly."

He rubbed his arm annoyed. "So?"

"They use the secret portal," Daniel said.

Sean nodded. "Excellent and they escape once again."

"What about the warlock?" Syrah asked.

"Ah, 'Your days are numbered,' says he and away he goes to his cave, thinking of new ways to capture the Trayon band." He began to play again.

"A true Pied Piper," Michelle said. "We should be worried that—"

"Shut up, Mich," Jessie said. "He's great. I wonder how much he charges for babysitting?"

"That was truly amazing," Teresa told Sean on their drive back.

He shrugged. "I saw a little hellion getting ready to tear a boy's eyes out and thought I'd better do something."

She frowned. "That hellion's my niece."

He nodded. "I'm not surprised."

"You had them under a spell."

"I thought I'd seen my wife."

She paused. "What?"

"That's really what you want to talk about. What happened.

She looked so much like Renee that I couldn't get my bearings. I'm sorry."

"She is beautiful."

"And she scared the hell out of me. It was the second time in two weeks I thought I saw her."

"I'm sorry I invited you."

"I'm glad you did. I want your family to know who I am."

"Even for a short while?"

Sean drummed his fingers on the steering wheel. "Yes."

"Do you have siblings?"

He nodded. "Five."

"A big family."

"Hmm."

"And I probably will never meet them."

"Not if I can help it."

He slowed the truck and stopped in front of a house that rose like a giant monument on a hill. In the dimming light they saw silhouettes in the windows. "Would you like to live in a house that big?"

"Is this a trick question?"

"No, be honest."

She thought for a moment then shook her head. "No, too many rooms to clean."

He tugged on her ponytail. "You'd have a maid, you ninny."

"A maid." She rested her arms on the dashboard. "You know we had a maid once, but she quit after a month because she had nothing to do. We did everything ourselves." She stared at the house for a long moment then sat back and smiled. "I like your house."

"It's big."

"I know."

"And ugly."

She playfully tugged on his beard. "Like you and I think it's wonderful."

He grinned and started the truck. "I don't feel like taking you home yet. Let's go to the cinema."

"And see what?"

"Whatever's playing."

What was playing was one of the worst films they had ever seen called *Woe to Life*. It was so bad, Sean actually laughed through all the dramatic scenes. Even the climactic moment when the heroine lost her entire family in a stove explosion. Teresa nudged him, warning him to behave, but that only caused him to laugh harder. Fortunately, nobody paid attention. The two other couples were high school students too busy making out to care.

"That was dreadful," Teresa said. They sat in his truck looking at the other cars in the parking lot. Teresa was finishing an ice cream sandwich and Sean a packet of chocolate covered raisins. "But you were worse."

"I couldn't help myself. It was so bad it was painful. I couldn't decide if the script was bad or the acting."

"It was a mixture of both. When she threatened to kill herself when the waitress bought the wrong order, I thought that was a bit overdone."

"I think someone trying to kill themselves after watching that movie would be more realistic. The love scene was okay."

"What love scene?"

"The one in the bathtub."

"That was a love scene? I thought he was doing some strange form of CPR."

Sean looked astonished, then laughed. But all his good humor left him when he dropped Teresa home. "I really hate leaving you here. You have a great family. Why aren't you with them?"

"Uncle Darren and Louisa are my family and they need me."

Sean lifted a sly brow. "I need you. Want to move in with me?"

She made a face. "No," she said then got out of the truck.

"Okay, then just stay the night."

"Another time," she said. "I have things I have to do," she added when Sean followed her to the front door.

"Relax, I won't stay long."

When they entered the house, they found Louisa sitting on the sofa, her hand in a bag of potato chips. The remnants of a sandwich, bag of Oreos, Twizzlers and muffins lay around her like casualties of a child's sleepover.

"Louisa, what are you doing up?"

"I was waiting for you."

Teresa began to clean up the mess. "You shouldn't eat all this junk food."

"I was hungry." She sent Sean a look. "You hardly stop by here anymore."

"I've been busy."

She patted the seat beside her. "You're here now."

"But I can't stay long."

"I know I'm the size of a cow, but I'm still a woman."

"You look great," Teresa said.

"Hardly anything fits." She held out her arms. "I had to borrow one of your shirts."

Sean sent Teresa a look, but she ignored the insult. "We can go shopping. We can buy you some clothes and get your hair done. Would you like that?"

Louisa looked at her unsure. "Are you serious?"

"Yes."

"Then I'm there." She stood up. "I'll leave you two alone."

Once she was out of hearing, Sean said, "I don't like the way she talks to you."

Teresa shrugged. "It doesn't bother me. She's been hurt. I know it's hard for her seeing us together, especially if..."

"If what?"

She cleared her throat. "I've never asked you this before because what you did before we met is none of my business, but... I know you liked Louisa. And she likes you."

Sean rested his hands on his hips and shifted his gaze to the piano. "And you want to know if I slept with her?" He looked at her. "The answer is yes. Is the baby mine? No." He folded his arms. "Louisa isn't nasty to you because of me, there's another reason."

"She's brokenhearted. The father of her child abandoned her."

"That's still no excuse—"

"I can handle her. Besides, if you saw how Aunt Margaret treated her, you'd understand why she's like this."

"I know and I still don't like it."

"She's never been loved," Teresa said remembering the vision she'd seen of Louisa as a little girl. "Truly loved. And if I can show her what true love is, she can change."

Sean shook his head. "I'm surprised you've survived this long being so naïve. You put your hopes in the wrong things."

"So I shouldn't hope in you? Are you warning me off again?"

He gathered her in his arms and held her snugly. "No. I've decided to keep you even closer."

TERESA CALLED Michelle the next day, "It's an emergency, I need to go shopping with Louisa."

"How is that an emergency?"

"None of her clothes fit."

"So what?"

"I don't want to go alone and I thought a shopping spree would be fun for her."

"Should I repeat my first question?" Michelle said in a bored tone.

"She's been unhappy and I'm trying to lift her spirits. Please help, I'll be forever grateful...unless you have something else scheduled this weekend," she said, knowing her sister rarely did.

Michelle sighed. "I'll see if I can string Jessie along. You know how she feels about shopping."

"Good and schedule something at Kayla's."

"At this late date?"

"Pull some strings. I know you can."

CHAPTER 24

"Doesn't she know the meaning of the word moderate?" Michelle complained as Louisa tried on a silk maternity dress.

"This is making her happy," Teresa said.

"Yes, at the expense of *my* checkbook. Why am I paying—"

Teresa patted her sister's arm. "It's for a good cause," she said, not wanting to explain that she wasn't making enough yet for this little extravagance. She had some of Bess's money left, but wanted to hold on to it as a reserve.

"I suppose I could write this off as a charity," Michelle mumbled.

Louisa's mood improved immensely and she felt like a star when they took her to Kayla's salon and treated her to a manicure, pedicure, make up tips and a perm.

Afterwards, Jessie took them all to lunch. Jessie tried not to show any expression when Louisa ordered five appetizers and two entrees. After clearing her plate, she excused herself to go to the restroom.

"Well, she is definitely well fed," Michelle commented.

"She's eating for two," Teresa said.

"Right. Two hundred," Jessie muttered.

"Stop complaining. You know you can afford it."

"That's not the point. It's bad manners to spend someone else's money with such abandon."

"Do you know who the father is?"

"She won't say."

The conversation stopped when Louisa returned to the table. "Sorry," she said. "I have to keep going. Sometimes I feel like a leaky faucet."

"Yes, well. How do you feel now?" Teresa asked.

"Great. I don't know how to thank you. It's such a shame we aren't closer. We could do this more often."

Michelle coughed; Jessie stared out the window, Teresa smiled wearily.

"You guys are so lucky. This is how I want to live. Fancy clothes, great hair, expensive restaurants."

"We work hard," Michelle said.

"Yes, but you both married money and don't have to."

"But as you can see that is not always the best route," Michelle said. "I'm separated from my husband."

Louisa shook her head. "But that's because you did it all wrong."

Michelle stiffened.

Louisa didn't notice. "If he cheated on you, you should have just turned the other way while he signed your checks and if he was bad in bed, you just get a lover—same goes if he was boring, dumb or immature."

"James was none of those things."

"Then why are you separated?"

They all looked at Michelle expectantly.

"None of your business," she said.

Louisa shrugged, unfazed. "Your problem is that you think too much. I on the other hand, have plans."

"And what are those plans?" Jessie asked.

"I'm going to marry money like you."

"You won't have time right now," Michelle said. "You'll have to take care of the baby."

"No I won't. He'll eventually take care of both of us."

Michelle leaned forward. "You're playing a dangerous game."

Teresa looked at her confused. "What game?"

Michelle kept her gaze on Louisa. "He's married, isn't he?"

Louisa slowly blinked, bored. "What if he is?"

Michelle glanced down at Louisa's swollen belly, then back at her face. "And you think having a baby will change that?"

"I already have another option."

"What?"

Louisa flashed a cool smile. "None of your business."

"It will be if you get Teresa involved."

Louisa's smile fell. "What does Teresa have to do with anything?"

Michelle's gaze sharpened. "You tell me, Louisa."

Louisa swallowed, suddenly feeling uncomfortable. Michelle was sharp and she hadn't expected that. What could she know? She couldn't know anything. She couldn't know that she'd been giving Thomas key information about Teresa's business. She was just bluffing. She had to play it cool. "I don't need another woman to catch a man. My face has always gotten me what I wanted and hasn't stopped." She nodded at Jessie. "I'm sure you understand about going after what you want."

"I don't know what you're talking about."

Louisa rolled her eyes. "Oh, come on. Everyone knows that you set out to get Kenneth because of a bet. But I bet you only used that as a cover. What caught your interest first? His money or his looks? You're going to have to share some of your tricks with me."

Jessie tapped her finger on the table, trying to curb her temper. "I didn't use any tricks."

"Hello, ladies. Mind if we join you?" Kenneth said, approaching the table with Syrah who beamed at her two aunts.

"Well, speak of the devil," Louisa said, looking at Kenneth with an intense there's-a-handsome-man interest.

Kenneth shook her hand. "I don't believe we've met. I'm Jessie's husband—"

"Kenneth Preston," Louisa said holding both his hand and gaze longer than she needed to. "Your pictures don't capture you. Even the bad ones."

Jessie nearly leaped to her feet in rage at the subtle mention of the scandal, but her husband lightly touched her arm as he sat down with a smile. "Thanks," he said simply, diffusing the tension. "This is our daughter, Syrah."

Syrah smiled briefly.

Louisa smiled. "So Kenneth, how would you suggest a girl catch a rich man?"

Michelle choked on her drink, Jessie crumpled her bread-sticks and Teresa groaned.

Kenneth kept his smile in place. "I'm not sure I follow you."

"Well, everybody knows that Jessie went after you because of a bet. Come on, be honest, were you a little embarrassed that you fell for it?"

This time Kenneth couldn't keep his wife seated. Jessie jumped to her feet and leaned over the table, bristling with rage. "You're disgusting. I did not marry Kenneth because of a bet or because of his money. I married him because I loved him. But someone like you wouldn't understand that." She tapped the table. "Do you know why you're here? Because we feel sorry for you. And if you weren't family,

I couldn't care less. You have a pretty face, but you've got nothing else. Your mother can't even stand to look at you and now I know why."

"Relax, Jas," Kenneth said, reaching for her hand.

Jessie yanked it out of reach. "Don't touch me right now," she warned, keeping her gaze on Louisa's face. "You're raw, you're vulgar and that's why you're alone." She grabbed her handbag and stormed out.

Louisa lifted her drink and took a sip. "Guess I hit a nerve."

Kenneth and Syrah said their goodbyes and immediately followed Jessie. Michelle studied Louisa. "Well done."

"What?" Louisa asked, looking the picture of innocence.

Michelle glanced at Teresa then shook her head. "Never mind. I think this day is over."

"Louisa's up to something," Michelle told Jessie and Kenneth later that day as they sat in their living room. She'd stopped by their house, determined to share her concerns with her sister. "I don't know what it is, but she's planning something."

"I don't care," Jessie said.

"You should care. If you weren't so hot-headed you'd see she was provoking you on purpose."

"Why?"

"I don't know," Michelle said with a note of frustration. "I can't believe Teresa's been able to stand being with her this long."

"Teresa is attracted to broken people. First Sean and now Louisa."

"I trust Sean more than Louisa," Kenneth said.

"You trust a man who has no past?" Michelle said. "At least we know Louisa's."

"Sean's past is spotty," Kenneth corrected. "But a man has a right to his secrets."

"Not when it involves my sister." Michelle toyed with the ring on her finger. "But I know Louisa is a bigger problem."

"What do we do about it?"

Kenneth shrugged. "Wait for something to hit the fan."

LATER THAT NIGHT, Kenneth slipped into bed next to his wife, unable to stop replaying the scene at the cafe. "So when are you going to tell me about Sean's reading?" he asked her as she rested her head on his chest. The light from the table lamp next to him pushed away the shadows.

Jessie grimaced with chagrin. "You saw that, did you?"

He chuckled. "I know you."

"You're right about the secrets, but Louisa's more dangerous to Teresa than he is."

"Why did you let her get to you?"

"I'm sorry," she said, lightly trailing her fingers along one of the scars on his arm. If she'd been anyone else, the motion would have bothered him, but her touch made him feel less self-conscious about them.

"I'm not asking you to apologize, I want to know why."

"Because I don't want you in any way to think—"

"Do you think I doubt how much you love me?"

He felt her stiffen. "Do you?"

"Should I?"

She shook her head. "No," she said.

But when she hesitated, he felt himself grow tense, whispers of his own worries coming to the surface as his gaze swept the large, exquisitely decorated room. He wondered if it was enough, if she was unhappy. "Do you doubt that I love you?"

She shook her head again and looked up at him. "It's not that."

He searched her gaze. "Then what is it?"

She sat up and folded her arms. "I hate that people can mock us, I hate what Louisa didn't say."

He sat up also, feeling the tension in him ebb as he tenderly brushed some hair from her cheek. "And that was...?"

"Why you married me."

He sighed. "Jasmine, I thought we were past this. You know—"

She pressed a finger against his lip. "I know why and that makes me happy, but sometimes the fact that other people don't makes me angry."

He moved her hand. "If you're happy, who cares what people think?"

"Wow, that's amazing coming from you."

He grinned. "When it comes to you, I don't care what people think."

Jessie bit her lip. "And what do you think about Louisa?"

His grin fell. "I don't like her."

Jessie groaned. "And that says a lot. Why doesn't Teresa see what we do?"

"Because for some reason she sees what she needs to— someone to rescue."

"I know and that worries me. I need to make her see the truth."

"I know she's not perfect, but she's not that bad," Teresa said.

She, Jessie and Michelle sat in the living room of the family house having tea and biscuits. Jessie had asked Teresa to come over to apologize for storming out, then revealed her real reason. Her worry about Louisa.

"We don't want you to live there anymore," Michelle said.

"Just a little while longer. She has nobody else and—"

"She deserves to stay that way."

"Look, we have each other," Teresa said, determined to make them see Louisa's plight. "You don't know what it's like to have nobody."

"You said Sean knows her, right?"

Teresa set her tea cup down. "Is that really why you brought me here? To tell me how much you hate Louisa, distrust Sean and want me to give up my store and come back and live with Michelle?"

"We didn't say anything about your store," Michelle said. "We're proud of what you're doing."

"And Sean's not such a bad guy," Jessie said, ignoring Michelle's look.

"Louisa tried to kill herself," Teresa said, remembering the sight of her cousin floating in the water. "No one should feel that isolated in this world. If I'm her only friend, then so be it. I'll help her any way I can."

"Even if she hurts you? Even if she doesn't care?"

"Yes, I'll love her until she learns to love herself and I love Sean too."

Jessie tucked her legs underneath her, dipping her biscuit in her tea. "Oh."

"I hate when you do that," Michelle said, motioning to Jessie's tea.

"It tastes so good," she said, putting the soggy biscuit in her mouth.

Teresa tapped the side of her cup until her sisters looked at her. "Did you two hear what I said?"

"Does it matter?" Michelle said.

"He used to be a surgeon."

"And Stalin used to be a teacher. What does Sean do now? If we're to believe he was a surgeon."

Teresa sipped her tea. "He was and he now volunteers at a clinic and helps me at the shop."

Michelle folded her napkin. "But you don't know how he makes his living?"

"I'm sure it's legal. I know you don't trust him, but I wish you two would trust me. I know what I'm doing."

Jessie glanced up at the ceiling, not knowing what else to say, and turned to glance out the window. She narrowed her eyes. "Who owns a blue Toyota with Pennsylvania license plates?"

The three sisters stared at each other as a horrifying realization struck them.

"Aunt Yvette," they chorused in a scandalized whisper.

"I am out of here," Jessie said, leaping to her feet. "She's not catching me to tell me how to run my life."

"Come back here," Michelle ordered. Unfortunately, Jessie had already made it to the back door when the doorbell rang.

Michelle muttered a curse under her breath, opened the door and plastered on a smile. "Aunt Yvette, what a surprise!" She hugged her. "And you brought cousin Olivia, how lovely." She nearly choked on the lie.

"Look, who we caught trying to sneak away." Aunt Yvette laughed, pulling on Jessie's sleeve.

"I was just getting something from my car," Jessie said.

Michelle grinned wickedly. "Of course you were. Pity you didn't make it."

"I see you have tea all set up," Aunt Yvette said, taking a seat. "It's as if you knew we were coming."

"If we knew you were coming, we wouldn't have been here," Jessie mumbled.

Michelle nudged her to be quiet. "Why don't you get more

hot water?" She lowered her voice. "In your case, you could just blow on it."

Jessie headed to the kitchen.

Teresa and Michelle sat in front of their aunt; ready for the verbal attack they knew was inevitable. Aunt Yvette was their mother's older sister and more into propriety and family values than their mother had been. Her eldest daughter had married well, so she felt it was her duty to assess everyone's future and obligations in upholding family connections. She was a thin woman with tiny eyes, a long haughty nose and heavy eyebrows. She wore a cream dress and a grey spiral hat tilted to the side.

"So how are you doing, ladies?" Aunt Yvette asked, tugging off her driving gloves and smoothing them in her lap.

"Just fine, Auntie," Michelle answered. "How are you doing?"

She clasped her hands together. "Absolutely splendid, thank you."

"I'm glad to hear it."

An awkward silence descended.

Jessie came in with more hot water. She placed the teapot on the table, then collapsed into a chair.

"You still move like a man," Aunt Yvette scolded. "Must you be so graceless? I'm surprised you didn't plod down the aisle when you were getting married."

Jessie took a deep breath, choosing not to respond.

"How is your husband?"

"He's fine, thank you."

"Does the beast still force you to work?"

Jessie folded her arms, trying to keep her temper. "I like to work, Auntie."

"Of course you do, dear," she allowed with a quick nod. "That's the acceptable answer nowadays, isn't it?"

"No, I—"

"My dear Celena doesn't have to work. Her husband provides her with all her needs."

"Kenneth provides for me and Syrah just fine."

"Of course he does." Her smile was the equivalent of a patronizing pat of reassurance on the cheek. "Celena's husband just bought her a delightful new dining room set. You must stop by to see it. It's the envy of the entire neighborhood."

The sisters nodded.

She adjusted her hat. "Belinda's getting married by the way."

"Is the marriage arranged?" Jessie asked.

Michelle pinched her.

"Of course it's not. I agree that Belinda isn't as social as I would like, but she has successfully snagged a very eligible man. He's from Germany, but nobody's perfect. He will treat her well."

They all murmured their congratulations.

"Bridesmaids have already been selected of course, but we'll still find some role for you ladies to play."

"Actually, I think I'll be busy," Jessie said.

"But I haven't told you the date yet."

"Right, but the year's pretty busy and next year—"

"I'm sure you can make it. It's next August. We'd like to use the same wedding planner you used."

"Actually, Kenneth scheduled everything. You'll have to ask him."

Aunt Yvette smiled. "Your humor is so unique."

"I wasn't joking—"

"His name is Brenton, or some such ridiculous name. I already told her that the children must have proper names. Oh, I am so happy. Now with Celena and Belinda matched up there's only Winston and Olivia. Then of course you two." She nibbled on a tea biscuit. "But enough of this chatter, I've heard news that I found both disturbing and intriguing."

"Kenneth and I were not having sex in the Long Creek Park fountain, it just looked that way from a distance," Jessie blurted.

Aunt Yvette gasped horrified, Olivia blushed prettily. Teresa and Michelle's mouths dropped open.

Jessie smiled sheepishly. "Just joking. I thought I'd add a little humor."

Aunt Yvette sent Jessie a censured look then focused her attention on Teresa. "As I was saying, I heard that you've decided to play nurse to some girl living in South Bank."

"Yes, Louisa. She's our cousin."

Aunt Yvette smoothed out her gloves, choosing her words carefully. "I know, dear, but her relationship with you need not be acknowledged so publicly."

"But she's family—"

She held up her hand for silence. "And I also heard that you were seen with the outsider."

"His name is Sean Casey."

"Yes, I know, but I don't wish you to converse with him until I can discover more about him. I'm sure if your parents were here, they would agree with me."

"Not Dad."

"Yes, well, your father was an exception when it came to good judgment."

Teresa bit her tongue trying to refrain from saying anything.

"You must think of your family ties, your name. One stain is enough." Aunt Yvette didn't look at Michelle, but everyone knew to whom she referred. Michelle was the first in the family ever to separate from her husband, let alone talk about divorce. Michelle didn't seem affected by the statement.

Michelle refilled her teacup. "I suppose I am the stain?"

Aunt Yvette sat straighter, adjusting her hat. "You married into a very prestigious family and ruined that opportunity and now you two are condoning your sister's indiscretions," she said.

Michelle sipped her tea. "What century is this again?"

"What did we do?" Jessie added.

"You invited him to your home." She lowered her voice. "Olivia told me he attacked her." Olivia opened her mouth, but her mother waved her finger. "Quiet, dear. I know that's what you meant."

"He accidentally spilled curried chicken on her," Teresa clarified. "Because he tripped over her purse, which was left in the way."

Aunt Yvette stiffened. "Olivia told me that he was uncouth, rude and—"

Olivia opened her mouth again, but Michelle spoke first.

"Auntie, we recognize that this man is not..." Michelle paused, searching for the right word. "Cultured. However, he is completely harmless."

Teresa and Jessie stared at Michelle in shock, wondering why she'd chosen to stand up for Sean.

Aunt Yvette nodded. "I agree."

"You do?" they chorused.

"Yes. Olivia, show them the box."

Olivia opened a box she was carrying and showed them a pink silk blouse, inside was a note that read:

I hope this is adequate compensation for your ruined blouse.

Sean

"Wasn't that gallant of him?" Olivia gushed. "I couldn't believe it when this was delivered to my door. I saw the exact same copy and it cost—"

"Don't be vulgar, Olivia," Aunt Yvette snapped. "You know we don't discuss the price of things. However, this changes things considerably. It shows some breeding and money. Now there are rumors that he may be one of the Caseys of New York."

"So?"

"So, I'll—"

"Let's leave the poor man alone," Jessie said. "He obviously wants to remain private for a reason, and Teresa only sees him socially."

"So he's free?" Olivia asked. "Do you know where he lives? I'd love to thank him."

"That's enough of that," Aunt Yvette said. "I've said my piece." She rose to her feet, went to the door and stood in front of it, waiting for someone to open it for her. Michelle looked at Jessie, but she folded her arms like a petulant five year old and shook her head. Teresa busied herself with clearing the table. With a checked sigh, Michelle did the honors. "I am staying in town with Olivia for a while if you need to reach me," she said.

"Thank you," Michelle said for all of them.

The sisters waved as they watched their relatives drive off.

"My only concern is that they're staying in town," Jessie said once Michelle had closed the door. "That Olivia is such a big mouth. I knew I shouldn't have let Kenneth invite her."

"I can't believe she didn't hear that Sean's Teresa's boyfriend," Michelle said. "Not that he made it very obvious. I can understand her confusion."

"I can't believe you stood up for him," Teresa said to Michelle.

Michelle tugged at the cuffs of her jacket. "The woman annoys me. I couldn't give her the satisfaction of being right. But please, for the love of God, please don't tell her that you're in love with him. Then she may never leave."

Louisa was watering the pots of purple flowers that lined the shop's windows, while Teresa tended to the front landscape of circular bushes and daffodils when they heard Sean's truck drive up. Although the store was doing well, and her manager and clerks were keeping customers happy, Teresa didn't have money in the budget for a gardener so she decided to take care of the plants herself with Louisa's help.

"Someone's in a good mood," Louisa said, watching Sean approach with a certain swing to his step.

"I'm in a very good mood," he said.

"What happened today?"

He stopped in front of her and leaned against the side of the building. "I just came back from white water rafting, the rush was exhilarating," he said, easily slipping into their old game.

She twirled one of his curls around her finger. "Alone?"

"Her husband thinks so."

Louisa laughed. "I've missed that. For a moment I thought you weren't going to be fun anymore."

"Why don't we go for a drive by the bay?" Sean offered in a soft voice. "It's a nice day."

Louisa smiled up at him; that's when Teresa saw it. The magic—He was in love! He had never looked at Louisa that way before, with such gentle admiration, sexual heat. Suddenly Teresa's eyes were opened, the translucent gauze lifted. Teresa looked at Louisa as he probably saw her: a beautiful young woman with luxurious hair pulled back in a braid and brilliant brown eyes.

She wore a soft peach dress that complimented a mother figure ripe with child. Sean could explain away staring at Olivia but the look he gave Louisa was undeniable. He'd stayed away from the store since the incident at her sister's party and now she knew why. Just as she'd feared, she'd healed his heart so that he could give it to someone else.

Teresa felt her heart split and melt.

"That sounds wonderful," Louisa said.

Sean turned to Teresa. "What do you think?"

"I'm sure she would prefer to stay here with her weeds," Louisa said.

Sean sent Teresa an amused look, a smile on his face.

She was unable to reply to Louisa's teasing with a witty remark. She felt worn and old, like something that had been around too long and needed to be replaced, she was no longer useful. "Right, I like my weeds," she said in a dull voice.

The teasing glint quickly left his eyes and his expression grew concerned. Teresa saw this and offered him a reassuring smile. "You two have a good time."

"We will," Louisa said, heading inside the shop. "Let me just get my bag and touch up my makeup."

Teresa went back to her weeding. "You're staring at me," she said after a few moments, feeling his eyes on her.

"You're angry."

"Yes."

"Why?"

"Because you lied to me."

"Lied?"

She ripped off her gloves, gripped them in her fist and turned to him. "Yes, you said you'd never fall in love."

He stroked his beard, amazed. "Damn, is it that obvious?"

As obvious as the sun in the sky, Teresa thought, feeling the weight of her sadness. She'd hoped he would deny it. "Olivia was looking for you. Do you want to be found?"

He squatted down in front of her and cupped her chin. "What's wrong?"

There would be no more moments like this, quiet moments that only she and he occupied. Even alone, someone else would fill his thoughts. *Oh no, she was going to cry.* She could feel the tears building up like a dam waiting to break. She blinked her eyes and plastered on a smile. "Nothing."

His eyebrows furrowed. "Don't smile at me when you're on the verge of tears."

Teresa's smile wavered. "Really, I—"

"And don't tell me nothing's wrong. I sent the blouse to Olivia because I want your family to like me, okay?" He threw up his hands in surrender. "All right, I admit. Seeing Olivia did something to me, I couldn't help—"

"You don't have to explain it to me. I know."

"No, you don't know—"

"I'm ready," Louisa said.

Sean looked up at her with regret. "Sorry, we'll have to go out another time."

She folded her arms, annoyed. "Having a lover's spat or something?"

"Yes," he said.

"No," Teresa countered.

Louisa made a face and went back inside.

Teresa stood. "Just go with her."

Sean stood too, resting a hand on his chest. "Do you think this is easy for me? Falling in love with you was not part of the plan, but once I saw your cousin, and then your brother-in-law tried to warn me off, something inside me just changed."

Teresa stared at him. "Wait, what?"

"He tried to warn me—"

"No, not that," she said waving her hands. "Did you say you loved me?"

Sean blinked. "Isn't that what we're talking about?"

"But you were looking at Louisa in a way I'd never seen before. You look so in love."

He blushed, tugged at his collar and lowered his voice. "I fall in love hard, okay? It's not something I'm proud of, but I can't help myself." He glanced at a caterpillar inching its way up the side of a pot, avoiding her gaze. "I'll try not to be so obvious, but I'm not good at it."

Teresa stared at him not knowing whether to scream or to cry to hug him or to dance. "You're in love with me?"

"Yes," he said looking at her, his eyes heated with emotion. "I was going to wait for tomorrow, but I might as well do it today."

"What?"

He took her hand in his and held her gaze as he got down on one knee. "Ask the woman I love to marry me."

CHAPTER 26

Teresa stared down at him. "What?"

"I've never been so sure of something in my life," Sean said, slowly rising, holding her gaze. "I've tried to fight it, but I'm not going to do that anymore. Because for the first time in a long while, I feel free. After your sister's party and thinking I saw Renee again, I thought I wouldn't be able to sleep. And I couldn't. But not for the usual reason. I kept thinking about you. I didn't care about her anymore. With you I don't feel broken. When you took me to your sister's party, you weren't ashamed of me. You fit into my life and fit into my home and I want to share all that I have with you. So, will you be my wife?"

Teresa continued to stare at him, dumbstruck.

"I know I have to win over your family, but I'll make that my mission." When she still didn't speak, he said, "Please say something, my heart is beating so fast I can hardly breathe."

"Can I ask you something?"

"Three questions."

"Only three?"

"I can make it two."

"And I can say n—"

He pressed a finger against her lips. "Okay, ask away."

"How do you make your living?"

"I had a lucrative medical practice and invested wisely. I also have other business assets."

"Do you want children?"

His voice caught. "Yes, some day."

"Will your family like me?"

"I don't care."

She shifted her gaze to the shop, unable to hold his gaze her heart dancing with joy, but her head conflicted at the same time. "Both of our families will think we're crazy."

"Only because they don't know we were meant to be together, but you knew that from the beginning." He stood behind her and wrapped his arms around her waist. "I'm sorry I didn't recognize you that first day," he said in a low voice, the hair of his beard brushing against her cheek. "Will you forgive me and marry me anyway?"

She turned in the circle of his arms and met his gaze. "Yes."

THEY ONLY HAD to wait forty-eight hours for their marriage license, then decided to marry in secret with Bertha as their only witness. She was initially against the idea.

"You should tell your sisters," Bertha said when Teresa approached her with their plans as they shopped for items in The Crabapple.

"I just want to enjoy this," Teresa said. "The outing with Louisa was such a disaster and I want my wedding day to be special."

"Did you ever consider that your sisters may be right about Louisa?"

Teresa grabbed a carton of coconut milk and put it in her basket. "I don't know why everyone is against her."

"And that's a sign."

"What?"

Bertha shook her head and looked at Teresa with pity. "You're so busy seeing Louisa's pain, you don't see the pain she causes." She held up her hand. "I will be a witness to your marriage; I just hope you don't regret it."

But Teresa was in heaven on her wedding day. After the brief ceremony, Teresa moved in with Sean, telling Louisa and Darren she was staying with friends.

Sean carried her bags to their bedroom. When she stepped into the room, the late afternoon sun filtering through the blinds, she noticed the bed now had two pillows; then she saw the red silk nightgown.

She rushed over and lifted it off the bed. "It's gorgeous." She turned to him. "But I didn't get you anything."

He grinned. "Put it on tonight and I'll be a happy man."

"I MADE DINNER," Sean said after Teresa had put her things away and joined him in the kitchen. It had light wood cabinets and dark flooring. The stove was yellow, as was the refrigerator and looked like they would fit in perfectly in a 50s kitchen. She'd get them replaced.

Teresa grinned. "Ooh...my husband can cook."

"I prepared some stew for dinner," he said, unable to hide his pleasure at her calling him 'husband' as he opened the fridge. "I just need to heat this up." He put the pot on the stove while

Teresa sat down at the wooden table. She rested her arms on the table and the salt and pepper slid to one side. She lifted her arms and they slid back in place.

"The table's a bit unsteady," he said.

"So I've noticed."

She saw a piece of paper off to the side, folded it and slid it under the short leg then watched him at the stove. She had never imagined him as a cook, yet he seemed comfortable gathering all the ingredients for his stew.

"You can get dishes from up there." He pointed to a cabinet behind her.

She opened the cabinet and found six green plates, six bowls and six glasses. They all looked brand new. Unfortunately, they sat on a shelf she could not reach.

"Need help?" Sean asked smugly.

"No," she said, pushing a chair next to the counter. She climbed on the chair and retrieved the dishes, placing the rest on a lower shelf she could easily get to. She returned the chair, set the utensils on table and then sat down. Sean brought over the pot, and even that looked new. She guessed he'd gone shopping.

He picked up her bowl and ladled a healthy serving of stew. It smelled delicious, but when Teresa looked down, she grimaced. The stew was a clear brown liquid, resembling dirty water with chunks of meat and vegetables in it.

She picked up her spoon then paused, watching him cut a loaf of Jamaican hardo bread, a white bread that's slightly sweet. "Did you make this stew horrible on purpose just so that I would cook?"

He went to the fridge and pulled out the butter and put it on the table, looking offended. "This is the best dish I make."

She failed to cover a grin. "Oh, sorry."

He sat down and grunted.

She took a small sip, letting the stew rest in her mouth a while then swallowed. In spite of its appearance, it tasted remarkably good—warm, solid, surprising like its creator.

He grinned. "It tastes even better when you dip the bread in it," he said.

"Hmm, this is delicious. I owe you a big apology."

"That's what happens when you judge things solely based on appearances."

Teresa broke off a piece of bread and dipped it in the stew. "Lesson learned, professor." She winked at him. "Anything else you want to teach me?"

"I have a lifetime to do so."

After dinner, Sean gave her a full tour of the house. To her relief he was very lenient with whatever changes she wanted to make to the house.

He had more land than she'd imagined. He pointed in the distance to a couple of small houses. "I own those too and the tenants pay me rent."

Teresa was impressed. "Another income stream?"

He shrugged then knelt down to grasp a clump of soil. "I know you love to garden." He let the soil fall through his fingers. "You can grow whatever you like. I'm sure nothing will die here."

She looked at the vast property full of potential, her mind already thinking of the many plants she could grow, for a moment wishing her parents could be there to see it. She took Sean's hand in hers. "You don't know how happy this makes me."

A sexy grin spread on his face and he gently tugged her back inside the house. "You can always show me."

SHE WAS in The Crabapple looking at large aloe vera stalks when someone bumped into her, which wasn't uncommon in the small aisles, so she apologized without looking up.

"Do you think my wife will like this?" the man said with a hint of a Spanish accent as he looked at a bottle of hot sauce.

She turned and saw an incredibly good looking, light-skinned man wearing dark sunglasses who looked completely out of place in the tiny shop. He looked like a Bedford resident or a tourist who'd lost his way, with his clean-shaven face, short-cropped haircut, khaki pants, pressed red shirt and expensive Italian shoes. Behind him she saw Camille Faulkner giving him a once-over and couldn't blame her.

"If she likes a kick with her meals," Teresa said, "she'll devour it."

He glanced at her basket loaded with hardo bread, guava jelly and other items. "You certainly know what you're doing."

"I'm cooking something special for my husband. Blue cheese and herb butter on crusty bread, and later sorrel sauce with white fish, and pasta followed by a mango sorbet."

The man licked his lips. "Wish there was a place I could buy that. Sounds delicious."

Teresa grabbed a jar of ginger sesame seed sauce. "Put this on chicken or salmon and you'll cook like a chef."

"Thanks," the man said, then turned down another aisle.

She caught up with him again while leaving the store and saw him walking towards an old truck. "You drive that?" she asked, surprised by the contrast.

"Yes," he said pulling out his keys.

"You know that's amazing. It looks just like Priscilla. My husband's—" Her eyes widened as she put the pieces together—the build was the same, even some of the movements, but she'd been thrown off by the accent and the hair. She spun around and gaped at him. "No."

Sean's face split into a wide grinned. "Yes."

Teresa playfully hit him on the arm. "Why did you trick me?"

He laughed and pushed his sunglasses to his head. "Because it was fun."

"What happened to you?"

"I thought I'd go for a haircut."

"But you don't look like yourself," she said, letting her gaze trail the length of him. "And those clothes."

"Business."

She walked around him. "I don't believe it. You look a little scary."

"Scary?"

"Like you don't belong here. You look like you should be driving a sports car, wearing a gold watch with a hot babe by your side."

He kissed her. "I've already got the hot babe. The rest I don't need. I'll meet you at home."

Teresa stamped her foot like a frustrated five year old. "And now you know all about my surprise."

"Don't worry," he said, getting into his truck. "I'll pretend I didn't know."

And he pretended well, but Teresa still didn't know how to feel. He was beautiful to look at, he always had been. But without the facial hair, she saw the cold cut of his chin, his chiseled cheekbones.

"I can always grow it back," he said.

"No," she said quickly not wanting him to feel uncomfortable. "You don't have to. I'm just getting used to your new look."

He swallowed a piece of fish then said, "Whatever you're thinking, you're right."

"How do you know what I'm thinking?"

"Right now you're wondering who the hell you married."

"No...well maybe a little."

"I'm not going anywhere. My life is here. My life used to be about cars, big houses and beautiful women and proving I was the best thing to ever walk the earth. You wouldn't have liked me much back then. But after life humbled me, I wandered for a while. I came here to escape until I met you. And I've never been the same. I met with my attorney today to put things in order with my trust and put you in my will. I'm also looking into opening a practice. This place needs one."

"That's wonderful," Teresa said.

And it was then she realized how much he'd help legitimize her business. Just like Helene, her husband was a doctor, and with a medical practice they could educate people on how to care for themselves. Helene couldn't look down at her anymore.

He pulled something out of his pocket and rested a small box with the Fedor Malenkov Jewelers logo on the table. "That's not all I was up to."

"What is it?"

Sean lifted the box and wiggled it. "Do you want to know how to find out? You open it."

Teresa snatched the box from him. "Why do you always have to answer questions like that?" she said, setting the box aside.

"You're not going to open it?"

"I'll open it later."

"Why not now?"

Teresa fought to keep from grinning. "It's not going anywhere." She playfully slapped his hand away when he reached for the box. "I'm almost finished eating."

Sean narrowed his eyes. "Now, you're the scary one."

Teresa straightened in her chair as if she were Aunt Yvette, set her utensils down and wiped the corners of her mouth with her napkin. "Things like this must take time," she said, mimicking her aunt's haughty tone. "I have to give it my full attention. We Cliftons know a little something about gems," she said, giving him a significant look. "I hope I won't be disappointed."

"Really scary," Sean said, suddenly looking unsure.

Teresa slowly lifted the box and stared at the golden hue of a pair of amber stone earrings sitting on a black velvet bed. She snapped the box close. "Just as I thought, absolutely tasteless. Pearls would have been better," she said then lifted her utensils and began eating again. When she finally looked at Sean, she saw an expression of both surprise and horror. She burst into laughter.

"I'm just joking. They're gorgeous."

Sean grabbed the front of his shirt as if he were afraid his heart would stop. "That was terrifying. You do that too well and almost sounded like Renee."

"I had to get you back for ruining my surprise," Teresa said, opening the box then lightly touching one earring with her finger. "They're stunning."

"Amber is important to my family."

"I can tell. Do you know how much this costs?"

"I should hope so," Sean said with a laugh. "I was there when I bought it."

Teresa stood and went over to a mirror on the side wall and put the earrings on, feeling like a wealthy woman. "Thank you."

Sean got up and stood beside her. "Every moment I'm with you, you make me glad I decided to remarry. My first marriage was miserable." He rested his hands on her shoulders and looked at her reflection in the mirror. "And you're my second chance."

And for the next week, Sean made sure to let her know how important a second chance meant to him—not just with special gifts, or surprises, but telling her so in different ways— Teresa was in heaven, satisfied that all her dreams had come true. Until a letter arrived, sending her crashing down to earth.

CHAPTER 27

"What is it?" Sean asked when he heard Teresa gasp at the sight of the letter she held in her hand. It was from Valley Ray Corporation.

"A cease-and-desist notice about my peppermint hand gel," Teresa said, collapsing into a kitchen chair as if she'd been punched. "It says I don't have the right to sell them."

Sean took the letter from her and read it then swore. "Did you register for a patent?"

"No, the formula was just a trade secret. I didn't tell anyone."

"Somehow they found out and patented it as theirs."

"What does that mean?"

"That you can't fight this."

"But the product was one of our bestsellers. How could they know all the ingredients?"

Sean was determined to find out, but when he spoke to the store manager and staff they all pleaded innocent. Although some of them had helped Teresa make the initial batch, no one knew the full mixture enough to give the information to a rival.

"They already make enough money, why are they picking on us?" the manager said, his toupee slightly skewed. "At first I thought Teresa was crazy not carrying their line, but that other brand we carry works just as well and our customers have been happy."

Sean patted him on the back. "Thanks, we'll just have to make do."

The manager nodded then left to clear the shelves.

"This will hurt business," Sean said as he and Teresa watched the staff remove the peppermint hand gel from the shelves. "But you'll recover."

Teresa gripped her hands. "They stole this from me, but I don't know how."

"Unfortunately, they did it legally. There's no way you can prove your position in court. We'll need to come up with something else."

Teresa fought back tears, knowing that wouldn't be that easy.

Louisa lay naked on her side under the soft hotel sheets, her body warm and wet from lovemaking. The light from the table lamp was low, casting a dull glow over the green and gold carpets and drapes. She could still smell his aftershave on the pillows. The hotel wasn't their regular meeting place, but being with him was all that mattered. She was glad the baby weight hadn't turned him off, but she still knew her days were numbered. The bigger she got, the more awkward it could be, but at least she knew she didn't have to make him come to keep him close. Now he was devoted to her.

She rested a hand on her protruding stomach and sighed with contentment. Being pregnant wasn't so bad and she actually looked forward to soon holding her baby. Teresa had helped her feel beautiful again with the shopping spree and spa treatment and even made motherhood sound like fun, with talks about nurseries and baby clothes, although Louisa hadn't wanted to set up a nursery yet since she didn't plan to stay there. She hadn't expected to miss her. The cousin who'd made her laugh when she'd felt the baby kick, who'd gone with her to several doctor's appointments.

She'd been there for her like no one ever had. She felt sort of empty not having her around, fussing over her. She'd gotten used to her calm ways and unrelenting kindness.

Louisa sighed. She felt a little bad about pissing off Jessie at the cafe, but that couldn't be helped. Michelle couldn't know what she was up to. She had to do whatever she needed to do for survival. She wasn't just thinking about herself anymore. She had a family to think about now. Fortunately, she was a good liar and no one suspected her. She was glad she'd made Thomas happy with the information she'd given him. It hadn't been easy piecing together the torn notes Teresa had tossed aside and watching her when she didn't think she was looking, and asking seemingly innocent questions. But she'd done it all for the man she loved. She looked over at him as he straightened his tie while he looked at himself in the hotel mirror. He was so handsome and smart. Soon she'd be wearing his ring.

"So what you gonna do?" she asked him, grabbing her bra and putting it on.

"Do?"

She slipped on her panties, then jeans, glad for the maternity give her old jeans hadn't provided. "In a couple of months this baby is coming and we'd better start making plans. When are you going to leave her?"

"Soon. The information you've given us has kept us busy with negotiations. I didn't want to distract her right now."

Louisa pulled on her blouse. "Maybe it's good that she's busy so she won't bother us. You told me—"

"To wait, and you're doing that just fine."

She lifted her shoe then threw it back down. "But I'm tired of waiting. I want to be with you."

He crossed the room and took her hand. "Look, in a year—"

"A year!" She yanked her hand away. "What do you expect me to be doing for a year?! Do you know what I risked for you? I betrayed my own cousin to get you what you wanted. I'm not waiting a year."

"Don't excite yourself. It's not good for you or the baby."

"Don't you dare tell me what I need," she said, resting a hand on her hip. "If you don't do right by me, I'll tell your wife and anyone else who will listen. I'll also tell them about your wife's connection to Valley Ray and how they *really* got the patent for their new gel."

He rested his hands on her arms. "Baby," he said in a soothing voice. "You're getting upset for nothing. You know it's complicated. A divorce can be costly and I want to be able to care for you in the way you deserve."

"You better not be seeing someone else."

"Why would you think that?"

Louisa flashed a sour grin. "Because I know you, Thomas. You didn't change hotels for no reason."

"I thought you'd want a change." He stroked the side of her face. "You're so beautiful, how could I want to be with anyone else? You're more than enough for me." He kissed her. "Why don't you trust me?"

Louisa slid her hand down his back, pushing down her suspicions. He loved her. He'd said so. She wouldn't have done all that she had otherwise. "I just want to be with you."

"And you will," he whispered against her lips.

But Louisa wasn't completely satisfied with his answer, and knew she had to do something to make sure he kept his word.

Helene greeted her husband at the door with a face that looked like thunder. "I got a phone call today."

Thomas stepped into the foyer and closed the door behind him with a soft click. "From whom?"

"When I give you permission to play, I expect you to keep your bitch on a leash."

He opened the hallway closet. "What are you talking about?"

"Some woman called me claiming she can make trouble for our business."

"It's nothing."

"Don't brush this aside. This strategy is working. Teresa's little shop is scrambling. We've already doubled our sales this month. In a couple of weeks we can be back on top and no one will even remember her.

But—"

"But nothing," he said hanging up his coat. "I said I'll handle it."

"I don't want you to handle it," Helene said in a clipped tone. "I want it gone. Do you understand me? She knows too much. Give her what she wants and get rid of her."

Thomas closed the closet door and shook his head. "I can't do that."

"Why not?"

He walked past her.

Helene stared at his back and swore. "You got yourself an AON, didn't you?" she asked.

He turned around. "A what?"

She slowly walked up to him her heels clicking on the floor. "An 'all or nothing'," Helene clarified with a bored look. "She wants the house and the family, doesn't she? Didn't I tell you to be careful of those ones? How can a smart man be so stupid?"

"She's young."

Helene rested a hand on his chest. "Poor thing, they are always your weakness." She slid her hand down to the front of his trousers and gripped him in warning. "But she better not be pregnant or I'll have your balls in a vice. Is she?"

"Is she what?"

"Don't play dumb with me, honey. It's too late for that."

Thomas held her gaze. "She just wants to get married."

Helene loosened her hold and pressed her lips against his. "Then you'd better change her mind and send her on her way," she said in a light voice that suddenly hardened along with her gaze. "Before I intervene."

Thomas didn't sleep that night. Instead he stared up at the dark ceiling, wishing for sleep that eluded him. His wife couldn't know about the baby, and he knew he couldn't keep Louisa quiet for long. How could a piece of sweet ass cause so much trouble? He didn't have much time. He could hold her off for a couple more months, but after that he wasn't sure. Louisa was a wild card; that was what had attracted him to her at first. Hell, she'd been good for his ego. But now she was a liability. All he needed was her arriving on his doorstep with a baby in tow. He'd underestimated her. He'd hoped to convince her to take his money and disappear, but the bitch wanted a family, and to get the information he wanted, he'd played along.

Helene would never forgive him if she found out, and he needed Helene. Helene was his life. He loved her. Stepping out on her was just what he did, but he always came back because she was his heart. She'd been by his side for years and knew him. She was his rock. He didn't care about Louisa threatening his business, but threatening his marriage had been a mistake. That was something he'd have to stop.

Sean looked at the disposable cell phone he'd bought, then looked out the window of the Virginia motel where he planned to make his call. He knew he was taking a risk contacting his brother, Robert. Both his younger and older brother, Evan, owned a top investigations firm and Sean would do anything to help Teresa find out how Valley Ray had gotten the ingredients for her peppermint gel. Even if it meant being found by his family, but he'd still take precautions to make that difficult for as long as possible.

He sat on the too soft mattress and glanced at stain on the orange patterned carpet the cleaning crew hadn't been able to get out then dialed.

"I need you to look into a company called Valley Ray," he said the moment Robert answered.

"Sean?" Robert said dropping his voice as if he didn't want to be overheard. "Where are you now? What—"

"I don't have time for questions. Just get everything you can about this company and their new gel," he said then briefly gave him more specifics.

"How am I supposed to reach you?" Robert asked once Sean had finished.

"I'll get in touch."

"And what do you expect me to find?"

"Something dirty."

CHAPTER 28

Teresa tried to keep the morale up at the store, although it was a struggle. She saw Louisa looking extra dejected as she setup a display. "Don't worry," she said, keeping her voice bright. "We're not going to close."

"It's not that," Louisa said. "I don't feel well. I just ate something bad I guess."

"I'll make you something to help you feel better," Teresa said then later came out with some ginger lemonade. "Here, I'll finish this."

Louisa sat in a chair, took a sip and shook her head. "Why are you always so nice?"

"What?"

"How can you be smiling and talking to customers and making this for me when Valley Ray did what they did to you?"

"I don't have a choice. Sean's looking into it."

"It's not going to help."

Teresa turned from the display and looked at her curious. "Why? Is there something I should know?"

Louisa looked down at her drink. "No."

"He's—"

"You two seem to be together a lot lately," Louisa said, changing the subject. "And he's hotter than even I thought. I don't know who got him to shave his beard." Her eyes twinkled. "Or maybe I do. Are you really staying at a friend's house?" When Teresa didn't readily respond, a smile touched her lips. "Do your sisters know?"

"I'm going to tell them."

"Why keep it a secret? Who cares about you living with a man?"

Teresa knew it wasn't safe to tell Louisa the truth yet. "They don't like him."

Louisa's smile grew. "Even better."

"But now that you know my secret, tell me yours."

"What secret?"

"Who the father is."

"You'll find out soon."

"Is he married like Michelle said?"

Louisa finished her drink. "You know, you probably should sell this stuff," Louisa said, standing and holding the glass out to her. "I feel so much better. I should get back to work."

Damn, she was starting to feel guilty, and she never felt that, Louisa thought as she left the store and headed for her car. Why did Teresa have to be so likeable? And sly? Who would have thought she'd have the courage to move in with Sean without telling anyone. Guess she wasn't the goody two shoes she first thought. Not that she could blame her. A man like Sean could make a woman do lots of things.

Her cell phone rang. She saw an unregistered number and knew who it was. "Hi, baby."

"I need to see you," Thomas said.

She met him at a hotel out of town that wasn't nearly as nice as the other two, but it was perfect for what he had in mind. And within minutes, all her feelings of guilt left when his mouth covered hers and he made love to her like he never had before. By the time she returned home, she already knew what her future would be. She saw Thomas holding their baby, counting its fingers and toes. She wouldn't have to live in this dump any more but would have a grand house and fine clothes.

She was lying on the couch when she started to feel strange. She sat up when a wave of pain hit. It frightened her because she knew she wasn't due for another two months. She gripped the cushions, knowing something was wrong. She called out her father's name, but realized he wasn't home yet. She dialed Teresa's phone, then disconnected when she got no answer. With shaking fingers, she dialed the ambulance, hoping they would get to her in time.

She felt another wave of pain, feeling her body betray her as it tried to rid itself of the life forming within her. She felt the wetness between her legs, glanced down and saw the blood, a silent scream catching in her throat. She didn't want to lose her baby.

But she knew that was exactly what was happening and the realization collided with the stark reality of her fate: She'd made the wrong decision. Thomas had done something to her, she didn't know what, but she could feel the poison taking over. Had it been on his lips? On his hands? She didn't know how he'd gotten it inside her, but she could feel herself dying.

She glanced at the empty space across the room where Teresa used to wash dishes in the kitchen, tears filling her eyes. She didn't want to die. She whimpered Teresa's name as a child would whimper for their mother. She realized how much she'd taken her for granted. How her cousin, not Thomas, had made her want to live again. How her constant care and presence had become special to her.

Teresa had shown her true love. And she'd betrayed that pure love for a man who'd lied and deceived her. But she wouldn't let him win. She crawled over to the table, grabbed her handbag and pulled out a pen, but finding no paper, she started to write his name on the wall, but she could only manage TH before the pain overwhelmed her. And as she slipped into darkness, she cursed the shadows that embraced her and prayed for forgiveness.

TERESA DIDN'T EXPECT to see the bright red and white lights of an ambulance clashing with the darkness outside Louisa's house. A slight summer breeze rustled the leaves of the surrounding trees mingling with a cacophony of voices. Teresa jumped out of her car and raced to the door. She'd seen Louisa had called her cell phone, but when she hadn't been able to reach her, she decided to check in on her since she knew she hadn't been feeling well. She dashed up the porch steps and opened the door.

Sean stopped her the moment she stepped inside. "You don't want to see this."

"What happened?" Teresa asked then looked past him and saw a large pool of blood. Fear gripped her heart. "Wait, what's going on? Where's Louisa?"

"It seems she went into labor early and hemorrhaged."

"Excuse me," a curt male voice said.

Teresa looked up and saw a man and a woman carrying a

stretcher. She felt Sean move her to the side, because she couldn't move on her own, as they carried a body covered by a sheet.

"No, no!" Teresa cried, leaping forward, her fear turning to horror. "Not Louisa. She can't be dead. It wasn't supposed to end like this."

Sean held her back, but she yanked herself from his grasp. "No, don't touch me."

He stared at her, the pain on his face echoed in his voice, "Teresa—"

"But I just saw her. She was fine. She had a little indigestion or something. Oh god, how could I have missed it? I was supposed to save her. If I'd been here—"

Sean reached for her, but she moved out of his reach. "You wouldn't have been able to do anything."

Teresa stared at him, her hands clasped together, her eyes beseeching him. "She's not dead, right?" she asked in an urgent whisper. "Tell me she's not dead."

Sean pulled her close and held her, wishing he could.

CHAPTER 29

Only Teresa shed a tear at Louisa's funeral and for her unborn child. Everyone else looked as if they'd rather be somewhere else. Especially Aunt Margaret, whose cold gaze bore into the wooden box surrounded by flowers, as if she could make it vanish with the power of her eyes. Once the service was over, Uncle Darren and Aunt Margaret approached Teresa, carrying two suitcases.

Teresa hung her head. "Aunt Margaret, I'm so—"

"Never mind," Aunt Margaret said. "You did your best." She shoved the suitcases at Teresa. "These are her things. I've donated her clothes, but didn't know what to with these. I don't care what you do with them." She turned and left. Uncle Darren gave her a reassuring pat on the arm, then followed his wife.

Michelle and Jessie came up to Teresa.

"I'll go get your things from the house," Michelle said.

"That won't be necessary," Sean said.

She sent him a glance, taking in his new clean-shaven look and crisp suit with interest. "And why would that be?"

"Because she's been staying with me...for awhile."

"I think she needs to be with family right now."

"And I think she'll do better with me," Sean said, taking one of the suitcases from Teresa.

Michelle lifted a brow. "So you think you know more than we do?"

"I just—"

"Michelle, please let's not argue about this," Jessie said looking around. "Not here."

Michelle shrugged. "It doesn't matter. Nobody cares that she's gone."

"I care," Teresa said in a fierce whisper, meeting her sister's gaze with tears in her eyes. "She didn't deserve to suffer like that. You didn't see all the blood—"

Sean placed an arm around her shoulders. "Darling, let me take you home."

Michelle stepped in front of him before he could turn. "*Darling?*" she said, mocking the word. "Oh, no," she said waving a finger at him. "I don't care what term of endearment you want to use with her, Teresa's home is with me." She looked at her younger sister and softened her tone. "I'm sorry. I shouldn't have said that about Louisa." She took her hand. "Now come on."

Sean shot Michelle a stern look. "I said she's coming home with me."

Teresa shook her head, pulling her hand from her sister's grip. "Please don't fight him. I don't—"

Michelle's voice hardened. "You're not thinking rationally right now and I won't let him take advantage of it."

Sean held his ground. "She's coming home with me. You can call her later."

"Your act is very impressive," Michelle said. "If I hadn't dealt with men like you before, I would almost believe your act of—"

"It's not an act."

"Because you're a man used to getting his way," Michelle finished.

"I do care," Sean insisted, his tone filled with emotion. "More than you know."

"And why should I believe you?" she shot back.

"Because I'm her husband."

Michelle didn't move. "What?"

Teresa touched the sleeve of his jacket. "Sean, let me—"

"If there's nothing that Louisa's death has taught me, it's that life's too short and I'm not going to pretend anymore."

Jessie's gaze shifted between Teresa and Sean. "You're married?"

"And you didn't tell us?" Michelle added, staring at her sister in disbelief.

"I was going to," Teresa said. "But then there was trouble with the store and then this and—"

Michelle held up her hands as if warding off something awful, and took a step back. "Fine, live your life. Obviously you don't need us anymore." She turned and walked away.

"Michelle!" Jessie called after her, but her sister kept walking. She sighed then turned to Teresa and placed a hand over her heart. "I'm so hurt I don't even know what to say."

Teresa tugged on one of her bracelets. "I knew you wouldn't have approved."

Jessie nodded. "You're right. We would have argued, we would have raged because that's what the Clifton sisters do. We would have done anything to try to change your mind, but," she said, blinking back tears although she managed to keep her voice steady. "We wouldn't have stopped you."

"I'm sorry," Teresa said, realizing how right Jessie was. Her sisters had been with her when she'd dared herself to jump in the bay, had helped her with opening her store, had taken Louisa shopping and not stopped her from moving in with Uncle Darren. They hadn't liked her choices, but they'd stayed by her side. She'd been so busy trying to show Louisa love that she'd taken them for granted. Bertha's warning had been right and she regretted leaving them out of an important moment in her life. "Forgive me."

"Of course," Jessie said giving Teresa's hand a squeeze. "But it's going to take awhile."

Teresa watched her sister leave, her heart aching with a new pain. "I've let everyone down."

"No, you haven't," Sean said taking the other suitcase from her and walking to his truck.

"Then why does it feel that way?"

"Married?" Kenneth repeated as he drove Jessie and Syrah back from the funeral. "Are you sure?"

"Yes," Jessie said, rolling down the window to let the summer air flow into the car. "That's what she said."

Kenneth started to laugh.

"What's so funny?"

"The bastard lied to me and I actually fell for it. Not marriage material my a—"

Jessie nudged him and glanced at Syrah in the rearview mirror.

"Butt," he finished.

"I wish I could laugh, but I don't think it's funny. It's going to take Michelle a long time to get over this."

"How did she take it?"

"About as calmly as if she'd heard we'd decided to turn the front lawn into a cemetery."

He sent Jessie a significant look. "And what about you?"

"I'm angry," she said, resting her arm on the window frame. "But I'm more hurt that she didn't trust us."

"Well, you don't have to worry. He loves her."

She looked at him surprised. "How do you know?"

"You couldn't see it on his face?"

"See what? I know he likes her a lot."

Kenneth's brows shot up. "A lot? He's completely devoted. Head over heels. I didn't know they were married, but the way he stayed by her side said a lot. And every time he looked at her, you could see the pain on his face."

"You really saw all that?"

"Why would I make it up?"

"To make us feel better?"

"Teresa's my family too. I wouldn't say something I didn't mean."

Jessie twisted her wedding ring around on her finger. "They make a really odd match."

"He looks better than before," Syrah said from the backseat. "He's really good looking."

Jessie frowned. "Exactly. Too good."

Kenneth sent his wife a curious look. "What's that supposed to mean?"

"It means he doesn't belong in South Bank and it makes me even more suspicious about why he's there."

"Give him a chance, I think you'll see that your sister's made a good choice."

"We still don't know much about him. We both know he has secrets."

Kenneth nodded. "And it seems your sister was one of them."

CHAPTER 30

Teresa went home and cried. Sean wanted to hold her, but she wouldn't let him. She didn't want him to soothe her pain and calm her misery. She wept until she fell asleep from exhaustion.

When Teresa awoke the next morning, she realized she couldn't move. She became aware of the warmth of Sean's body, his slow breathing, as he held her in his arms. She didn't know when he'd come to her, but knew that she'd had a dreamless, healing sleep and felt renewed. She stared at the face inches from hers, lying on the pillow. He looked very young and defenseless in sleep, which surprised her, as had the strength of his anger when Michelle accused him of having another motive for being with her.

She hated how Michelle misjudged him. She remembered tearfully recalling the death of her parents and her friend Bess and how Louisa's passing tore open those wounds. But she knew his touch had stopped her from falling apart.

She tried to carefully ease herself out of his arms, but his eyes slowly opened.

"Ready to eat something?" she asked, sorry she'd woken him.

He shook his head and closed his eyes. Teresa slipped out of bed.

"Are you okay?" he grumbled against the pillow.

"I'm getting better," she said. Teresa changed and headed for the kitchen. She had just finished the pancakes when she heard the shower turn on.

Sean entered the kitchen just as Teresa set fruit on the table. He sat down, pushing hair from his forehead.

"I've ruined your morning by keeping you up all night, right?" she asked when she saw him twice reach for his orange juice and miss.

"You're worth it." He stared at her through half-closed lids. "But if I hadn't smelled the food, I'd still be asleep."

"I can reheat it for you."

"No need. I'm already up." He rested his chin in his hand. Teresa placed a plate in front of him, then sat down to eat. It took her a few seconds to realize he'd gone back to sleep.

"Sean?" She gently shook him. "Go back to bed."

He ran a hand over his face. "I'm all right now."

He yawned then began to eat.

"You don't have to stay up with me. I'm okay, really," she said, forcing a smile.

"Really?"

She nodded.

"Good." He sighed then stood and shuffled past her, placing a kiss on her cheek before he went back upstairs.

THE NIGHT WAS heavy and warm as Sean drove them home from watching fireworks on the bay for the Fourth of July. Twice she thought about calling Michelle, but knew her sister would need more time. She'd created another gel, but it wasn't selling as quickly as the peppermint gel had. She remembered getting her spirits lifted by visiting Second Chances bookstore and telling Pernelle some of her troubles, when Pernelle had seen Teresa looking at some business books.

"You married him?" Pernelle said, stopping Teresa halfway. She shook her head, perplexed. "Did you say you *married* Sean Casey?"

Teresa nodded surprised that was the only part of her story that interested her. But then she had to remember they had a history. "I know I should have told you since—"

"It's better that you didn't," she said, waving Teresa's words aside. She glanced at something outside the window. "I guess he's really gotten over her," she said in an odd tone.

"He's changed."

Pernelle looked at Teresa and her face brightened into a smile. "I guess what's past is past, right? No wonder you haven't stopped by like you used to. You shouldn't read books, you should write them."

But as Teresa sat beside Sean as he maneuvered the truck through the winding roads, she wondered what her next chapter would be. What would she do if the shop didn't survive? Would her relationship with her sisters ever be the same? She sighed, then paused.

"What's that smell?" she asked.

Sean looked at her. "What?"

"That smell."

He sniffed the air then shifted gears with a frown. "I don't know." He abruptly pulled over to the side of the road amid some honking protests.

He didn't want to worry her, but he had a feeling of dread.

Priscilla usually didn't disappoint him, but she wasn't moving or picking up as she should and he didn't like that smell.

"Get out of the car!" he ordered, unlatching his seat belt. Just as the words left his mouth, the front hood burst into flames.

He jumped out and ran. He was a few feet away when he realized that Teresa wasn't behind him.

He turned and saw her still trapped inside the truck, struggling with her seat belt as the flames grew. And as he rushed forward he died a thousand deaths angered that he hadn't fixed something so simple as a tricky seat belt. He swung open the door, the heat of the flames sneaking closer as they ran along the dashboard. Soon the fire would jump to her seat and engulf them both. He grabbed for the metal lock, but it wouldn't budge.

"Leave me," she said, sweat sliding down her face.

"Never," he said with fierce determination. If nothing else, he'd die with her. He tugged on the seat belt, hoping some super human strength would help him, but it wouldn't disconnect. He thought of the night he received the phone call that Renee had died in a fiery crash. He remembered seeing the wreckage of her burnt out Mercedes and the tiny charred remains that had been used to identify her.

He wasn't burying another wife. He saw the flames clawing at Teresa's jeans and tried one last tug, willing to rip the seat apart if he had to—the lock disengaged and broke free. He grabbed Teresa and pulled her out.

Within seconds the passenger side was engulfed in flames. Neither spoke as they lay on the ground, staring at how close they had come to death.

Following the terrifying event, Sean's sleepless nights

returned with a vengeance. Any time he closed his eyes, he saw Teresa trapped and her face would blend with that of Renee's, who looked at him with a cool smile. Teresa tried to ease his insomnia with an elixir she made, but it did little to help. He felt on edge.

"There's something wrong, Mother, I can feel it," Sean told Bertha as they sat in her kitchen the scent of spiced tea in the air. "There was nothing wrong with Priscilla before."

"At least you're all right."

He set his tea cup down afraid he would break it. The mechanic's conclusion that his truck had an undiagnosed leak that contributed to the fire didn't sit well with him. "If anything happened to Teresa because of me—"

"But it didn't."

"But it could."

"Do you still blame yourself for your wife's death?"

"I have to keep Teresa safe," he said glancing out the window, avoiding the question and Bertha's keen gaze. "I have this feeling that someone's trying to hurt her."

"Who?"

He shook his head. "I don't know. And I know it doesn't make sense."

Bertha fell silent, then said in a soft tone, "I can't help you if you don't tell me the truth."

Sean sat back in his chair, resigned. "I've started seeing her again. Worse than before. Every time I close my eyes I see her face and now I think I've actually seen her." He didn't want to share that several times he'd followed a woman, certain it was Renee, but she always eluded his reach. "I'm chasing shadows and ghosts."

"Or something you've always feared to be true."

A wave of apprehension swept through him, he didn't want

her to give voice to what had driven him to hide away. "I'm sure it's nothing," he said quickly. He glanced at his watch. He had to pick Teresa up from the store since he was driving her car. They would soon have to look at getting another car and this time he would make sure it was solid. He stood up and thanked Bertha for listening.

"You're not crazy, Sean," Bertha said, following him to the door. "If you believe nothing else, believe that." She touched his necklace and he thought he could feel the tiny amber stones heat up. "You are strong enough to fight this."

He thought of Bertha's words as he and Teresa drove up to their house. No, their *home*, Sean thought, looking at the structure in a new way. Rather than being the hideaway it had once been, now every room had a special meaning to him. He wouldn't let his nightmares steal what he'd fought hard to reclaim—a place where he belonged.

Teresa pointed to an unfamiliar vehicle in the driveway. "Looks like we have visitors," she said.

Sean parked the car in grim defeat. "Shit, they found me."

CHAPTER 31

"Who's 'they'?" Teresa asked unbuckling her seat belt.

He swore under his breath, wanting to break something, but he didn't want to upset her. "You'll see." He walked up to the door and put the key in the lock. "Follow my lead."

He opened the door and turned on the lights.

"No one's here," she whispered.

"They're here."

He went into the living room and turned on the lights. Although Teresa was prepared for a surprise, nothing could have prepared her for the two people occupying the living room. She gave a small gasp and bumped into Sean when she saw two giants who reeked of money and status.

One stood next to Sean's chair. He was the color of nutmeg with grey eyes and a thin mouth. A strong hand gripped a heavy wooden cane. He wore expensive pale jeans and a designer T-shirt. The man next to him was slighter in build, although just as impressive with brown eyes and a friendly smile. He took care with his attire, and she could see his sneakers were top of the line, and his blue shirt and trousers wrinkle free.

"Well, we didn't expect guests so let me get you something to drink," she said. Before anyone could disagree, she raced to the kitchen to collect herself, but didn't have the chance. She found two more guests in the kitchen.

A woman with frizzy hair and chocolate freckles on her nose stared at Teresa. A young man, who was rummaging in the fridge, closed it and stared at Teresa through his dark rimmed glasses while holding an apple in his mouth. Teresa stood speechless. Sean came up behind her and took her hand, leading her back into the living room. "Let's make some introductions."

"Who's that?" Grey Eyes asked, the cadence of his island lilt harsher than Sean's. He was now seated with his cane resting against the chair.

Sean took a deep breath. "What are you doing here?"

"Making sure you're all right," the woman said.

"As you can see, I'm fine."

"At last you got a haircut," Friendly Eyes said, rubbing Sean's head.

Grey Eyes looked at Teresa. "Why don't you introduce us to your—" He raised a questioning eyebrow.

"Wife," Sean said.

"Again?" Grey Eyes said in a quiet tone.

Sean didn't seem affected by the obvious disapproval. He turned to Teresa. "Let me introduce you to my family. That's my elder brother Evan." Grey Eyes gave a curt nod. "Then there's Robert."

He smiled flirtatiously and bowed over her hand. "They call me the robber of lonely hearts."

"You can call him something else," Sean said dryly. "I'll give you a few suggestions later."

"I'm Darcy," the woman said, taking Teresa's hand. The gesture was an attempt to put her at ease, but Teresa could feel the way her eyes measured her, wondering what had persuaded her brother to marry her.

"And the last one here is Patrick."

"I thought you said you had five siblings," Teresa said.

"Cameron couldn't make it," Evan said.

Teresa smiled. "It's nice to meet all the Caseys in one place."

"Caseys?" Evan said. "We're not—"

"Staying long, I hope," Sean cut in, sending his brother a look.

"I know this is bit of a shock," Teresa said feeling the sudden tension in the room. "Would you like a cup of tea? I'll go make a pot."

"We're not tea drinkers," Evan said in his gritty voice. "How about something stronger?"

"I'll get coffee then," she said and left the room.

"Who the hell is that?" Evan demanded once she was gone.

"I already told you," Sean said.

"And what's with this place?" Patrick asked, looking at the candles, the velvet pillows, and drying herbs. "You'd think we were in the presence of a witch."

Sean's silence said it all. Their eyes widened.

"You married a witch!" Patrick said, intrigued.

"She's not a witch," Sean said. "She's a healer."

Evan shook his head. "You've lost your damn mind."

"Yes," Sean said through set teeth, sending Robert a cold look. "I was crazy to call you. Did you find anything?"

"We're still digging," Robert said, unmoved by his brother's look. "It's a big company."

"And we like to be thorough," Evan added.

"This isn't a game," Sean said, annoyed by his brother's cavalier attitude. "I really needed your help. That company—"

"We're on it," Robert said. "I promise."

Sean rubbed his chin. "What are you doing here?"

"We already told you." Evan shook his head, looking around the room. "You've really gone off the deep end."

Sean glared at him. "That's right, or have you forgotten. I'm the one that's crackers. I'm the one who's haunted by his dead wife."

"And lying to his second. Why didn't you tell her your real surname?"

"I legally changed it."

"Why?"

"Why do you think?"

"You need to come back and seek help."

"Listen, I wanted a new life and I got one and—"

The conversation dropped when Teresa entered. She could feel the tension, but knew better than to say anything. They all took their coffee and ate their snacks and stared at her except for Patrick, who delighted in toying with a string of crystals hanging near the window.

"So how did you meet?" Darcy asked.

"I met him at the bay."

"And how long have you known him?" Robert asked.

"A couple of months."

Evan tapped the head of his cane. "How do you earn a living?"

"I used to teach piano. But now I own a store—"

Patrick spoke up. "You play the piano? Could you play something for us?"

His three older siblings glared at him, and the idea was dismissed.

"I guess I'll get dinner on," Teresa said.

"Don't bother. I'm already doing that," Darcy said. "Hope

you don't mind, but I've always made myself at home in Sean's house. We always know where he hides his key."

And Darcy's look told Teresa that Sean's family knew a lot more about him than she did.

"Why don't you go wash up?" Sean suggested.

It was clear they wanted her to leave, so that they could talk about her. Teresa bowed out gracefully and went upstairs, hoping another Casey wouldn't pop up.

Teresa went into the master bedroom, grabbed the phone and took it into the closet. She hit speed dial, desperate to talk to Jessie.

Michelle's voice came on the line. "Hello?"

She silently swore. She'd hit the wrong number.

"Hello? "

She took a deep breath. "Michelle...it's me."

Her sister's tone instantly changed. "What's wrong?"

She hadn't said anything, so how did her sister know? Because she just did, her heart replied. Michelle had always been someone she could depend on. She bit back tears, sorry that she'd hurt her.

"Is he there with you," Michelle said. "Is that why you can't talk? Is he cruel? Wait don't answer that, I'll—"

"No, no," Teresa quickly said. "It's nothing like that."

"Then what's wrong? Do you want me to come and get you?"

"Part of me wants you to," she admitted. "His family just showed up and they don't like me."

Michelle delicately cleared her throat. "Remember we aren't too fond of Sean either."

"I wish you'd give him a chance. He's not as bad as you think."

"Which is why you're talking to me instead of him. If you want me to say something nice, you're talking to the wrong sister.

But—" she said in a rush before Teresa could speak. "If you want a place to stay, you know you always have one."

"Thanks. I'm sorry about—"

"Don't. I don't want to talk about it right now."

Teresa switched the phone to her other ear. "There are a lot of things you don't want to talk about. It started when you left James—"

"Or when he left me," she said with a laugh that held no humor.

"He left you? You never said—"

"Because there's nothing to say. There's no mystery. No story. It was a marriage that ended. That's all."

"And more you're not telling us. How come you're the only one allowed to have secrets?"

"Why did you marry Sean without telling us? What drove you to buy a store and live with Louisa?" Michelle sighed. "Let's not fight, okay? If you need me and want a place to stay, you have one," she said, then disconnected.

Teresa hung up the phone, feeling drained. She drew her knees to her chest and rested her head. She'd never had a tense relationship with Michelle and didn't know how to handle it. She thought of calling Bertha but knew there wasn't much she could do to help. She opened the closet door. The first thing she saw was Mist, sitting staring up at her. Behind the cat were a pair of worn jeans. She didn't need to look up to know who they belonged to. She sighed and came out of the closet, pretending it was nothing out of the ordinary. She placed the phone on the nightstand.

"Now you know why I left them," he said.

"Your family doesn't like me."

"They don't know you well enough not to, they just don't trust you."

"Dislike and distrust feel the same. Now I know how you feel," she said putting on a brave face. "Quick, tell me more about them."

"There's not much to say. Evan and Robert own a private investigation firm. Patrick's in high school and loves tennis. Darcy owns a fitness spa."

Teresa looked down and tugged on her loose top. "Oh dear, no wonder she's disappointed," she said with a laugh. "Maybe I should start eating more carrots."

Sean didn't smile. "That's not funny."

Teresa thought so, but decided to change the subject. "How long are they planning to stay?"

"Probably until I can get rid of them. I'll try to make that as soon as possible."

"What are you cooking?" Darcy asked Teresa the next morning as Teresa stood next to the stove cooking a mixture of sliced potatoes, scrambled eggs and red peppers.

Darcy looked at the mixture and shook her head. "Sean doesn't like that."

"He usually eats it."

"He is probably being polite. He usually doesn't like his vegetables mixed with his main meal."

"But—"

"Sean's not here anyway. He left you a note to say he's running some errands, so you can keep that for yourself. I'll make something for the rest of us."

"But—"

"No worries, I'll be careful."

Teresa finished her cooking, storing some in the fridge just in case Sean wanted it later. She ate alone in the dining room while the Caseys took over the kitchen. Once she'd finished, she sat in the living room and hemmed a shirt Sean had bought, Mist curled up at her feet.

"What have you got there?" Robert asked, taking a seat in front of her.

"I'm just hemming."

"I hope that's not Sean's shirt you're fussing over, he hates a woman who bothers his things."

"But he—"

"Won't tell you of course, but he likes being independent."

"I see." Teresa smiled, trying to keep her temper, annoyed that Sean hadn't taken her with him. She decided to work in her garden. They could fill up the house, but at least nature gave her space and the warm summer wind could warm the coldness of worry creeping over her heart.

That space closed when Patrick walked up to her and said, "We've been hard on you."

She didn't reply. He sat down, chewing on a pear. *Did the kid ever stop eating?*

"You're just so different than Renee it's hard to get used to. She was—"

"Awful. I know."

His brows shot up. "Is that was Sean told you?"

"Yes." She paused. "You mean that's not true?"

"Not the Renee we knew. She was beautiful, fun and charming. She was the kind of woman you wanted to be around because she just glowed."

"Oh," Teresa said feeling her heart sink. She'd believed Sean saying *she* was his second chance. But had he chosen her only because she was so different than his first wife? Had he lied to her?

"No," Patrick said as if reading her thoughts. "I know why Sean likes you. You're nice too. I like you."

"One of the few."

He shrugged, then took another bite of his pear. "Sean wasn't himself after Chloe." He paused. "He told you about Chloe, right?" he asked suddenly looking anxious.

"Yes."

He visibly relaxed. "Yes, that tore us all up, especially him but then when Renee died..." He let his words trail away. "Maybe that's what he wants to believe, that she was awful, because she hurt him so much. I think he has to be angry with her."

"For dying?"

"No, for killing herself."

CHAPTER 32

Teresa could barely focus over the next few days. Renee had killed herself? Why hadn't Sean told her? She wasn't ready to ask him. She didn't want to deal with his lingering feelings for her. But she didn't think Patrick was lying. Why would the Caseys see Renee in one way and Sean see her in another? Even Pernelle had liked her. What had caused her to take her life? Did Sean blame himself? Was that why he thought he saw her?

"Ask him," Bertha told her as they sat on her porch drinking mint lemonade they'd made; Bertha provided the freshly squeezed lemons and Teresa did the rest.

"I'm afraid to."

"Why?"

"Because I don't want to hear him lie to me or say what he wants me to hear."

"Which is?"

"That he's happier with me than he was with her. You're the one who told me he had a deep sorrow."

"Teresa, I need you to trust Sean more than you've ever trusted anyone. If you can't handle this, then leave him now."

"Why would I leave him?" Teresa asked, surprised by her friend's words.

"Because maybe you don't love him enough. Staying by his side may cost you and you might resent it."

"Bertha, what are you saying?"

"I'm saying that Sean loves you, but it comes with a price. He knows it and I've tried to help him, but..." She shook her head. "I've told you, I see something shadowy around him. He sees it too, images of his wife."

"I know. He's told me."

"Then if you truly love him, you won't doubt him. You'll be able to ask him questions and face whatever he has to say. Be careful about listening to others and hearing what you want to hear."

"I do love him," Teresa said, a little offended that Bertha casted doubt on her feelings.

"It's not enough to say the words," Bertha said, then tapped Teresa's chest with her forefinger, "if you don't feel that certainty with all your heart."

"You're right," Teresa said, then finished off her drink. "This was delicious. I'll have to take some back to Sean." Bertha poured what was left of the lemonade into a thermos. Teresa was not eager to return home, at least not yet, so she went to Second Chances hoping Pernelle could fill in some gaps about Renee.

But Pernelle seemed reticent as they sat in the back of the bookstore.

"Is it true she killed herself?" Teresa asked. "You said that he left her or vice versa."

"Yes, well from what I know they had a major argument and

then the accident happened. They ruled it a suicide because there were no skid marks at the crash site and mechanical error was ruled out. What's that?" Pernelle asked, looking at the thermos.

"Oh, just some extra mint lemonade for Sean. It's his favorite."

Pernelle grinned, her expression strangely brighter than usual. "You must make him happy. I knew you'd be good for him. Didn't I tell you?" She stood up. "Well, come with me I have a new selection of romances and fantasies that just came in. You can just leave your things here and get them later."

A half hour later, Teresa left the bookstore with five more exciting reads and feeling more relaxed. Pernelle was right. She did make Sean happy and she knew he wasn't lying about that. They were meant to be together. Her good mood rose higher when she got home and the house was empty. Sean sat alone in the kitchen. "Are they gone for good?" she asked.

He gave her a sad smile. "I wish. They'll be back later, but at least we have some time alone."

She poured the lemonade from the thermos and handed him the glass. "Here. I just came back from Bertha, we made a fresh batch."

He finished the drink in one gulp then set it down. "Hmm... delicious as always." He stood up and kissed her. "Thanks."

"Can I ask you something?"

His phone rang. He checked the number. "Sorry, darling I have to get this then I have some papers I have to look over. But we'll talk later, okay?"

"Okay," Teresa said, watching him dash out the room.

To Sean's relief, the call didn't last long, but his family had returned so he knew his plan to skip looking over the papers and be with Teresa were dashed. He hoped to quickly look through some of his financials then have some time to talk to Teresa or at least take her for a drive. He didn't like leaving her alone with his family for too long. As Sean climbed the stairs to his study, the steps seemed to lengthen and shorten. He shook his head trying to orient himself.

When he reached the top of the stairs, he felt dizzy and a sharp pain hit him in the stomach—like someone had grabbed his inside and was trying to rip out his intestines. He fell to the ground in agony. He heard the front door open and close, but couldn't cry out...his throat was tightening and his tongue felt like it was covered in paste. He heard the sound of a cane against the steps and his brother's heavy footsteps. The cane dropped to the floor and someone was holding him, calling his name. The pain tore through him then darkness descended.

Downstairs, Teresa emptied the thermos then noticed that their birdbath was empty. She filled the thermos with some tap water and refilled the bath. She watched a robin and two cardinals go up to the bath and take a sip. Then the birds began to convulse and all three fell down dead.

CHAPTER 33

Teresa didn't realize she was screaming until Darcy and Robert were by her side, holding her up.

"What's wrong?" Darcy asked.

"They died...the birds...died."

"These things happen."

She shook her head, frantic. "No, you don't understand. They drank the water and—"

She wasn't able to finish because Patrick came rushing out, his eyes wide behind his glasses.

"Come quick! Something's wrong with Sean."

They all raced upstairs where they found Evan on the ground in the bathroom with Sean's limp body in his arms.

Robert and Darcy rushed towards him. "What happened?" Darcy demanded.

"I found him on the ground in pain," Evan said. "He cleaned out his insides and now he's barely breathing and burning up with fever."

"We need to call a doctor," Robert said, lifting Sean in his arms.

Patrick went to the phone.

They rested Sean on the bed, stripping him of his clothes. Teresa stood near the door.

"It's some sort of allergic reaction," Evan said.

Darcy and Robert shared a look then turned to Teresa.

Darcy's eyes narrowed. "An allergy he seems to share with birds. What did you give him?"

"It was just something Bertha and I made," Teresa said in a small voice. "Lemonade."

"What did you put in it?"

She hesitated, her mind suddenly going blank as she tried to think of all the ingredients. Her silence was enough to prove her guilty.

Evan's eyes bore into hers. "I swear to God, if my brother dies—"

"You pretended not to know who he really was, didn't you?" Darcy said. "You waited until he put you in his will—"

"I didn't try to kill him," Teresa said, horrified by their accusations. "Bertha and I have made this before and we drank it today. It was harmless."

As if to combat her claim, Sean's entire body began to shake. Evan held him and soon the trembling stopped.

"Harmless you say?"

"The ambulance is on its way," Patrick said holding the phone. "Is he still breathing?"

"Barely."

Teresa moved towards the bed, desperate to get to Sean. "Let me touch him, I can sense—"

Robert blocked her path. "We'll take care of him."

She tried to move around him. "But I just need to—"

"Leave," Evan said.

"Please let me help him. I can—"

Darcy grabbed Teresa's arm and shoved her back with such force Teresa hit the wall, causing a picture to shake. "Stay away from him."

Teresa stared at the four pair of eyes knowing she couldn't fight them, a chilly black silence coursing through the room. "I didn't try to kill him, I wouldn't—"

When Darcy reached for her again, Teresa held up her arms in surrender. "Okay, I'll go," she said and turned to the door. "But—"

Darcy didn't give her a chance to finish. She shoved Teresa out of the room and slammed the door.

Teresa wanted to break down the door and defend herself. She wanted to scream and fight them, but she knew that wasn't what mattered. It didn't matter that she was an outsider or even that they thought she had tried to kill him. What mattered was saving Sean and finding out how this had happened.

She couldn't explain what had gone wrong. She and Bertha had both enjoyed the lemonade so much, there was hardly any left for Sean. Just enough for a small glass. Teresa raced down stairs and grabbed the thermos. She had to find out what went wrong. She had to clear her name, Bertha could help her. Unfortunately Bertha wasn't home and she couldn't reach her by phone. She called Dr. Knox, relieved when he picked up after the second ring.

"Thank goodness," she said. "I need another favor and fast."

"What is it?" he said with a note of caution.

"I need you to check—"

"Leave it alone, Teresa."

She paused surprised by his curt tone. "What?"

"I can't help you. I can't check anything for you, just leave things as they are."

"But this—"

"Is bigger than you. Leave it alone. Don't look too deep."

"But I—"

"I'm sorry, I have to go," he said then disconnected.

Teresa stared at the phone perplexed. Why didn't he want to help her? What did he mean she shouldn't look too deep? She briefly squeezed her eyes shut and took a deep breath. Sean was sick and she didn't have time for more questions. She needed answers. She grabbed her car keys and headed for the door. She had to go to someone with more insight.

DETECTIVE HARTNETT HID when he saw Teresa burst into the police station looking like a wild woman. He saw her rush up to the front desk and ask for him. He caught the officer's eye, from where he was standing, and shook his head. The officer told her he was out. She asked a few more questions, but the officer made it clear that Hartnett couldn't be reached. She then lowered her voice so he couldn't hear the rest of the conversation, but from the mumbling he could tell she was talking fast and the expression on the officer's face made Hartnett know that whatever she was saying sounded interesting.

The officer was trained to look interested, even when he wasn't, but this time his expression wasn't fake. He really was listening to her every word. She then shoved something at him, which he took, using a pen to hold it by the handle. She said something else then dashed off. Hartnett half smiled, imagining her grabbing a broom and flying away.

Once she was gone, he came out of hiding. "What was that all about?"

The officer held up a thermos he'd put in a plastic bag. "She thinks someone tried to poison her husband. She wants us to test this."

"Are you serious?"

"She seemed very serious, sir."

"I don't know why she keeps dropping things off here."

"She seemed pretty desperate. I think we should look into it."

"Why? It's probably a waste of time."

"What if it's not, sir?"

Hartnett sighed. The officer was right. He needed to put an end to her hysterics. "Fine, send it to the lab. We'll see what they find."

TERESA LEFT THE POLICE STATION, not knowing where to go next. She knew she couldn't go home yet. Sean was likely at the hospital by now and she doubted his family would allow her to see him. She drove to Long Creek Park and wandered around. As the sun beat down around her, she could hear the fountain, the rush of bicycle wheels whizzing past, laughter and people enjoying ice cream snacks, sunbathing and the smell of food drifting through the air from a local food truck. But she felt cold inside not knowing who to call or what to do. Her sisters couldn't help her.

"Teresa!" Kenneth's bright friendly voice said behind her.

She spun around and saw that he was on a late afternoon break, a half-eaten meal in his hand.

"I thought it was—" he began until he saw her face. His expression changed. "What happened?"

She stumbled towards him then stopped, tears suddenly blinding her. "I'm in so much trouble. I don't know what to do."

Kenneth reacted immediately. He threw the rest of his lunch

away in a garbage bin and led her over to a bench. When he spoke, he kept his voice steady. "Just tell me what happened."

Teresa nervously tugged on her bracelets. "This is all my fault. They think I tried to kill him."

"Who?"

"Sean."

"Who thinks that? Where is Sean now?" Kenneth took a deep breath then gently covered her hand. "I don't want to rush you, but you have to tell me everything. Start from the beginning."

"There's not much to say," she said thankful for his presence, but knowing there wasn't much he could do. She looked away from him and saw a squirrel peek its head inside an empty potato chips bag. "I visited Bertha and we had some mint lemonade and she put some in a thermos, which I gave to Sean."

"And now he's sick," Kenneth concluded.

Teresa shook her head. "No, it's worse than that, it killed the birds."

"Birds?"

"I used the same thermos to fill the birdbath. The birds drank the water and died. Now his family won't let me near him."

"We know you didn't do anything so there must be another explanation."

She turned to him intrigued. "What?"

"Someone tampered with the thermos."

"But it was with me the entire time."

"Are you sure?"

"Pretty sure."

Kenneth frowned, rubbing his chin. "Pretty sure isn't definite. Are you sure you never left the thermos?"

She shrugged searching her mind. "Just when I was in the book- shop."

"Where is the thermos now?"

"I gave it to the police."

Kenneth swore.

Teresa stiffened. "I did something wrong again, didn't I? I should have come to you first and—"

"No, no," he said. "You did what you had to."

She jumped to her feet. "But I keep making things worse. I have to go talk to Pernelle at the bookshop."

"Wait," Kenneth said, standing too. "Let me go with you to the hospital so we can explain to his family what you think happened."

Teresa shook her head. "I can't face them, yet. If he dies...."

"He won't die," Kenneth said, with more hope than conviction.

HE COULDN'T FIGURE out where he was. When Sean opened his eyes, the light in the room was dim and the walls seemed far away, like he was in the middle of an auditorium. He knew by the stark white walls and crisp, scratchy sheets that he wasn't at home. He heard the whisper of footsteps, then two faces peered over him.

"How are you feeling?" Darcy asked, touching his forehead with cool fingers.

"Better," he managed, his voice hoarse. He struggled to sit up feeling that something was missing. When he glanced around the room at his family, he figured out what it was. "Where's Teresa?"

"She's out," Darcy said quickly.

"She's gone," Evan corrected.

Darcy sent him a harsh glare, which he ignored. Sean stiffened. "Gone? What do you mean she's gone?"

"I mean she left you."

"Evan!" Darcy warned. "He doesn't need news like that right now."

The warning tone in her voice alerted him that something was wrong. He had to be careful until he knew the full story. Teresa's freedom—and maybe even her life—was at risk and he had to do his best to save her. Although Evan was no longer a cop after a bullet shattered his leg, his instincts were on alert and Sean knew his brother would have Teresa in jail before he knew it. "I don't believe you." He turned to Patrick. "Is it true?"

"I'm sure she's coming back."

Sean sighed, wishing he had more strength. "How long have I been here?"

"A couple of days," Robert said.

"I want you to find her. I need to see her and—"

"What's the point?" Evan cut in. "She tried to kill you."

Sean scowled. "What are you talking about?"

"She put something in your drink. She wouldn't admit it, but we guessed."

Patrick shook his head. "No, she said—"

"Shut up," Evan said.

"What did she say?" Sean asked his younger brother.

"She said she didn't do it," Patrick said in a soft voice.

Evan gripped his cane. "And then she did a runner."

"Well maybe if Darcy hadn't pushed her—"

Sean shot his sister a glance, anger piercing through him. "You *what*?"

"I was trying to protect you."

"By attacking my wife?"

"She kept trying to get near you."

His hands shook as he imagined the scene in his mind. Teresa trying to touch him and his family pushing her away. "So you kept her from me!"

"Keep your voices down," Robert said.

"She may be dangerous," Darcy said.

"She didn't do anything. It was my fault," he lied.

They all stared at him, then Evan finally said, "How is it your fault?"

"The doctor had prescribed pills for anxiety and I probably took too many."

"Then why did she run?"

Sean met his brother's hard stare. "Oh, maybe because you accused her of trying to kill me."

"Or maybe because anxiety medicine is not what they would find in your system and she knew that. She even took the thermos. We nearly lost you. It's only because they were able to flush out most of the toxins that you survived."

"You have to find her," Sean said.

Evan tapped his cane. "We plan to."

"How?"

"There's a warrant out for her arrest."

Sean grabbed the lapel of his brother's shirt and pulled him close. "Don't lie to me."

Evan easily loosened his hold. "I'm not lying. Your wife has a history. She did quite well after the death of a friend of hers and some say she was the last person seen with her cousin Louisa before she died. The police were only too eager to listen. Especially when they got back the lab report on the thermos."

"Teresa would never hurt anyone. Louisa hemorrhaged."

"And people at the shop saw Teresa giving her cousin the *same* lemonade she gave to you."

"So what? They're just gossips trying to make connections that don't exist. Get me my trousers, will you?"

"You're not going anywhere," Evan said.

Sean pushed back the sheets. "Watch me."

Evan stopped him with the tip of his cane. "If you fall on your face, I'm not picking you back up again."

"That's fine," Sean said, moving with a great amount of will. He knew he didn't have the strength to make it even a few feet, but he had to do something.

"There's nothing you can do," Darcy said, gently pushing him back. "The police are already looking for her."

He glared at her. "I won't press charges."

"With a past like yours, will it even matter?"

Sean felt his insides grow cold. His sister was right. All the things he hadn't told Teresa about—the loss of his practice, his insomnia and his brief stay in an asylum—could all be used against her if his family deemed him incompetent. He felt his heart begin to race; his joy was being taken away from him, again, just as it nearly had been when the truck caught fire.

"Sean, are you all right?" Darcy asked.

He knew he was breathing too fast by the sudden concern on his sister's face, but he didn't care. He had to think. He knew Teresa was innocent and if he couldn't protect her, someone else had to.

"We're not doing this to hurt you," she said.

"The fact that they haven't found her, means she knows what she did and doesn't want to get caught," Robert added.

Evan shook his head in pity. "You need to rest and regain your strength. She isn't worth it."

Sean squeezed his eyes shut, the rage in him hot and acidic. She was worth everything to him, but he knew he couldn't make them understand. He gripped his hands into fists, until he felt his fingernails impaling his palms.

"Sean?" He felt the light touch of his sister's fingers on his shoulder. "You're scaring us."

Don't touch me, he wanted to say but fury made him mute. He wouldn't let them hurt her. Where would she go? Who would she talk to? He took a deep breath. He had to be calm and think. He had to know what Evan was thinking in order to outwit him.

Sean slowly opened his eyes, regaining control of his emotions. "Have you talked to her sisters?"

A smooth, cold smile touched Evan's mouth. "Don't worry. We plan to."

CHAPTER 34

"You have two visitors."

Michelle listened to her receptionist with a dispassionate ear. Somehow she knew they would eventually come, especially after learning that her sister was a suspect wanted by the police, but she pretended to be surprised. "Who?"

There was a delicate pause. She heard the receptionist ask the visitors their business, but she could not understand their reply "They say they're relatives. Evan and Robert...uh...Casey."

She gave a deep sigh, slowly putting her papers away. "Send them in."

Michelle wasn't sure what she was expecting when the doors opened, but nothing could have prepared her for the two handsome giants that came through her door like renegades on the scent of a traitor.

One had a cane and a decided limp, this however did not lessen the overwhelming presence that surrounded him. His hair was black, contrasting eerily with his silver eyes and brown skin. He studied her, not with absent curiosity, but intense judgment. She had met his type before, therefore she was not uncomfortable under his glacial gaze. It was the other one who garnered the most attention. His stance was much more relaxed, but not less threatening. His brown eyes were frank and assessing. A small smile danced on his lips as if he was aware what impression his presence made on her.

"Please take a seat. Or perhaps you would like to go to the conference room?"

"This is fine," the one with the cane said, taking a seat.

"Would you like something to drink?"

"No, thank you."

"If you could tell me—" Michelle's statement was cut off when her receptionist buzzed her again.

"Yes?"

"Your sister is here to see you."

Michelle's pulse quickened and she suddenly wished she hadn't put her on speaker. Could Teresa have come out of hiding to see her? She felt the men's gaze on her. "Okay, send her in."

Jessie burst into the room. "I just spoke to Kenneth about a strategy and—" Her eyes widened when she saw the two men. She shut the door and rested against it. "Oh no. Sean's dead and you want to charge Teresa with murder. I knew—"

"Jessie, sit," Michelle ordered, sending her sister a warning glance. "I doubt that's why they're here."

Jessie found a seat and sank slowly into it looking chagrined.

"So," Michelle said. "How is Sean by the way?"

"Still weak," Brown Eyes said before the other could speak. He sent his brother a stare that indicated he would handle things. The other man lifted his shoulders an infinitesimal amount in a show of acquiescence. Brown Eyes leaned forward and smiled engagingly; Michelle felt her face grow warm. "Before trying to deal with the matter at hand we should introduce ourselves. I'm Robert and this is my brother Evan."

"Nice to meet you—both," she added, tearing her eyes away from him to include his brother, whose expression had become oddly neutral. "I'm Michelle, and this is my sister, Jessie. Now with the formalities out of the way, how can we help you?"

"We'd like to know where Teresa is."

"So would we."

Robert sighed disappointed. "So she did run off then."

"No. She went to find her...." Michelle floundered.

"Friend," Jessie said.

"To find out what went wrong," Michelle finished.

Evan nodded, watching the woman with a studied impassioned gaze. Jessie would be a poor liar, but he was certain Michelle was not. Her gaze was too intelligent, he decided to reveal what they knew. He tapped the head of his cane. "You can stop lying to us. Does your sister dabble in witchcraft?"

Jessie stiffened. "Now listen here, Captain Ahab—"

"Quiet, Jessie," Michelle said.

Jessie sat back in her seat.

"No, whatever unfortunate rumors you may have heard are false," Michelle said determined to set the record straight. "She is not a witch. Some may think Teresa is one because she's...special."

"So it's not true that your sister deals with herbs and oils and rituals and she," he nodded in Jessie's direction, "can read stones? I'm afraid I haven't uncovered your special talent yet," he said, sending Michelle a significant look.

Robert grinned. "We did our homework."

"Teresa occasionally makes medicinal drinks," Michelle said. "but they haven't hurt anyone."

"Of course," Evan said, doubtful.

Michelle could feel her sister's temper rising at Evan's blatant distrust. She decided to change the subject. "When we find Teresa, what message do you have for her?"

"I suggest you encourage her to turn herself in."

Robert spoke up. "Also, Sean wants to see her."

"She won't see him," Michelle said.

"Why not?"

"Guilt," Evan muttered.

Jessie opened her mouth, but Michelle's cold stare stopped her. "Is he convinced of her guilt?" she asked.

"Yes," Evan lied.

"No," Robert countered. "He wants to know what happened."

"Are you convinced of her guilt?" Michelle addressed the question to Evan.

"Unequivocally."

"Wow, that's big word," Jessie said. "You must be proud of yourself."

His jaw tensed.

Michelle clasped her hands together on her desk. "Why are you two determined that my sister is the only culprit? Your brother has a past. Perhaps it's caught up with him."

"No, Sean doesn't have enemies like that," Robert said.

"Our sister has no motive," Michelle countered.

"Really?" Evan said. "We think she has several million reasons."

Michelle looked bored. "That's just sloppy."

Evan blinked. "What?"

"Your entire rationale is sloppy," she said with a wave of her hand. "If my sister wanted to kill your brother, she would have done it in a clean efficient way that no one would have detected. How you were able to convince the police to waste their time on this, I don't know, but I am disappointed that this is your conclusion. However, let me make things clear. My sister does not, would not, nor ever will, need your brother's money. Do you think you can manage to put two brain cells together and come up with another theory?"

"You say you know a lot about her and yet you don't know where she is," Evan said.

"And you think I'm lying?"

He nodded.

"Once again, you'd be wrong." She flattened her hands on the table. "Let's be honest with each other. We like your brother even less than you care for our sister. Shut up, Jessie," she said when her sister opened her mouth. "He came here with no background and a lot of secrets. Why my sister fell for him still amazes me, but she did. If...when I get in contact with her, I will make sure that she turns herself in and clears up this misunderstanding." She stood, walked to the door and opened it. "You can tell Sean we wish him well."

Evan walked to the door and stopped in front of her. "For his sake, or your sister's?"

Michelle only smiled.

Teresa knew she was taking a risk, sneaking into her house, but after watching it carefully, she knew it was empty and she needed to see something. After her talk with Kenneth, she'd gone to see Pernelle to see if someone else—-an angry patron or other disgruntled worker—could have tampered with the thermos, thinking it was hers. Unfortunately, Pernelle wasn't there.

Since Sean's poisoning, she'd ended up hiding in Bertha's attic, without her friend knowing, after discovering that she was wanted by the police. She knew she couldn't hide there forever, but she wasn't ready to turn herself in without evidence to prove her innocence or at least find another suspect. And she decided not to contact either of her sisters because she didn't want to get them involved.

Something about books and the bookshop kept bothering her and she felt that the answer was here. She opened the front door and Mist came up to greet her, but she couldn't offer much affection as she raced to their utility closet. She pulled out Louisa's suitcase. She'd started to go through some of the items, but had stopped because it had become too emotional.

While hiding at Bertha's place, a book kept rising in her thoughts for some reason. She quickly shifted through Louisa's things and found it. An old, out-of-date book of herbs. She remembered flipping through it, then discarding it after seeing the area Louisa had highlighted about inducing an abortion.

She'd felt pity at Louisa's naiveté that such a mixture would work, but now seeing the book, she felt anger. She remembered Louisa telling her that '*She* had said it would work'. Louisa hadn't gotten the book on her own, someone had recommended it. Perhaps someone who worked in a bookstore. The same bookstore where she'd left her thermos unattended.

Pernelle? Could it really be? Had she betrayed her? But why? She couldn't understand the motive, but the means were clear. Pernelle had acted a little strange after their last meeting, more reserved than usual, though her smile had been the same. Had Sean been right? Did she trust too easily and not know how to read people? She'd thought Bertha was being too harsh with her cruel comments about the vibrant, pretty woman, but she'd warned her about how dangerous she was. Soon Bertha's words about Louisa echoed in her mind: *You're so busy seeing her pain, you don't see the pain she causes.*

She'd been so blind. She'd never once questioned the real

reason Pernelle didn't want to see Sean. Just as she never once questioned why Louisa had left her alone at Preek's Bar. Blind trust was as dangerous as blind love.

Teresa packed up the items and returned to Bertha's house. She was relieved to see the house was dark and sneaked inside as she had before. She made her way to the staircase and had her hand on the railing and was halfway to the landing when the hall lights came on.

She spun around and saw Bertha at the bottom of the stairs. "Bertha, I—"

"I know why you're here," her friend said, looking at her in a cool, detached way Teresa had never seen before.

"I just need to hide here for a few more days."

Bertha shook her head. "You will not run away from this, the police are on their way."

A cold knot formed in her stomach and her legs gave way. She sat down hard on the step beneath her. "You betrayed me?"

Bertha walked up the steps and took her hand in a strong warm grasp. "I'm doing this for your sake. You must stop running and face these accusations. You must prove them wrong."

Teresa met her friend's earnest gaze and saw her friend's unwavering love. But at that moment, her actions hurt too much for Teresa to feel it.

"Will you abandon Sean like this?" Bertha continued. "A handler must be used like a violin, he will die without you."

"Someone else can use him."

"I said 'you' not 'use.' He needs you."

"He may die because of me. And his family won't even let me near him and now the police—"

"This is just the beginning, not the end. You must be strong."

She jumped to her feet, pushed past Bertha and raced down the stairs. There was still time to escape. "I'm not strong," she said. She felt weary of fighting. Weary of trying to prove people wrong. Maybe they were right. She was a murderer. She was a dangerous witch. She hurt everyone she cared for. Her touch was poison. She'd brought shame to her family and they'd be better off without her. She briefly considered running to the bay and finding the perfect peace Louisa had tried to find under the waves.

She ran to the front door, then halted when she heard the sirens of the police cars and the sound of their tires as they sped up the driveway.

She turned to run to the back door, wondering how far she could get, hoping the darkness would shield her.

"Think of your sisters," Bertha said in a quiet voice that could be heard over the sirens. "Think of Sean. Think of how much he loves you. How much you love him."

Teresa froze with her hand on the door handle, she rigidly held her tears in check. "No."

"The moment you step out that door, you're sentencing him to death. You hold his heart, his soul. Your destinies are intertwined. I told you, you were in a battle. It is time to wear the armor that his love has helped you create. You must fight your way back to him no matter what it takes."

Teresa heard the knock on the front door and the voice of the police.

Bertha lightly touched her shoulder. "Surrender, Teresa. That's the only way you'll be free."

CHAPTER 35

He smelled her perfume first. A light, exotic scent that hinted of cool breezes and hot spices.

Sean opened his eyes from a drug-induced sleep and saw a beautiful woman with long dark hair staring down at him. The sight of her perfect face turned his insides into icicles.

"Hello, Sean," his wife said. His dead wife. But she wasn't dead. Just as he'd always feared. He blinked, wanting it to be a dream, but this nightmare was all too real. She hadn't died in that accident. The sight of her took him back to that fateful night—their shouting argument and her constant accusations.

"I know you're seeing someone," she said, meeting him as he came through the door. "Why won't you admit it?"

"I'm not seeing anyone." He closed the door behind him. "How many times do I have to tell you?"

"You really expect me to believe that a good looking man like you doesn't have something on the side?"

He rubbed his eyes. He'd had a serious medical emergency at the hospital and had been running on three hours sleep over the last three days and had started seeing double. "We had a crisis."

"Tell me her name!"

It had become a common accusation after Chloe's death. He knew Renee's father's infidelities against her mother were what fueled her suspicions against him, and he did have some minor flirtations with nurses when his ego needed boosting, but he never crossed the line. That didn't matter. No matter how he tried, he could not love her enough. He couldn't give her enough —not enough money, jewels and definitely not enough attention. "Let's stop this."

She stared at him as if he'd struck her. "You're not leaving me."

He walked into the kitchen. "It's not working anymore."

She followed him. "Don't say that."

He opened the fridge and grabbed a bottle of water. "Why not?"

"You bastard. You care about everyone else. Everyone sees you as the hero. Why would you want to leave me?"

He slammed the bottle down and spun to look at her. "Because staying with you hurts too much."

"If Chloe had lived."

He squeezed his eyes shut. "Stop that."

"It's true."

He opened his eyes and looked at her with sadness. "It's not true."

"I won't let you leave me." Tears glistened in her eyes. "I love you too much to see that happen."

"If you loved me at all, you'd trust me."

She spun away and grabbed her car keys. He'd been too tired and angry to care, not knowing what would happen several hours later. How she would leave him. How she would make him feel guilty and realize that he hadn't loved her enough, that his career had always meant more to him. He felt as if he had killed her because they had once been friends, once been happy together and he replayed in his mind what he could have done or said differently.

He couldn't believe she was dead and it was a month later, when he thought he'd seen her again. She'd passed by his office window. At first he thought it was a trick of a light, but then the occurrences seemed to increase until he couldn't focus anymore.

Soon he started drinking and seeing her more. He moved away, but she followed him. By the time he moved to South Bank, he'd spent two years of wandering. His mind telling him that she wasn't dead and that he'd never escape her, but his heart hoping he'd find solace somewhere. Now he knew his head had been right. She hadn't died.

He didn't move, he didn't want to give her the pleasure of seeing how much her cruel joke had unnerved him. "What do you want?"

"That's not an original question," she said, taking a step back. She slowly walked around his bed, staying out of reach. Just as she had throughout their marriage. But there was something different about her movements, something more practiced and staged.

"What did you expect me to say? I've always suspected you weren't dead."

She smiled. "You always were a clever man." She tilted her head in pity. "Too bad no one else believed you. And soon you didn't even believe yourself."

"What do you want?"

Her smile fell and venom filled her tone. "I'm already getting what I want. The chance to see you suffer. This all wouldn't have happened if you hadn't tried to forget about me. I watched you with your different women, but I knew none of them could satisfy you like I could. Teresa was a shock. I knew she'd be useful somehow when I first met her at the bookshop, but I never knew how much. I thought it rather funny that she had a crush on you, but then you decided to get married." She clicked her tongue. "And now poor little Teresa is in so much trouble. Just imagine what would happen if you were to die..."

Sean held her gaze. "That's not going to happen."

"No, that won't be half as much fun. Teresa's a lot more fun especially now that her shop is closed."

He stiffened. "What?"

"Oh, yes you haven't been listening to the news. Her shop was vandalized. Words like 'Witch' and 'Killer' were spray painted on the windows. Just imagine all the pressure she must feel. No one would be surprised if she chose to end it all."

"Teresa wouldn't do that to me."

"But only you'd know that. Don't worry, I'll be more considerate in making you a widower the second time around," she said walking to the door. "This time I'll give you more than just ashes to bury," she said then left.

Sean couldn't move fast enough to catch her. When he finally managed to make it to the hall, she was gone. He walked up and down the corridor, but she had vanished.

"Sean," Darcy said coming up to him, holding a candy bar she'd gotten from a vending machine. "What are you doing up?"

Sean headed back to his room. "I need to be checked out now."

"You'll be checked out tomorrow."

"That will be too late. She was here. *Is* here."

"You need to calm down," she said, reaching for him.

"Renee was just in my room," he said, moving away from his sister's attempt to subdue him. "I have to find Teresa. Renee's behind all this."

"Sean—"

A nurse with broad shoulders and sandy colored hair approached them with a look of concern. "Is there a problem?" he asked.

"Yes, my brother's hallucinating about his dead wife."

"She's not dead! She was just here." He pointed to his room. "Didn't you see someone come out of there?"

"No," the nurse said. "But we've been busy."

Sean leaned against the wall, using all his might to stay upwards. "I have to get out of here, I have to find Teresa."

"You need to rest," the nurse said.

He pushed himself from the wall and stumbled back to his room, holding onto his IV drip for support. "I can't rest knowing she's out there and Teresa's not safe." He made his way to his bed and sank down into it. "I have to see her. I have to do something."

"Get back in bed," Darcy said. "And I'll call Evan and see if he has any news about her."

"I'm not crazy. I told you she wasn't dead. She was standing right where you are."

"Right," Darcy said in a soothing voice and he knew she didn't believe him. And as he was trying to convince his sister, he saw, too late, what the nurse was putting in his IV. Drowsiness soon over took him and any protest became a mere whisper on his lips.

"He should be getting better," Darcy said in a low voice as she hovered by Sean's bed. It had only been a week since their arrival, but felt like years. He was finally out of the hospital, but although he was on antibiotics, due to a touch of pneumonia, he wasn't recovering as fast as the doctors had hoped.

"He'll get better," Evan said, pulling up the sheets to Sean's chin after he'd pushed them aside in his sleep. "Give him time."

"Maybe we should let him see her," Robert said, leaning against a far wall and watching them with a pensive look.

"No," Evan said.

"Do you think there's something to all this?" Patrick asked, standing at the foot of the bed, looking around the room at the candles on the windowsill and the pressed herbs on the table in the corner. "Maybe she is a healer."

"No."

Robert frowned. "We can at least let him know that she's out on bail. His worrying is making him ill."

"I don't think that's enough," Patrick said. "He needs to see her."

Evan headed for the door. "I said no."

"We'd watch her," Patrick added. "We wouldn't let her be alone with him. I think—"

Evan stopped in front of his youngest brother and pinned him with a hard, glacial gaze. "The matter is finished," he said. He glanced at the bed. "He's not seeing that woman until he's well. He's stubborn, but so am I," he said then left.

Once Evan was gone, Robert approached the bed and lightly tapped Sean on the cheek until his eyes opened. "Come on and eat something."

"I need to see Teresa," Sean said in a gravelly voice.

Robert looked up at Darcy and Patrick for guidance. Sean had been making the same request nonstop. "You will, but not yet. You need to get your strength back."

"She's safe with her sisters," Darcy added.

Sean gave a weak shake of his head. "She's not safe. Renee is out there."

"If you were stronger, you could help her," Darcy said.

Sean closed his eyes. He knew she was right, and he wanted to be strong, but every day without Teresa by his side he felt as if he were dying. He couldn't seem to fight it. No matter how much he tried to will himself, his body wouldn't listen. He found himself clinging to the memory of her smile, of her touch, even her tears.

The thought of her crying somewhere alone tore at him the most. He remembered holding her after Louisa's funeral, but he couldn't hold her now. But instead of his memories strengthening him, he felt his energy drain away. When he opened his eyes again, he saw Patrick pacing back and forth in front of his bed.

An idea started to form. His youngest brother was the weak link.

"You like Teresa, don't you?" Sean said.

Patrick paused a beat, pushed up his glasses, then started pacing again.

"I know you can help me."

He shook his head. "No, I can't."

"Teresa really is someone special. She can make me better."

He stopped and stared at him. "How?"

"Help me go see her."

He scratched the back of his head, looking unsure. "I don't have my license yet."

Sean managed a slow smile. "I know that, idiot. I can drive, I just need help getting to the car. We can slip out once everyone's asleep."

But sneaking out proved harder than he thought. First his siblings stayed up two hours later than they usually did and Sean's body felt weak from the exertion of just getting dressed, let alone making it down the stairs. Twice he had to shush Mist from meowing at him, only silencing the cat when he picked him up.

They made it to the foyer without incident until Robert turned the corner holding a handful of sugar biscuits from the kitchen for his late night snack.

He lifted a brow. "Should I pretend I don't see you?"

"Please," Patrick said.

He walked past them and headed up the stairs.

Sean and Patrick both breathed a sigh of relief and disappeared into the still night air.

THE SOUND of the doorbell woke Michelle from an unsettling sleep. She grabbed her robe, stumbled to the door, turned on the outside light and looked through the peephole. "Yes?"

"Can we come in?" a young man said.

Michelle became more wide awake. "First I need to know who you are."

Teresa came up behind her. "What's going on?"

"Some kid's at the door."

"At this hour? Should I call the police?"

"If he was planning to rob us, I doubt he'd use the doorbell."

Teresa looked through the peephole then gasped. "It's Patrick," she said swinging the door open. "What are you doing here?"

"Sean had to see you."

Teresa eagerly looked past him, but didn't see anyone. "Where is he?"

Patrick took a step back and glanced to his left.

Teresa and Michelle stepped out the door and saw Sean leaning against the wall, as if it was the only thing holding him up. His hair was unruly and there was the shadow of a beard, making him look like an escaped criminal if it hadn't been for the cat he cradled. Teresa rushed towards him, shocked by the state he was in, but when she reached out to touch him, she stopped herself.

"You brought a cat?" Michelle asked.

"He wouldn't be quiet otherwise."

Teresa took Mist from him. "You shouldn't be here."

He gazed down at her through half-closed lids. "I had to make sure you were safe."

"We told him you were," Patrick said with a note of frustration. "But he wouldn't believe us."

"Come inside, it's a chilly night," Michelle said.

Teresa sent Sean a worried look. "I think our couch is too small for you, can you make it up the stairs?"

"No," Patrick said.

"Yes," Sean said.

Michelle shook her head, when he grabbed a chair to steady himself. "If you collapse—"

"I won't," he said in a sharp tone.

Teresa led him to her bedroom, casting nervous glances at him every step of the way. She'd learned more about him over the last several days, from what her sisters had discovered and from what his family had shared with the police, than the entire time they'd been together and she was still trying to process it all. His given name was Ryan Hamilton, but he preferred to use his middle name—Sean. He was wealthy, but came from a family that was worth a lot more. He'd married just before medical school and the marriage had lasted six years.

After being released on bail, and sharing her suspicions about Pernelle with her lawyer and the police, Teresa had tried to contact him, both by phone and in person, but his family wouldn't let her. Soon Michelle—seeing how unhappy her efforts were making her—convinced Teresa to stop trying.

"But I have so many questions," Teresa had told her one day while they were in the kitchen, unable to share her desperation to see him or hear his voice. "And now that—"

Michelle remained adamant. "Until this whole issue has died down and he's well again, I think it's better this way."

"I need to see if he's okay."

"We know he's out of the hospital. That's enough."

But it wasn't enough. And now as she looked at Sean, she wished she hadn't listened to her sister. She wished she'd fought harder to see him.

"He still shouldn't be this weak," Teresa whispered to Patrick once they'd gotten Sean settled in her bed. Mist curled down beside him.

Patrick nodded, for a moment looking younger than he actually was. "That's what has us worried."

"Is it some lingering effect of the poison?"

Patrick shook his head. "No, it's the pneumonia."

CHAPTER 37

"Where are you going?" Michelle demanded when Teresa abruptly turned and left the room.

Teresa held up her hands. "Just leave me alone." She headed down the stairs.

Michelle instructed Patrick to stay with his brother, then followed Teresa. "You're acting weird. You haven't touched him once since he got here."

Teresa shook her head. "I'm not getting near him, not yet. I'm not going to touch him, I'm not going to feed him, I'm not doing anything. Tomorrow morning we're sending him home or to the hospital."

"Why?"

"He has pneumonia."

"So what?"

Teresa stopped walking and stared at her in astonishment. "How can you say that?"

Michelle blinked, not understanding Teresa's expression then rolled her eyes when she did. "You can't still be blaming yourself for Mum and Dad. It wasn't your fault. Everybody knows that."

"It was just the beginning of things going wrong. People thought I hurt Bess, I know you heard the whispers..." She let her voice trail away and bit her lip. Bertha had been wrong. Surrendering hadn't made her feel free, she still felt imprisoned.

She still remembered the cold feel of the handcuffs on her wrists, the smell of the cell where she'd been held. The suspicion felt right to her guilt-ridden mind and although she'd given enough evidence for a strong defense, she didn't trust herself to help him. Sean was here, they were together, that was enough.

"The whispers came from people who don't matter," Michelle said. "From people who don't know you as much as we do. Bess had a heart attack. Our parents were older and had underlying conditions. I saw you, I know how you cared for them and made their last days special."

Teresa headed to the living room and turned on the lights. "Well, I don't want to make Sean's last days special."

"Don't twist my words around. He's overexerted himself. He's probably dehydrated and needs nourishment, but he's not going to die."

Teresa sat on the couch. "How do you know that?"

"He's young and—"

"Pneumonia doesn't care how old you are."

Michelle took a deep breath and sat down beside her. "Teresa—and I really hate to say this but I will—you're what he needs."

"No, I can't. I destroy everything I touch."

"That's not true."

"I tried to help Louisa and look at how that turned out. And my store—"

Michelle sat back and stared at her for a long moment. "When did you become so arrogant?"

"What?"

"When did you think you were supposed to know everything,

succeed at everything, hold life and death in the palm of your hand? You don't know everything, that's not what life's about. You do your best and you love your hardest and that's it. That's all you can control. What happened to Louisa was tragic, but it wasn't your fault and making it your fault is making you think you're more important than you are."

"So I'm not important?"

"No, not on the level you want to be. To the rest of the world you're a nobody. Forget about gaining their acceptance and applause, you'll never get it. That's why in the blink of an eye your shop can be littered with foul words and people can turn their backs on you. That's why his family was so quick to jump to conclusions and believe the worst about you, the same with the police. All because you're not important—to them.

"But to the people who love you, you mean the world. You were one of the most popular piano teachers around with students who adored you, The Garden Society loved your oils and creams, and friends like Bertha don't come by very often." Michelle paused. "And I don't like Sean, but he took a risk coming all this way to see you, the least you can do is take care of him."

Teresa looked away. Tears welled in her eyes. "I wanted to prove that I was better than Helene at The Wright Herb Store. That the Valley Ray supplements didn't do what they claimed, but I didn't. The last thing I did for Sean was pour him a drink that nearly killed him. I can't stop replaying that moment over and over in my mind."

Michelle grabbed Teresa's chin, forcing her to look at her. "Then don't let that be your last memory with him. You have the power to change that. Put the kettle on and make him something that will soothe him, nourish him, and heal him. And once you pour him that drink, you can focus on the *real* reason he came to see you."

Teresa frowned. "What's that?"

"To have you by his side."

TERESA RETURNED to her bedroom and saw Patrick fast asleep at her desk, his glasses set off to the side. She tried to nudge him awake so she could lead him to the guest bedroom, but he just turned his head and continued to sleep. So she put a blanket over him.

She then turned to Sean, whose large frame made her queen-size bed look like a twin. Mist lay curled up at his side. She placed several candles around the room and lit them to center herself and give her the courage to perform the task at hand. She bit her lip then stood at the side of her bed. It had been less than two weeks since she had last touched him, but it felt like years. And who would she be touching? Ryan Hamilton? Sean Casey? A mixture of both or someone completely different? Could she give him what he needed? Bertha had once asked her if she were strong enough to carry all his sorrows and she'd arrogantly said yes. Would she be able to prove it now? She reached out a trembling hand, then gripped it into a fist and withdrew it.

"Are you afraid to touch me?" Sean said in a deep tone.

Teresa looked at him, startled. The glow of candlelight cast soft shadows on his face, highlighting his eyes. And in them she saw the man she'd met at the bay, the man who Camille had taunted at the Crabapple, the man who had held her after Louisa's death—the man she'd married. In his gaze, she saw their children and the future they would share. She knew then that he'd never be a stranger to her. He'd always be the man she loved. She sat down beside him. "You're supposed to be asleep."

"I can't sleep," he said, then rested his hand on her arm. His hand was cold, but she didn't recoil from his touch. "There's something you need to know—"

"You can tell me later," she said, caressing his cheek. "I'm not going anywhere. Take off your shirt."

Sean flashed a grin, then looked over at his brother. "Are you sure that's a good idea?" he asked, handing her his shirt.

She sent him a mock look of censure. "We're not doing that."

He sighed with feigned dejection. "Okay."

She bit back a laugh. "I can't believe you're thinking about that right now."

"I'm sorry about your store. We can—"

Teresa shook her head, stopping him. "That's okay. I don't need to own a store anymore. Seeing you well again is all that's important to me right now."

His eyes darkened with emotion. "I've missed you more than I can say."

"Me too. And I won't leave your side again. No matter what." She reached and grabbed a small bottle of oil and spread it on her hands. "Now lie back and just close your eyes."

"First, I have to tell you—"

"First you have to let me take care of you, then you can take care of me." She nudged him with her elbow. "Relax, unless you don't trust me."

He narrowed his eyes. "That's a low blow."

She grinned, knowing he'd feel guilty about his family's treatment of her. "Whatever works."

Sean lay back. Teresa massaged the oil over his chest, sensing his anxiety and fear. The anxiety she could expect, but the fear surprised her. She knew that was what was draining him of his energy more than the virus. With each stroke and touch she let her heart speak, determined to rid him of the toxins caused by stress, worry, anger and fear. Soon she felt his body relax and surrender and he drifted off into a welcome sleep.

"Wow!" Patrick whispered.

She glanced up and saw him staring at her in amazement. She grabbed a towel and cleaned her hands. "You should be asleep."

"I had to see this," he said looking at the candles around the room before letting his gaze return to his brother. "He was right. He needed you. He hasn't slept this peacefully in days."

She started towards the door. "Now let me show you where you can sleep."

Patrick shook his head. "Nah," he said pulling up the blanket around him. "I like being here." He rested his head on his makeshift pillow and closed his eyes.

Teresa shook her head, then picked up Mist, who briefly protested, and set him on the ground. She blew out the candles then got into bed next to her husband.

And that night she dreamed. She saw her parents in the distance across a field and called out their names, but they didn't turn. She ran towards them, but they remained out of reach. She felt her legs turn to jelly, but arms caught her before she fell. She looked up and saw Sean. "What are you doing?" he asked.

She shifted her gaze towards the horizon. "My parents still won't forgive me."

He gave her a strange look. "What do you mean? They've been behind you the entire time."

Teresa spun around and saw her parents smiling at her. She stared at them frozen in shock.

"We've been saying your name," her father said. "But you

could never hear us or feel our touch. We could never get past the wall you put up."

Teresa felt a fresh breeze touch her skin as if the walls of an invisible box had shattered around her. She took Sean's hand in hers and faced her parents without fear or regret, finally feeling truly free.

Thomas cracked the shell of his hard-boiled egg with the edge of his spoon, feeling a sense of satisfaction. The last couple of days had been great. Helene had been in high spirits since Teresa's store had been forced to close. He knew Teresa's arrest wasn't the only thing that had done damage to her store's reputation, and he wouldn't be surprised if his wife hadn't helped in getting some tongues wagging. He glanced across the circular table at her as she read the morning paper and finished her orange juice, the light from the breakfast nook windows bouncing on the cutlery and her glass.

"They found her," she said.

"Who?"

Helene looked up at him then tossed him the paper. "The one who looks like *your* type."

A sliver of unease swept through him as he looked at the beautiful image on the front page. She certainly was his type and he'd had a taste of her, but he knew his wife didn't need to know that. He remembered the fear that had gripped him when he'd first learned Pernelle was a 'person of interest' in the Casey poisoning. He'd hoped she'd disappear before anyone could reach her, because if she talked she could take him down with her.

"What's wrong?" Helene said in a sharp tone.

He swallowed and pushed the paper away, desperate to hide his worry. "Nothing."

But Helene knew him better than that and she kept her gaze on him. "What did you do?"

He'd gotten too cocky and talked too much. Louisa had been right about him having another woman, but he'd needed the stress release and Pernelle could ride him like no other. He probably shouldn't have told her about Louisa and what a problem she'd become to him. But that wouldn't have been bad if he hadn't gotten tipsy and told her how he'd killed her. But his nagging conscience hadn't let him keep his mouth shut, and after a hot lay and a couple of cold drinks, he'd told her everything.

"So what happened?" Pernelle asked, stroking the inside of his thigh, just the way he liked it.

"With Louisa?"

"Yea."

"I took care of her."

"How?"

"You'd never guess."

"No," she said sliding her hand higher up his thigh. "That's why I'm asking."

He felt his lower half come to attention and looked down with a grin. "With him," he said laughing. "He did all the hard work for me."

She frowned. "I don't understand."

So he told Pernelle about the undetectable poison he'd put on the tip of his condom. He knew it would attack her system faster vaginally than orally. It was a revelation he should have kept to himself.

"Thomas!" Helene said, banging the table with her hand. "What did you do?"

He sighed, weighing his options. It would be Pernelle's word against his and he'd gotten rid of the proof. Women were known more for poisonings than men. He was a doctor with a reputation, he had that in his favor. She couldn't hurt him. He calmly folded the paper. "I told you, 'nothing.' Pass me the pepper."

But three hours later when the police arrived at his practice, Thomas knew she had talked and an hour after that, when he sat in an interrogation room and they mentioned Louisa's unborn child, he knew that everything he had tried to protect—his reputation and most importantly his marriage—was gone forever.

SEAN OPENED his eyes to the sight of soft lavender walls, dried flowers in a vase sitting on the windowsill, and a picture of a field of poppies swaying in a breeze. He smiled. Teresa's room fit her perfectly and he briefly imagined her as a little girl gathering flowers in the garden or running with a kite along the bay. He turned to her as she slept beside him. She was safe and he planned to keep it that way. He felt renewed and invigorated, although not one hundred percent. But he felt strong enough to protect her. No one was taking her away from him again. He pushed her hair from her face and she opened her eyes. "I didn't mean to wake you," he said.

"That's okay," she said, sitting up and stretching. "I need to make breakfast."

Sean shook his head. "No, you don't have to."

"Yes, I do. Especially once he wakes up," she said jerking her head in the direction where his brother slept. "Go take a shower and freshen up. You look like a wild man."

He grabbed her wrist before she could stand. "I am a wild man. And you have to stay with me because Renee—"

"You can tell me at breakfast."

His grip tightened. "No, I need to tell you now. We have to leave here. Renee is still alive and—"

She covered his hand with hers and flashed a sad smile. "Renee is dead."

Sean swallowed feeling suddenly ill. She didn't believe him. "Teresa, I saw her."

"No, you didn't."

Was he going crazy? Had it all been a dream? Why was Teresa looking as if she pitied him? Had his family gotten to her and convinced her that he was delusional? But he wasn't. He knew the danger was real. "Please listen to me," he said trying to keep the panic from his voice. "I saw her at the hospital. The woman in my room—"

"Was not Renee," Teresa said in a soft voice. "Her name is Pernelle Hall and the police are looking for her." She turned when she heard a soft knock on the door. When she opened it, Michelle stood there with a grin. "She's been caught. It's in the paper," she said handing the torn article to her.

Sean looked at the two women confused. "I don't understand. Who?"

Teresa returned to the bed and pointed to the picture. "Does this woman look like Renee?"

He nodded.

"She had some plastic surgery, but she's not Renee and she's in custody right now for trying to kill you."

"But that doesn't make sense. How do you know that?"

"I put some pieces together, but it started with a book of Louisa's I found. It started making me think about my conversations with Pernelle and how she said she knew you, but never wanted to see you. And she had a strange reaction when I told her we were married. But things didn't come fully together until I realized the only place where I'd left the thermos was in the back of the bookstore where Pernelle had access."

Sean shook his head. "But I don't know her. Who is she?"

"An obsessed fan of your wife, which isn't uncommon for TV personalities. She did everything she could to be like her. After your wife died, she made it her duty to keep her memory alive. At first, just dressing and looking like her until she'd convinced herself she 'was' her and then she started stalking you. She didn't want you to forget Renee, since she felt that you were the cause of your wife's death.

"In her delusion, you and Renee were to be united forever, you were to love no one else. The fact that you'd remarried and moved on with your life broke her hold on reality. She couldn't face the fact that Renee was truly dead, so she had to make you pay. She distracted me and put something in the thermos knowing I was going to give it to you."

Sean held the paper in his hands and stared down at the image. "Renee's really dead?"

"Yes."

He felt a fresh wave of grief that she had truly been dead all these years and regretted his hatred towards her, then he felt a sense of relief. That chapter of his life was finally closed. He put the paper down, turned to Teresa and wrapped his arms around her. She was safe and she'd remain that way. His past couldn't hurt her. "Thank God," he whispered and when she buried her face in his neck, he could feel the sweet wetness of her tears.

"Come on, you need this as much as she does," Sean said parking his truck in front of Bertha's house.

"Bertha doesn't need anything."

"I know it wasn't easy for her to make the decision she did." He lifted his hand to knock.

Teresa turned the doorknob. "Why bother?" she asked, stepping inside. "She probably knows we're here."

"Yes, she does," Bertha said from the other room. "Come and join me."

Teresa and Sean found her in the sitting room, a bowl full of ripe mangos on the center table. "Help yourself," she said.

"No thanks," Teresa said sitting.

A soft smile touched her lips. "You think they'll be sour?"

"I'm sure they're wonderful, Mother," Sean said, taking one then placing a quick kiss on her cheek.

She looked up at him in approval. "You seem to get better looking every time I see you."

He sat beside Teresa and grinned. "You helped me find the right remedy."

Bertha let her gaze shift to Teresa. "But your wife is still mad at me."

Teresa sighed. "I'm not mad."

"Of course you are. I pricked your pride. I forced you to depend on others. You are the one who likes to do the rescuing, but it made you uncomfortable that you had to be rescued by the powerful lawyers your brother-in-law could afford. That you had to stay with your sister, Michelle." She looked at Sean. "Even that he had to make his way to you."

Teresa toyed with her bracelets, annoyed that her friend's logic made sense. "I know."

"You two must promise me one thing. That no matter what happens, you will always turn to each other."

CHAPTER 39

"Consider it our apology," Evan said.

Teresa looked down at the manila envelope Evan had carelessly tossed on top of the piano keys, barely missing her fingers. She'd been playing for Sean, who lazed on the couch with Mist resting on his stomach. They had been enjoying time alone—Patrick and Darcy had gone for a walk—when Evan and Robert had returned from an errand.

Sean sat up, sending his brother a look. "Because saying 'I'm sorry' is too hard for you?"

"We did what you asked," Robert interjected before his brothers could argue. He sat down across from Sean. "You were right about Valley Ray."

Teresa opened the envelope and took out the papers inside. "What is it?"

"Proof that Valley Ray is very dirty. We had some supplement bottles tested and none of them had the herbs they'd stated on the label. Worse, they contained ingredients like pine nuts, which some people are allergic to."

"We've contacted the Attorney General with our findings,"

Evan said, taking a seat beside Robert. "They have a lot to explain."

Teresa gripped the paper, her mind briefly going back to Dr. Knox's report and how it had bothered her. She shook her head in disappointment remembering how he'd refused to help her with the thermos and had warned her 'not to look too deep'. "I knew it. I knew something was wrong."

"We also learned about a woman named Helene Wright and her connection to the company—she was their master herbalist," he continued.

Robert nodded. "She'd provided the company with the ingredients for the peppermint gel and was given a sizable payment, which wouldn't have drawn much interest if Thomas's affair with Louisa hadn't intrigued us.

"We spoke to his lawyer and although he admits to the affair and getting information from her, he continues to vehemently deny killing her."

"Which is no surprise," Evan said.

Teresa sighed in agreement. She was still reeling from the discovery that Louisa had been in a relationship with him, and that Pernelle had been as well. Pernelle had also admitted to sabotaging Sean's truck and putting poison in the thermos.

"When we spoke to Helene, she denied knowing anything about Valley Ray's fraudulent practices, but her connection to the company will impact her reputation since she didn't disclose to her clients her financial tie to the company. Plus, it's possible that the supplements had been designed not to work so that a third party pharmaceutical company that both Thomas and Valley Ray have interest in could benefit from his patient referrals."

Teresa shook her head, stunned that a doctor would think

more about making money over the health of his patients. "I can't believe it."

"That's just the beginning," Evan said with a note of caution. "Nothing's been proven yet."

Robert looked at her, his friendly brown gaze a little unsure. "But is this enough to make you forgive us?"

Teresa smiled at him without hard feelings, relieved to be finally vindicated. "Absolutely."

THE CRY of a seagull could be heard overhead as a warm August evening settled over the bay and the canopy that housed a large table decorated with candles and an assortment of dishes including jerk chicken, coconut shrimp and sautéed zucchini.

"Only my husband would want to host a farewell dinner for the very people who tried to put you in prison," Jessie said to Teresa and Michelle and their cousin BJ as they stood a few feet outside the canopy, watching Kenneth say something to Evan and Robert, making them laugh. "He's so damn likeable."

"Plus they're family now," BJ said, watching Darcy look out over the water. "It's good to get on with them."

"Especially since there are so many of them," Jessie said with a grimace. "Every time I turn the corner there's another Casey."

"Hamilton," Michelle corrected.

"Oh, yes," Jessie said, slapping her forehead. "I keep forgetting."

"I don't," Syrah said, picking up the Frisbee she'd been throwing to Patrick that had landed at the adults' feet. "Their name is the same as the county."

"County?"

"Yea, Hamilton County. You know the one people call South Bank."

BJ paused and sent Jessie a look. She snapped her fingers. "I knew that pendant looked familiar."

BJ shook his head. "You don't think—?"

"What?" Michelle asked when Jessie remained quiet. "What do you think? What are two talking about?"

"There's an old photo of the founder of Hamilton County wearing a pin on the lapel of his jacket," BJ said. "The design matches Sean's necklace." BJ looked at Teresa. "I knew there was something I recognized about that sketch when you showed it to me, but I never put it together."

"Are you sure there's a connection? It could be a coincidence and—" Teresa stopped when Sean joined them.

He looked at them acutely aware of their sudden silence. "I can feel my ears burning. Were you discussing me?"

"Yes," Michelle said.

"No," Teresa countered.

"We're curious about something," Jessie said.

He folded his arms, but the gesture was more relaxed than defensive. "What is it?"

"Are you in any way related to the Hamiltons of South Bank?"

He nodded. "Yes," he said then reached for Teresa's hand. "Now, can I steal my wife away for a few minutes?"

"No," Jessie said. "You can't admit to something like that and then just walk away."

"Why not?"

"You're really a descendant of the Hamiltons?" Teresa said. "I never would have guessed."

Sean's face split into a wide grin that hinted at a brutal, lust-filled, yet intriguing history. "Let's just say we're a side that they're not ready to claim."

Michelle sent him a significant look. "And you're behind the recent influx of money in that county, aren't you?"

He shrugged. "I know some people who'd like to give the place a chance. It can be revitalized." He held up his hand. "And that's all the questions I'll answer for now." He took Teresa's hand. "Come on."

Teresa followed, now understanding his interest in jobs and possibly opening a practice. She wondered if he would be open to having part of his practice devoted to the use of alternative medicine.

"What are you thinking?" Sean asked when they were far enough away from the others.

"How much you like to be alone."

He turned to her and winked. "Not anymore."

Teresa stopped walking and wrapped her arms around his neck, sending him a mock look of rebuke. "I'm glad."

"Me too," he said with feeling, his steady gaze giving voice to what no words could say. He kissed her.

Teresa drew away and turned to the water, where the sun's rays danced along the surface. "I'm so happy. Sometimes I wonder if this is all just a dream."

Sean wrapped his arms around her waist, clasping her body tightly to his. "No, Sweets, it's all very real."

Martin lay face down on an old cot, his back raw from the lashings by his new master. He briefly thought of the girl he'd claim as his woman and the child she now carried. He now had a reason to live and dreamed of the day when he could turn his rage into something that would defeat this injustice. But he'd be patient.

He reached into his pocket, although the action pained him, and pulled out the object he'd kept for years. He'd never forget his friend's kindness and wished there was a way he could repay him.

He glanced down at the amber stone in his hand. It was a sacred stone to him now. A stone he'd pass down through his family. And as he gazed at the stone, he wasn't to know that the importance of the amber stone would stay within his family line for generations, traveling lands and oceans. It would survive the heartbreak of separations, wars, and the joys of freedom, along with tales of a friendship and a chance at a new life.

ABOUT THE AUTHOR

Dara Girard, an award-winning, national bestselling author of more than forty novels, from romance to suspense, loves telling stories.

Born in the US to immigrant parents, Dara enjoys pulling from her Jamaican, British, Nigerian heritage and exposure to various cultures to bring what reviewers and fans call "vivid emotional stories" to life. She is best known for her popular Henson Series, the mysterious Clifton Sisters, and the fun Black Stockings Society.

You can write her at:
contactdara@daragirard.com
or
P.O. Box 10345
Silver Spring, MD 20914
If you'd like to receive a reply, please send a self-addressed stamped envelope.

Visit her website to sign up for her newsletter and get sneak peeks, monthly updates on new releases, and special offers.

For more information visit
www.daragirard.com

DARA GIRARD

The Sapphire Pendant